by Mary Brinker Post

MATT REGAN'S LADY

Doubleday & Company, Inc., Garden City, New York

by Mary Brinker Post

MATT REGAN'S LADY

PRESCRIPTION FOR MARRIAGE

ANNIE JORDAN

for Harry and Sylvia

"I SLEEP, BUT MY HEART WAKETH."

IN any work of fiction that hopes to bear any relation to life, real people must form the basis for believable characters. This is true of the characters in MATT REGAN'S LADY, yet none is based solely on any one particular person, but is a composite of several. Only two characters in this novel are taken straight from life, and I feel sure that Milly and Bob Brinker will be pleased to find themselves once more aboard the *Kelpie*, sailing up their beloved Puget Sound.

MARY BRINKER POST

Acknowledgments

I AM greatly indebted to my parents, Robert and Millicent Brinker, for invaluable background material about early days in Seattle, the lumber industry, and First Hill Society.

My thanks, also, to Miss Louella Clancy, librarian of the New Milford Library, for assistance in obtaining research material through inter-library loans; to the University of Washington Library; to my sister-in-law, Nellie Sloan, for help with research; to Stewart Holbrook for advice; to my editor, Lee Barker, for help and encouragement.

Matt Regan's Lady

One

WHEN the first hansom cab drove up the long circular drive-way to the Compton mansion on Boren Avenue, Genevieve Lansing, one of Terry Compton's "bosom friends," who was watching from Terry's upstairs bedroom window as lookout, squealed, "Oh, Glory be! Guests are arriving already! And you're not dressed yet, Terry. What a *faux pas* to be late for your own debut, darling!"

But as Terry and Mable Fisher, who had been hooking her up the back, rushed to peer over Genevieve's shoulder, they recognized the three men emerging from the cab as the hired musicians, not guests at all.

"Don't they look just like *undertakers?*" cried Genevieve. They did indeed, in their somber black derbies, long black overcoats buttoned up in spite of the mild early fall evening, with their odd-looking black instrument cases. "What if there are really bodies in there, instead of fiddles?" Gen whispered lugubriously.

"Oh, stop it, Gen!" Mable reproved her sternly. "Can't you see that Terry is nervous enough already?"

"*Are* you nervous, Terry?" asked Genevieve hopefully, turn-ing from her vantage point on the red-cushioned window seat.

"Whatever for? I should think you'd be *swooning* with joy at making your debut. My beastly parents are too *miserly* to give me a coming-out party this season. *How* I wish I had a rich, doting papa like yours!"

"I'm not at all nervous," said Terry, and up to then she hadn't been. She'd been chattering excitedly away with her two boarding-school friends who had come early "to help her dress," had been twisting and turning, shrieking that she wouldn't be able to *breathe*, while Mable hooked her into the wasp-waisted, rustling, pale blue *mousseline de soie* gown, which had come all the way from Marshall Field in Chicago. Her father had sent for it himself, refusing to believe that a Seattle dressmaker could do justice to this crucial occasion.

But presently, hearing the musicians tuning up in the music room which opened onto the huge drawing room, cleared now of most of its massive furniture, with the Brussels carpet taken up and rolled away for dancing after the reception, Terry's hands went cold as ice and she felt the perspiration prickling suddenly in her armpits.

How *can* I go through with it? she thought, as she pretended to be trying to decide between the pearl necklace her father had given her when she graduated from Wolfe Hall in June, and the fashionable rhinestone dog collar Isobel had presented her with that morning as an eighteenth birthday gift. She knew it would please her stepmother if she wore the dog collar, but she loved the pearls. And she desperately wanted to please her father.

"Oh, by all means, the dog collar, Terry. They're all the rage," urged Genevieve, holding it up to her own pretty white throat. "Aren't you the lucky girl, though, with parents who *shower* you with jewels!" Envy glittered in her hazel eyes, though her little pink mouth smiled at her reflection in the dressing-table mirror.

"The pearls belonged to my grandmother, Gen, and they

aren't actually mine to keep. My daughter will have them, or my son's wife—if I ever marry and have children."

"Just listen to her, Mable. *If* she marries—why with your looks and your papa's money—and after this coming-out party, you'll have the pick of the eligible men, darling!" Gen's eyes sparkled maliciously. "Mama says that's the whole point of a debut, to parade your daughter's charms before the stag line, hoping one of them will take the bait."

"Honestly, Gen, you can say the *nastiest* things." Mable's face was pink with annoyance. "It isn't like that at all. A debut is to present a girl to society."

But Terry was hardly listening to them, too absorbed in the terror that was slowly creeping over her. How shall I ever face all the people who will come to stare at me, to pass judgment? What if I don't pass and nobody likes me or asks me out this season? What if none of the young men dance with me more than the once that's expected of them, or don't call on me afterward?

She thought of the great, empty drawing room with its gleaming waxed floors, the heavy old-rose plush curtains drawn over the tall windows, the stiff, gilt chairs set against the wall, the hothouse roses and ferns sent by Mr. and Mrs. Struther, her sponsors, and those her father had ordered, massed on the mantel and on the big table where the punch would be served, and then the most terrifying thought of all came. What if no one ever arrives, and the musicians play while the flowers droop and Gen and Mable watch for carriages in vain and I stand in the receiving line, wilting like the flowers, with no one to receive!

She suddenly swayed and caught herself from falling by clutching the edge of her dressing table. Mable immediately took her arm and made her sit down on her bed, chafing her wrists.

"Oh dear," she worried, "maybe that waist *is* too tight,

Terry. Perhaps I could undo one or two of the hooks and if you don't turn your back it won't show."

"Heavens!" said Genevieve, putting down the dog collar reluctantly. "I do hope you'll be all right. A friend of Mama's fainted *dead away* at her coming out, right in the receiving line."

There was a sharp rap on the door and Terry's stepmother, handsome in mauve taffeta, with the Compton diamonds glittering in her ears and at her throat, swept into the room, breathing rapidly from her hasty climb up the stairs.

When Merritt Compton married her, seventeen years before, she had been a dainty blond with a peaches-and-cream complexion, soft blue eyes, and a waist he could span with his hands. She was still a pretty woman, without a line in her smooth face or a gray hair in her blondness, but her Pennsylvania Dutch heritage of plumpness (her mother had been a vast woman, weighing close to two hundred pounds) and her own predilection for good food had blurred the figure her husband had once admired, coarsened the small Dresden-china face. By rigid corseting, she was still able to maintain the hourglass silhouette fashionable now in 1904, but she suffered for it, longed for the moment when she could escape to her room, strip off her armor, and let her prisoned flesh overflow comfortably in a peignoir.

"Oh, Mrs. Compton," cried Mable, her honest, plain face anxious. "Terry's dress is so tight she can scarcely breathe. What if she faints during the reception?"

"Nonsense," replied Isobel, looking enviously at her stepdaughter's tall slenderness. "She won't faint. She doesn't even have to wear a corset. If anyone faints, I'll be the one. Wait till you girls are my age and put on weight and have to be laced into the kind of contraption I'm wearing."

"Why, Mrs. Compton," purred Genevieve. "You have a *lovely* figure for an older woman. I think it's ideal, the real Gibson Girl shape. I just wish *I* had more curves. Men don't

18

care for us bean poles." But she smiled at her reflection, switched the full skirt of her charming little white dotted-swiss frock, caught here and there with lovers' knots of bright green velvet. She'd begged for satin, but her mama had been right about the frock. It enhanced her soft, appealing look of helplessness, and while the men might be struck by Terry's magnificence, any wise girl knew they were charmed by femininity. She must remember to stand beside Terry to make sure they noticed the contrast.

Mable, who looked even less attractive in the fussy pink silk with its high net collar and long, tight sleeves which her mother had made for her (Mrs. Fisher disapproved of "low-necked" gowns) than she did in shirtwaists and suits, gave Gen a shocked glance. "The right kind of man is more interested in a girl's *character* than in her—her shape," she said primly.

"Not the kind I'm interested in!" laughed Gen, tossing her head.

"It's high time you girls stopped chattering about men and got downstairs," said Isobel, with a smile for Gen's giddiness. She was fond of Genevieve, who reminded her of the girl she had been, and often wished her husband's daughter, instead of being tall and big-boned like Merritt, were like Gen, dainty and feminine. It would be so much easier to find her a husband. Yet she had to admit, as Terry stood up and went to the mirror for a final glance at herself, that the girl had her own "style," even if it wasn't quite in fashion.

Terry turned to her with a shy smile. "Do I look all right, Isobel?"

"You look very nice. Turn around and let me see the back."

Actually, Terry looked stunning. The pale blue accentuated the transparent whiteness of her skin, deepened the gray of her eyes almost to violet. Against the pastel color of the gown, her heavy chestnut hair, parted in the middle and done in a chignon low on her neck, glowed with mahogany richness. Out of the froth of white net ruching that edged the décolletage, her splendid white shoulders and full throat rose proudly.

The word that came to Isobel's mind was queenly, which, of course, was ridiculous, considering who her mother was. It must be the Compton blood coming out in her, she thought, and of course, they taught her at boarding school to carry herself well. Who would have dreamed the gangly, awkward, scared ten-year-old that Merritt brought home to me eight years ago would turn into this handsome creature!

But the awkward, frightened little girl had not completely vanished, for she looked out of the young woman's shining eyes pleadingly, as Terry stood humbly waiting for her stepmother's approval. Again, as so many times, Isobel was ashamed of the old resentment of the child Merritt had fathered by another woman, but was unable to surmount it to give the girl the warmth of affection she needed.

To hide the conflict within her, Isobel went to the dressing table, picked up the single strand of pearls. "Aren't you going to wear these? They'll be perfect with that dress."

"Not the dog collar?" Terry asked. "I thought—Gen said——"

"Nonsense, these are real, the dog collar is only paste. Besides, your father will be expecting you to wear them. Bend down so I can fasten them around your neck."

Her hands were warm on the girl's neck and when she had fastened the pearls she gave her a friendly, little pat that sent the color rushing to Terry's cheeks. "Oh, Isobel," she cried impulsively, turning to clasp her hand, "I hope I won't disappoint you and Father tonight."

Had she been her own daughter, Isobel would have embraced her, told her she was lovely and would have a great success, but the unpremeditated little pat was all she could bring herself to do for Terry. Disengaging her hand, she said, "Nonsense! Come along now, your father is waiting downstairs and people will be arriving any moment."

Isobel led the way and the girls followed. Merritt Compton, pacing in the great hall below, his hands in his trousers pockets because his wife had cautioned him not to smell up the place with his nasty old cigars for *once*, heard the soft rustle of skirts and turned to watch the pretty sight of the four ladies in their party dresses descending the stairs.

He was a big, handsome man, well over six feet, with a loose-knit, rugged frame, a commanding nose, a hard mouth, and deep-set, very dark brown eyes. His broad, intelligent brow and brooding eyes were those of a thinker, but the strong, willful chin, the purposeful set of the broad shoulders, the restlessness of his rangy body marked him as a man who thinks on his feet, follows up split-second decisions by vigorous action. Women admired the way he wore his clothes, and it was true, he looked as completely at ease in tails and a wing collar as he did in tweeds or riding pants and a lumberjack shirt.

Oh heaven! he thought, as he saw poor, homely Mable in her modest finery trailing down the stairs, what on earth did Terry ask her for? She looks like a member of the Ladies' Sewing Circle, which she probably is. Still, her family is solid, George Fisher is in the bank and it will do Terry no harm for Seattle society to see the daughter of a deacon in the First Baptist Church in the receiving line. Either Terry is a good deal smarter than I thought, or it's simply schoolgirl loyalty, and knowing my girl's honesty, it's more likely the latter.

That Gen Lansing is a pretty little kitten, and knows it, too, he observed, as she minced demurely behind his wife. But I wouldn't trust her too far, if I were Terry—little kittens grow up quickly to be cats. How is it a girl like Terry picks her friends? Mable Fisher, homely, but probably honest as the day is long, and Gen Lansing, already preening herself for the evening's conquests by making eyes at an old dog like me——

And then he had eyes only for Terry, coming last, slowly, as if reluctant, running her hand along the bannister, her face averted until she stepped into the hall, lifted her head and sought his eyes.

As their gazes met, a surge of love, pride, compassion filled Merritt Compton's heart. He thought, how utterly beautiful she is and how completely defenseless. She doesn't know she's a beauty and she's scared and uncertain. And as he proudly recognized his own blood in her, traced himself in the noble bearing, the long-limbed slenderness, the broad forehead, he saw, too, her mother's clear, gray-eyed gaze, the soft, full, warm mouth, the richness of chestnut hair that once he had buried his ardent face in, and knew a stab of pity and regret. Poor Maizie, I wish you could see our daughter tonight, realizing, even as he thought it, that it was the last thing in the world he wished. And then Terry was beside him, her cold, tense hand in his, her eyes searching his face for reassurement.

He wanted to clasp her in his arms, he wanted to tell her she was the loveliest thing he'd ever seen, he wanted to promise her that as long as he lived no one would hurt her, to tell her that none of his power and money meant anything except what they could do for her, the only child he would ever have.

"Father," she said softly, "will I do?"

And all he could say was, "The Marshall Field dress is quite a success, Terry. It was well worth what it cost."

"Thank you, Father," she murmured, looking down at the dress, and he knew that he hadn't said the right thing, he hadn't given her the confidence she was asking for. But with Isobel watching and listening, the color too high on her plump cheeks, her china-blue eyes bright with jealousy, it was the best he could do.

Terry turned to follow the others into the drawing room, but he caught her arm and held her for a moment. Isobel and the girls were already on their way and Compton bent suddenly and kissed his daughter's cheek, pressed her hand. "The dress is lovely, Terry, but the girl wearing it is much lovelier," he whispered. "I'm very proud of my only daughter."

For a moment tears shone in her gray eyes and then there was the scrape of carriage wheels outside and she hurried to join Isobel in the drawing room, but not before she had given him a quick, dazzling smile of love and gratitude.

It was her father's almost reluctant praise, his hurried, embarrassed kiss, not the Marshall Field gown (which was destined to be copied by all the best dressmakers in town), nor the real pearls glowing softly around her throat, nor the charming old-fashioned nosegay of tiny pink rosebuds and maidenhair fern in a white lace-paper frill presented to her by Mr. Struther with a whispered compliment as he took his place in the receiving line beside his wife, the formidable Theodora Struther whose word in Seattle society was law, that gave Teresa Compton the courage to stand for an hour and a half, pressing the white-gloved hands, meeting the polite smiles and the curious eyes of Seattle's First Hill elite.

Without the miraculous reassurance of that stolen moment in the hall, she would never have survived Mrs. Struther's abrupt scrutiny when she swept into the drawing room where Terry, Isobel, and Merritt were waiting in ill-concealed tenseness, while Mable and Genevieve whispered together in a corner.

Isobel knew quite well that without Mrs. Struther's approval Terry would never be received by "the right people" in town, and up to the last minute they hadn't been sure she would accept Merritt's invitation to sponsor the girl.

Merritt knew it too, and while he could count on Manley Struther's support, he was also aware that Theodora disapproved of him. As he waited while Hannah took their wraps in the hall, a muscle twitched uncontrollably in his bronzed face and he promised himself that if Struther's wife didn't treat Terry right she and her husband would live to regret it.

Terry knew nothing except that her father and Isobel were uneasy and tense and that if Mrs. Struther didn't pass favorably on her no one else would. Then Isobel was saying in her sweetest tones, "This is our daughter, Teresa, Mrs. Struther," and Terry braced herself for the fateful moment.

Theodora Struther, majestic in an ancient purple velvet which she wore to all coming-out parties as a sort of badge of her power and of her indifference to changing fashions, whipped out the lorgnette which had been lurking in her capacious bosom and stood for a full moment staring through it at Terry.

Terry stared gravely back at her, unconsciously holding her head high, so that Mrs. Struther, herself a tall woman, met her eye to eye. The lorgnette went back into its nest and the keen eyes sparkled. Mrs. Struther held out her gloved hand and clasped Terry's. "Well," she said in her ringing voice, "so you're Merritt Compton's daughter, eh? You're much better than I expected. You're a fine-looking big girl. I like big girls. Can't stand those soft, simpering little things. They smile and flutter their eyelashes and I know quite well they're scared to death of me. You don't flutter."

Suddenly Terry smiled and Mrs. Struther was reminded of the handsome, reckless young man who had scandalized Seattle long before he became Terry's father. "To tell the truth, Mrs. Struther, I was scared of you, too."

"*Was*, you say. But you're not now?"

Terry shook her head. "No, not since I've met you. I think people must be afraid of you because you're honest and say what you think. But I like that. The people who really scare me are the ones who don't say what they think."

Mrs. Struther burst out laughing, wheeled, and poked her lorgnette at Compton's starched dress-shirt front. "I like this girl. She's good-looking and she's got character. If I'd met her earlier, you wouldn't have had to bully my husband into making me sponsor her. Just see you don't marry her off to the first tailor's dummy who asks her. She needs a real man. Now, bring me some champagne punch before the stampede starts."

Two

ONE minute the drawing room had been empty and waiting, with the white-coated waiter hired from the Rainier Club for the evening standing behind the great cut-glass punch bowl, patting a yawn and glancing at his pocket watch. The next, so it seemed to Terry, it was filled with chattering, laughing people, men in black tails and gleaming white "boiled" shirts, women in swirling, whispering, shimmering evening gowns, jewels glittering on their bare throats and bosoms, long white kid gloves reaching to their elbows, feathers, flowers, jewels in their high-piled hair, while above the hum and tinkle and chatter, the sweet, thin, half-sad, half-gay music of Vienna waltzes floated, drawing it all together, the lights from the crystal chandeliers imported from Paris, the flowers, jewels, perfume, the laughter, the whispered gossip, into a sort of enchantment that was almost too much for the young girl, for whom it had all been called into being, to bear.

Marguerite Brookes, society editor of the *Argus*, described it as a "glittering assembly of the flower of Seattle society, comparable to the most lavish New York soiree, and by far the most brilliant debut in many a season."

Her escort for the affair, Rolly Collins, the chubby, round-faced perennial bachelor who was the joy of every hostess's heart, murmured that, as usual, Merritt Compton had got what he wanted, and that he, himself, would collect a handsome pair of pearl studs from Hugh Deming as a result. "Hugh bet me the studs against my opal stickpin that Theodora the Terrible would never sponsor the girl. I reminded Hugh at the time that Struther, devoted as he is to his redoubtable wife, was too good a businessman to risk getting into Compton's bad graces by snubbing his—er—daughter."

"But she *is* his daughter, Rolly, isn't she?" insisted Marguerite. "She looks very like him. And the Comptons are certainly irreproachable, socially."

"Ah, yes, my dear, Terry is Merritt's child, but *not* by the well-upholstered Isobel. And one could hardly say that the woman who bore our lovely young debutante is irreproachable, socially or—er—otherwise."

"Shh!" cautioned Marguerite. "Here Terry comes now, with Annie Jordan."

"Mrs. Ed Bauer, you mean, dear. Remember our Annie lives on the First Hill now, respectably married to that rather dull but honest grocery dealer. But somehow, she's never lost the tang of the waterfront, and you know, I'm glad. She seems to bring a fresh sea breeze into our stuffy little gatherings which I, for one, find quite refreshing." He bent closer to sigh, "But dear me, how we are slipping, up here on the First Hill, when Annie, the daughter of a waterfront saloonkeeper, and Terry, child of Maizie La Tour, late of the Variety Theater, are admitted to our sacred groves!"

"I wouldn't start looking too closely into Seattle backgrounds if I were you, Rolly," Marguerite replied. "They say old Madame Struther, Theodora's mother-in-law, was a Mercer girl. And it's not many steps from trolling for salmon in the bay with the Siwashes to owning an Alaskan cannery, is it, dear? Just a couple of generations?"

Rolly's round face turned rosy pink, his blue eyes opened

wide like a baby who'd been slapped. Then he chuckled, bowed elaborately, and said, "Touché! Maybe that's why I'm so addicted to eau de cologne!"

The statuesque, red-haired woman in the low-cut black net gown that swept the floor kept her hand on Terry's arm and, instead of steering her past the two whose glances and whispers she hadn't missed, paused before them with a challenging smile.

"Marguerite Brookes and Rolly Collins, what have you got your heads together over now? Have you been gossiping about us?"

"Now, Annie, surely you know that gossip is all that makes social life bearable," retorted Rolly, beaming. "Besides, only the most interesting people get talked about."

"Rolly just now paid you a very sincere compliment, Annie," said Marguerite. "He said you were like a fresh breeze off the Sound. And he said something nice about Miss Compton, too, didn't you, Rolly?"

"I didn't, but I was about to," he responded cheerfully. "So I'll say it now to Miss Compton's face instead of behind her back. In a long and rather exhausting career of attending these ritualistic affairs we call debuts, I have seen dozens of pretty young things make their bow to society, but few have been as lovely and unspoiled as you, dear child."

"Thank you very much, Mr. Collins, but it isn't necessary to pay me compliments," said Terry, her clear gaze making him blink nervously. "You see, I haven't learned yet how to take them."

"I usually take most of what Rolly says with a grain of salt," Annie observed. Then she laughed and patted his arm lightly with her black lace fan. "Rolly and Marguerite are two of my best friends on the First Hill, Terry. They like to gossip, but they're loyal to the bone." And with a swift, direct glance at both of them, she nodded and moved away with the girl.

27

"Now just what did she mean by that last remark?" asked Marguerite uncomfortably.

"She meant to shame us for gossiping about a young girl who can't help her origin and who certainly is the freshest, loveliest creature I've seen since—well, since Annie Jordan bowled everyone over by coming to the Nesika Club Ball with Hugh Deming."

Rolly took out his silver cigarette case and offered it to her. More than one head turned as she took a cigarette and bent to the light he held for her. She was probably the only woman in polite Seattle circles with daring enough to smoke in public. But Marguerite had always done exactly as she pleased (which may have been why, at thirty, she was still unmarried), and also, her curious status as the daughter of a First Hill family who earned her own living writing for a newspaper absolved her from the usual conventions.

"Speaking of Hugh," she murmured as they made their way toward the punch bowl, "he's here alone. I guess Emily hasn't started going out again since the baby came. And about half an hour ago, I saw him having a very absorbing tête-à-tête with Mrs. Ed Bauer, who is also here alone."

"Now, now," chuckled Rolly, "gossiping again?" But he whispered behind his hand, "You know I've always wondered if there might be anything between those two. Remember the New Year's Eve party Annie gave the first year she moved up on the Hill? Well, I observed something very interesting——"

As Annie and Terry moved through the crowd to an open window for a breath of air, Terry said thoughtfully, "I suppose they were talking about my mother, weren't they, Annie?"

"I don't think they even know who your mother is, Terry," said Annie quickly. "Not many people do. It all happened a long time ago and people forget fast."

"I haven't forgotten her," replied Terry. "At least, I don't think I have. Sometimes, when I try to remember her, I can't. Other times, when I'm not even thinking about her, I remember exactly how she looked and what she said the day I went away with Father——"

"Shh, dear!" Annie put her hand on her arm gently. "There's a handsome young man coming toward us. I think he's looking for you to ask you to dance." And with a light, reassuring squeeze, she left the girl standing alone by the window.

"Miss Compton——?"

"Oh, yes——" Terry turned with a stiff little smile, the color washing over her face, suddenly aware that the dancing was about to begin again.

The orchestra had already played several waltzes and she had led off the first one with her father, who had swept her proudly out onto the floor, then smilingly relinquished her to Ned Deming, the son of his lawyer, Beauchamp Deming. She had been relieved to see Ned heading the stag line, since she knew him slightly from family dinner parties. He was a nice, easy-going, rather clumsy boy who set her immediately at ease by complaining that his wing collar was choking him. She had confessed that she could scarcely breathe in her tight-waisted dress and he had told her she looked "simply ripping."

One by one the well-bred young men had presented themselves as was expected of them, until the musicians, hot and thirsty, had repaired to the servants' dining room for sandwiches and beer. Now they were back, tuning up with "Waltz Me Around Again, Willie," one of last year's favorites, and the floor was filling up with circling, fast-stepping couples, while the non-dancers gathered around the punch bowl, drifted into the big dining room to sample the lavish collation of creamed oysters, deviled crab, chicken patties, and other delicacies, or lined up on the stiff chairs to watch and gossip.

The young man standing before her was, Terry thought, the handsomest, most elegant she had ever seen. He was slightly taller than she, his hair was dark, his skin rather pale. His eyes were almost black and they looked at her gravely, though his lips smiled as he bowed. "I haven't felt it proper to ask you for a dance before, Miss Compton. Being a stranger and a newcomer, I felt I should allow your friends that privilege first. But now, if you would do me the honor?" He held out his white-gloved hand and Terry, hesitating only for a moment, put hers into it.

"I should be pleased, Mr.——" She looked up at him, embarrassed at having forgotten his name, though he must have been presented to her in the receiving line. "I'm sorry, but——"

"Forrester, Halloway Putnam Forrester, Third. One of those awful traditional family names. But my friends call me Hal." He smiled as he led her onto the floor. "I'm not surprised that you don't remember my name, with all the people you must have met tonight. What an ordeal for you!"

"I was terribly frightened at first," she said. "But it wasn't as bad as I'd feared."

"But why should you be *frightened*, Miss Compton? Bored, exhausted, but not frightened." His voice was quite different from any she'd ever heard. He talked rather fast, ran his words together, had a most intriguing accent. He was completely poised and danced so well that she had no trouble following him, though her boarding-school dancing master hadn't taught her the latest steps.

"I guess I was afraid that people wouldn't like me," she said. "It's really quite awful knowing everyone will be looking at you and deciding your fate." Suddenly she colored deeply, took her hand from his arm, and pressed it to her mouth, staring at him in consternation.

"What is it, Miss Compton? Is something the matter?" he asked. His eyes were serious and, she fancied, interested and kind.

"Oh, I shouldn't have told you that, should I? I have an awful time remembering that I'm grown up now." All at once her embarrassment vanished and she smiled up at him as if he must be sharing the joke, too. "All of a sudden I wanted to

30

stop pretending and tell someone how I really felt, and because you're a stranger I took advantage of you."

"I consider that a compliment, Miss Compton. I'm sure that any man here tonight would feel honored at being your confidant," he replied soberly, not treating it as a joke, after all.

She looked at him with a faintly puzzled air. "Do you always talk like that?" she asked earnestly. "Or is it just something you put on for special occasions like this, like your dress suit and white gloves?"

"I beg pardon, Miss Compton, but I don't quite follow you. Are you referring to my accent?"

"Well, that's part of it. I noticed it right away and I like it very much."

"Thank you. I suppose, being an Easterner—some people call it the Harvard accent——"

"*Now* I know who you are, Mr. Forrester," cried Terry. "You're Erica Crawford's nephew from Boston."

"Not quite Boston, Miss Compton. Plymouth, to be exact."

"Where the Pilgrims landed!" she said, smiling up at him.

He shrugged. "So I understand. As a matter of fact, I've sat on the famous Rock and shied pebbles at the gulls. It didn't make me feel particularly historic."

"That's what I mean," cried Terry. "It's not just the accent. And I don't think it's put on." She gave him a perfectly dazzling smile and he suddenly felt a little weak. If he was different from the young men she'd known in Seattle, she was quite beyond his experience of proper young women.

When the music ended he still kept her hand tightly in his as he bent over her and said, half ironically and half sincerely, "I assure you, Miss Compton, that even if I wanted to, I should find it quite impossible to 'put on,' as you say, with you. Certainly not while you are looking at me with those beautiful, but disconcertingly honest eyes."

"Hey, Terry!" cried Ned Deming, coming up, red-faced, hot, and beaming. "Don't I rate something as a friend of the family? I've had only one dance with you." He clapped Hal Forrester on the back. "Hello, Hal, why don't you run along and peddle that Harvard culture somewhere else? There are hordes of lovely creatures panting to have a whirl with you. I see Gen Lansing right now without a partner."

Hal Forrester relinquished Terry's hand and bowed. "I recognize the prior claim of the friend of the family, but only on condition that the next dance after this is mine, Miss Compton."

"I'll be sure to save it for you," said Terry, and let Ned whirl her away in a lively schottische.

"I hope I didn't break up something serious," said Ned after a few minutes. She gave him a puzzled frown and he went on. "This Forrester guy, Mrs. Crawford's nephew, is all the rage with the ladies, I hear. But I swear, Terry, you've got him going. When I came up he was looking at you as if you'd mortally wounded him."

"Oh, Ned, how silly!" she cried, her heart beating fast and her cheeks burning. "He was only doing his duty, dancing with me."

"His duty didn't include holding your hand after the music stopped and looking like a dying seal when I came up and took you away from him, I guess," said Ned crossly.

"Ned," whispered Terry, unaware of his misery, but glad that she knew him well enough to question him. "Do you think he was—well—interested?"

Ned held her at arm's length and gave her a wry smile. "If he isn't, he didn't learn much at Harvard!"

"I don't know what you mean," she protested, her cheeks flaming.

"You'll find out soon enough. Rotten luck for me that I'm a friend of the family. I'll bet all you can think of when you see me is roast leg of lamb with mint sauce, and lotto in the parlor!"

"I think you're a dear," she laughed, and he rolled his eyes heavenward in despair.

Promenading with Ned as the music ended, she saw Mr. Forrester with Gen Lansing, saw her put her hand on his arm, smile up at him provocatively. He'll never come back for our dance, Terry thought. Not with Gen's claws in him. She's ever so much prettier than I am and she knows how to talk to men, how to flirt in a nice way, how to get them wondering about her. I think she was born knowing.

But he did come back, squeezing his way through the circle of determined young men besieging Terry for dances. When she saw him, the color flew to her face and she said to the others, "You see, I wasn't fooling you. I *do* have a partner for this dance," and held out her hand to the dark young man with the fascinating accent.

As he led her onto the floor, he said by way of apology, "My last partner wanted some punch. I was afraid you wouldn't wait for me and would give this dance to someone else."

"But I promised it to you, Mr. Forrester," she replied.

He smiled down at her. "Do you always keep your promises, Miss Compton?"

She looked up at him in surprise. "Yes, of course I do. Don't you?"

"A man of honor always does," he replied. "But women usually do only if it suits them to."

"You talk as if you didn't think women were very honorable, Mr. Forrester," she cried, with a faint smile and a little puzzled frown.

"It's not expected of them, Miss Compton, so long as they're beautiful and charming."

The music was a lovely, haunting waltz from a Victor Herbert operetta, new to Seattle, but familiar to Mr. Forrester, who'd heard it in Boston and who hummed it softly, gazing into Terry's eyes as they glided away. His arm was firm about her slender waist, her hand lay lightly on his black sleeve. His dark head bent to hers and her warm, open, flushed face was lifted to his gaze.

"What a handsome couple they make!" observed Erica Crawford, accepting a glass of punch from Merritt Compton. "Your daughter and my nephew, Hal."

Merritt followed her gaze. The young man's back was to him, but he caught a glimpse of Terry's smiling face. She's having a good time, he thought gratefully. She's not afraid any more, but happy and excited. Maybe she's even beginning to feel her power as a beautiful woman. Thank heaven it's all gone off so well. Everybody who counts, except a handful of stuffed shirts, is here and I've already had it from several people that Theodora Struther considers the girl her protégée.

"Yes, don't they?" he replied with a smile he was sure was fatuous, but he didn't care who saw his pride. "At the risk of sounding like a fond papa, I'd say they were the best-looking couple on the floor!"

"Terry is a lovely child, Merritt. And from the way Hal is looking at her, I'd say he's definitely smitten," laughed Mrs. Crawford.

"Tell me about your nephew," said Merritt, looking serious. "I understand his family is old Massachusetts stock. Grandfather once governor?"

Genevieve Lansing, who had been sipping punch with Ralph Greene, suddenly put down her glass, laid her small hand on his arm, and cried, "Oh, do let's dance. I can't bear to miss a moment of this heavenly music!"

She couldn't bear to stand there listening to Hal's aunt and Terry's father a moment longer. To hear them talk, Hal was as good as married to Terry already, which was absurd. This was only his second dance with her, and he'd been most attentive and flattering to Genevieve all evening. Of course, being the star of the party, Terry has the advantage over the rest of us, she thought angrily. But handsome as she is, if you like big

34

girls, she has no real *instinct* about men. If I want, I'm quite sure I can take him away from her. And I rather think I want.

Lifting her soft, pretty face to her partner, she cooed, "Oh, Ralph, you are the most *divine* dancer. I feel light as a feather with your strong arm around me."

"But you *are* light as a feather, Gen," he said, blushing with pleasure. "And pretty as a picture, too."

"Ralph, you're just a flatterer. I know you don't mean that, but it's nice of you to say so!"

"I *do* mean it, Gen. I think you're the prettiest girl here tonight," he protested.

She gave a little sigh. "Now I *know* you're a flatterer. How can you say that when Terry Compton, a real beauty, is the belle of the ball?"

Ralph's face got redder and he tightened his arm about her. "Terry's darn good-looking and a real nice girl, too. But honestly, Gen, I really think you're prettier. I like girls to be small and—well, sort of soft, and—well——"

"Feminine?" she prompted.

"That's it. Feminine. The kind you'd like to pick right up and carry off with you."

"Why, Ralph Greene, you *terrible* man! If you dare——"

Annie Jordan was in the ladies' retiring room behind the great hall stairway, powdering her nose and adjusting her seal-skin wrap, when Terry rushed in to have a tear in her skirt mended by Hannah's daughter, Sadie, who had just "gone into service" and was on trial as Isobel's parlormaid. Terry, flushed and laughing, urged Sadie to hurry.

"Now you jist stand still, Miss Terry, and stop hopping up and down or I'll be bound to prick you," scolded the maid.

"I'll try, Sadie, but I daren't leave my partner alone too long or someone will take him away from me," she cried.

Annie laughed. "Who is this much-sought-after young man, Terry?"

35

"He's the most fascinating man I've ever met, Annie. His name is Hal Forrester and he's from Plymouth, Massachusetts, and he has the oddest, dearest way of talking and he's very dark and handsome, and *tall*, praise be!" Her eyes shone and she put her palms against her hot cheeks. "I'm having such a whirl, Annie! He's danced every other dance with me ever since the first intermission and he'd dance them all, only I tell him it wouldn't be proper. And oh, Annie—he's so *wonderful!*"

"I'm so glad, honey," said Annie affectionately. "Then you're really having a good time at your party."

"Yes! Isn't it heavenly? And I was so scared that no one would like me."

Annie took her hand and squeezed it. "Ah, poor kiddie! As if anyone with any sense could help but love you, Terry. You just forget being scared and hold up your head and be your own sweet, lovely self."

"That's right, Miss Terry," said Sadie, biting off her thread. "Why, none o' them other girls that come tearin' in here, snappin' at me to 'do this—do that, and don't take all night about it' can hold a candle to you. In looks *or* manners."

"Oh, Sadie dear, thank you!" and Terry bent and hugged the little maid.

Annie picked up a thin, gauze scarf shot with silver threads and wound it about her head. She looked, Terry thought, like the heroine of a Graustark novel or like Milady de Winter in the Dumas books, only, of course, Annie wasn't wicked, but as kind as she was beautiful. "It's been a grand party, Terry. I'm so glad you asked me to come," said Annie.

Terry put out her hand impulsively. "Oh, but you're not going yet? It's still early."

"I left my poor husband in bed with a sore throat, which is why he didn't come with me. He *would* go hunting last week in all that rain. And I promised my little boys a picnic and a clam dig at Alki Point tomorrow if the weather's good. Good night, dear, be happy, and God bless you."

The handsome red-haired woman gave the girl a swift, warm hug, picked up gloves and evening bag, and with a smile for Sadie went out into the hall.

"*That's* a fine woman, Miss Terry," observed the maid. "Handsome, too. They say she come from the waterfront, but she's more my idea of a lady than some o' them First Hill snobs, beggin' your pardon."

Terry smiled as she pressed a chamois skin over her flushed face. "That's all right, Sadie. I was born on the waterfront, too." There was an odd little ring of pride in her voice and she met Sadie's gaze in the mirror squarely. "And you know, I think I'm glad of it."

"Good for you, Miss Terry. Folks hadn't ought to be ashamed o' their birth. I ain't, though when I was born my ma had to wrap me in an old quilt, we was that poor. In the old country, where my folks come from, a body couldn't never rise above hisself, but out here in God's country everybody's got a chance." Sadie smoothed out the folds of Terry's skirt and gave her arm a little pat. "Now you go on back to that young man afore he gets tired waitin' for ye."

As Terry stepped into the hall she saw Hugh Deming in his evening cloak, hat in hand, standing by the door, talking earnestly to Annie Jordan. She hadn't meant to spy on them, but suddenly she felt shy about going out again onto the dance floor where Hal Forrester was waiting for her. She stood quietly, gathering her courage, and she saw Annie lift her head and give the man bending over her a long, unguarded, tragic look. Then, for an instant, she laid her hand on his cheek in a brief gesture of tenderness and farewell and went out the door alone.

Terry, ashamed of having witnessed so private an encounter, turned quickly while Hugh was still standing sunk in thought, and as she stepped out into the drawing room, she had, for the moment, forgotten the young man waiting for her. They love each other, Terry thought, with a strange pang of sorrow in her heart, but they can never be together. They're both married and she has two little boys and his wife just had a baby. How tragic and romantic and beautiful——!

"Miss Compton! I thought you'd forgotten me!" cried the darkly handsome young man waiting for her at the threshold. He sprang forward and took her hand, which was cold and trembled in his.

She looked at him gravely. "I guess I did forget you for a moment," she said quietly, miles away from him. As she looked at him she wondered if he or any other man was destined to bring to her face that look of love and longing which she had just seen on the face of Annie Jordan, who was Mrs. Ed Bauer.

And then the music began again and she and Hal Forrester were flying away with it and she was laughing and happy and Annie's tragedy was not her tragedy, and she wished the evening would never end. She wished she might dance forever, while the young man of her choice pressed her hand discreetly but ardently, murmured compliments, and begged leave to see her again.

Isobel had already retired when Merritt came into their bedroom and began to undress. "Is Terry asleep?" he asked.

"I hope so," said Isobel, yawning and pulling the covers modestly over her bare arms and bosom. "I looked in on her half an hour ago and she was mooning by the window in her bathrobe. I told her it was 2 A.M. and time she was asleep. She said she was wide awake, but I stayed until she got into bed. You'd think, what with standing in the receiving line for nearly two hours and dancing all night, she'd be exhausted. I certainly am!" she added pointedly.

"It went off very well, didn't it, Isobel?" he remarked, sitting on the edge of their bed to take off his pumps and socks. "She was a success."

"Well, she certainly put Theodora Struther in her pocket.

How, I don't know, but the old battle-ax was singing her praises to everyone," admitted Isobel rather crossly. She was dead for sleep, but she knew that while her husband hardly listened to her replies, when he was wrought up about something he expected her to stay awake and listen to him talk to himself.

"She did, didn't she? Won the old girl over two minutes after they'd met." He chuckled. "And with that kind of backing, she's really in."

He stood up and hung his dress coat in their closet, came back into the room and began to unfasten his braces. Isobel, who had always found the spectacle of a man undressing in her bedroom somehow indecent and embarrassing, turned her face to the wall. Compton slipped off his trousers and draped them over the back of a chair. "She danced every dance, too, Isobel. Had the boys around her three deep."

"I thought she danced altogether too often with that good-looking, rather conceited nephew of Erica Crawford's. Unless, of course, he has serious intentions and you approve of him as a suitor," said Isobel. Actually, she'd been much encouraged by the young man's attentions and was only afraid her husband would find fault with him, since it was common gossip that he hadn't a dime and only a good family, an Eastern college education, and Mrs. Crawford's backing to recommend him. Plus, of course, a great deal of *savoir-faire* and charm.

"I intend to look more closely into that young man's background and prospects," said Merritt. He threw up the window, stood a moment breathing the foggy, chill air with its flavor of the tide flats which he loved, and which Isobel detested. Then he blew out the gaslight and got into bed beside her.

She lay still, hoping he would let her get to sleep and not talk all night. He reached toward her and patted her plump shoulder affectionately, which was his way of thanking her for having done a good job of Terry's coming-out party. All his thoughts were of his daughter and of the events of the evening.

39

He crossed his hands under his massive head and smiled into the darkness.

"You needn't worry about Hal Forrester's intentions, Isobel," he said. "He gave me his card as he was leaving and asked permission to call on my daughter next Tuesday. I think he's smart, ambitious, well-bred, and decent. Whether he's the man for Terry remains to be seen. After all, she's had little chance to meet young men until tonight. But if she cares for him and he measures up, I won't stand in their way."

Isobel sighed and said rather sharply, "I hope very much that Terry finds a suitable husband as soon as possible, Merritt. I think we'd all be happier and more settled."

Terry was not asleep. As soon as her stepmother had left, she got out of bed again, put on bathrobe and slippers, and knelt by the open window. She could hear the eerie hooting of the foghorns out on the bay, a sound she'd always loved, and smelled the wild, rank aroma left by the receding tide.

She was too excited to sleep; too happy and too sad, all at the same time. Her coming-out party had been a great success. Everyone, following Mrs. Struther's lead, had been so nice to her. She had danced every dance, and not only Hal Forrester, but three other young men, including poor Ned Deming, had asked to call on her. She was quite certain that she was in love and that *he* was interested in her. Life was opening up like a great, perfumed, glorious flower. She had never been so happy. She was so happy that she had to hug herself and then, suddenly, a wave of unbidden sadness swept over her, wrung her heart, brought tears to her eyes.

When Isobel had come in earlier, the sudden hope had risen in her that her stepmother wanted to sit and talk about the party, to share her triumph with her. But Isobel, patting yawns, had opened the window, turned back the covers, and told Terry she *must* get to bed. Her father had kissed her good night in the hall, told her she'd done him proud, and left her, while he went off to his study for a nightcap. Neither of them had cared about what had *really* happened to her tonight. Neither of them realized that she was longing to tell them, someone, anyone—but there was no one to tell.

"Oh, Mother," she whispered, staring into the dark. "Mother dear. Forgive me if I can't remember your face. But I do so wish you were here tonight. If you were, you'd sit on my bed and want to hear all about everything. I know you would. And I could tell you about Hal Forrester and you'd help me. You'd tell me what to do. Oh, have you forgotten me, too, Mother? Where are you tonight? Where are you?"

She leaned her head on her arm on the window sill and cried, being careful to make no sound. Presently, there were no more tears and, feeling spent but somehow refreshed, she got back into bed and began to think about the future.

Tuesday, that's only the day after the day after tomorrow, and then I'll see *him* again. What shall I wear? He'll be coming to tea, so I could wear the blue crepe de Chine, but no, he saw me in blue tonight. The rose linen, if it's warm? Or, if it turns cold and rainy, the French gray flannel with the rose braid trimming? Should I do my hair in a different way—a pompadour, which is so smart now? But I'm too tall for a pompadour.

I'll ask Hannah to make those wonderful little Swedish cakes and maybe Isobel will let me use the Minton teacups. But what if by tomorrow he's forgotten me? What if he didn't mean all the things he said tonight? *What if he doesn't come on Tuesday?*

Three

IT had rained, off and on, for nearly two weeks after Terry Compton's debut, a typical Seattle autumn, which annoyed visitors but which the natives took as a matter of course and went on about their business, cheerfully rearranging their plans. Lawn parties moved indoors, picnics turned into buffet suppers, yachting parties were postponed. No true Seattle-ite ever complained about the rain—it, like the quality of mercy, dropped gently from heaven, mild, beneficent, keeping the Northwest green the year round.

Probably the first test of Terry's New England-bred beau's devotion was when, on his second call, she calmly suggested that since the rain was diminished to a drizzle and she hadn't been outdoors all day they should go for a walk in Volunteer Park instead of sitting in the stuffy parlor, looking at the stereopticon.

"But won't you take cold, Miss Compton? It's so very wet out," he'd protested, to which she'd laughed and said, "Nobody ever takes cold here, Mr. Forrester. The rain in Seattle is *good for you!*" And bareheaded, disdaining his umbrella, with only a scarlet rain cape and toe rubbers, she'd sallied forth, lifting her face eagerly to the wind-scattered drops, breathing the damp, fresh air that did smell quite wonderfully of wet leaves and of the Sound.

"Ah," she'd cried, taking his arm and smiling up at him happily, "isn't the air marvelous? Doesn't it make you feel alive and happy?"

He'd been surprised to find that it did and he'd furled his umbrella, tucked it under his arm, and let her walk him through the rose garden in the park, where drops glistened on the rich green foliage and where, to his amazement, roses were blooming as profusely as if it were June.

Then the skies cleared to the bright, miraculous blue of October. The sun came out warm and dazzling. Mount Rainier emerged, shining and rosy white, like a god once more revealing his smiling face, and the predictions were for at least a week of fine weather.

The Condons' yachting party, which had been postponed, was definitely on again. By two o'clock of a shimmering blue and gold Saturday afternoon, more like July than October, after a gay luncheon at the Ratskeller, the four young couples and an extra man, Kate Condon's cousin from British Columbia who had popped in unexpectedly, assembled on Colman Dock to board the *Kelpie*, a small, trim yacht moored just beyond the pier out in the bay.

The snowy Olympics rose cloudlike from the dark green wooded peninsula across the bay, which was dotted with small craft, fishermen trolling for salmon, tugs hauling endless log booms to South Seattle sawmills, small island steamers making for Vashon and Bainbridge. The clear, bright air was traced with feathers of smoke from freighters low-slung with heavy cargoes of fish or gold or furs steaming down the Sound from Alaska, or up from the California coast with goods shipped round the Horn from the Eastern states: iron, steel, pianos, fancy dress goods, ostrich plumes, spices. All up and down Elliot Bay were these comings and goings, breathing a sense of vigorous life, activity, movement, trade, a sense of pulsing, swelling expansion, of communication with the farthest reaches of the world, which made the port of Seattle the most exciting place in the Northwest and which made Terry Compton, who recognized one of the tugboats, the *Tillicoom*, as one of those that hauled her father's logs, cry proudly, "Look, Hal. Isn't it thrilling? This is Seattle! Do you wonder I'm proud of my waterfront?"

He laughed. "What chance has a mere New Englander here? No wonder Seattle has grown so fast. You people have made your city a religion."

The crew of the *Kelpie*, two sailors in dungarees and red undershirts, was still taking on supplies, plying back and forth in a motor launch when the party arrived, so the young people amused themselves by feeding the gulls popcorn bought from a vendor who had materialized, sounding his inviting whistle, as soon as they piled out of their cabs.

The gulls, which had been squabbling over a bucket of garbage tossed overboard by the cook of the *Kitsap*, one of the North Star passenger steamers on the Alaskan run, which lay in the slip with a gang of sailors sluicing down her decks, rose in a body, screaming and beating the air with their heavy gray and white wings, to swoop upon the corn tossed to them.

Genevieve Lansing and Milly Fox shrieked in real or pretended terror and retreated from the greedy onslaught, but Terry, laughing, knelt at the edge of the pier, holding out a handful, coaxing one big brown fellow with a fierce yellow eye and a cruel red beak that had landed on a pile and was flapping his wings and screaming at her.

"Be careful, Terry," warned Hal, keeping his distance. "He looks hungry enough to eat you, too."

The gull suddenly hopped down onto the dock, waddled arrogantly toward her, thrust out his snakelike head, and gobbled up a mouthful, then shrieking hysterically as the West Seattle ferry blew her rusty-throated whistle for a landing at the next pier, took off into the air again.

"I must say, Terry," said Hal, taking her arm and pulling her away from the edge, "you Western girls are amazing. Or is it just you? I notice the others kept their distance."

"Oh, the gulls are old friends of mine," she cried, her eyes shining. "I used to feed them when I was a youngster. They're supposed to be horrible birds, scavengers, and the fishermen hate them because they peck the eyes out of the young salmon, but I've always liked them. They're so blamed independent and cheeky. And they're as much a part of Seattle as Puget Sound and the dear old Mountain. I missed them terribly when I was at school in Denver."

Two little boys ran shouting out onto the pier, handsome little fellows, about four and five, dressed alike in white sailor suits with blue collars and blue sailor hats with streamers. "Mama! Mama!" they shouted. "Lookit the gulls. Lookit the boats!"

Their mother hurried after them, calling to them not to go too close to the edge. She was smartly dressed in a dark gray tailored suit with a pleated jabot of Irish crochet at her throat and wore a dashing Knox sailor with a green quill on her flaming hair.

"Annie!" cried Terry, and went quickly to meet her. "Are those your little boys? They've got so big. Last time I saw them they were babies, in kilts!"

"Hello, Terry dear," said Annie Jordan, embracing her. "What are you doing down here on the docks?"

"Waiting to go aboard the *Kelpie*. We're all going on a week's cruise up the Sound with Dr. and Mrs. Condon. Come, I want you to meet a—a friend of mine." Her voice was suddenly warm and shy and Annie glanced up at the tall, dark young man, handsome in white duck, who had grabbed each of her two young hopefuls by the breeches, just in time to keep them from careening into the oily green water.

"Hugh! Joseph!" she cried, and, laughing, went forward to thank the young man and to scold the boys.

"Annie, this is Mr. Forrester," said Terry, her cheeks rosy. "Hal, Mrs. Bauer, one of my dearest friends."

Annie, with a lively youngster tugging at each hand, could only smile and nod. "Forgive me for not shaking hands, Mr. Forrester," she said, "but I'm afraid to let go of them for a minute." But as his dark eyes appraised her handsome figure and met her deep gaze, he was quite aware that he was being studied.

"They're splendid little chaps, but rather a handful, I should say," he remarked, smiling. "How about coming with me, boys? We've got popcorn up at the other end of the dock and you can feed the gulls, if your mama agrees."

"I'd be delighted, but only if you boys promise to do just as the gentleman says."

"Yes, Mama." And suddenly docile at being under male supervision, the children each took a hand and walked quietly along with Hal Forrester.

"What a very nice young man!" said Annie, smiling at Terry.

"I'm glad you think so, Annie!" Terry blushed and squeezed Annie's arm.

"Is he the one who gave you such a rush at your coming-out party?"

Terry nodded and whispered, "And he's been rushing me ever since—calls, flowers, candy. He took me to the Nesika Club Ball last Saturday, to Mrs. Crawford's dinner a week ago Tuesday. Then there was Mrs. Struther's box party at the Moore Theater last night to see David Warfield in *The Music Master*. We went canoeing on Lake Washington on Sunday week——"

"He's certainly not wasting any time," smiled Annie. "Are you being swept off your feet, or are there others in the picture?"

"Oh, Annie, three other young men called and sent me flowers after my party, and I like them very much, but"—her

46

eyes darkened and the color was high on her cheeks—"Hal is just wonderful, and it's all so thrilling!"

Annie gave her a direct, searching, oddly compassionate look. "Of course it is, honey. I'm awfully pleased you're such a success. But don't forget, Terry, marriage is forever. And love is terribly important."

"I know, Annie. I mean, I *don't* know, but that's how I feel about it, too." She looked down and her face was no longer flushed and excited, but thoughtful and pale. "It would be unbearable, I suppose, to marry a man and then find out you didn't love him."

"Not quite unbearable, Terry, but wrong and unfair to both parties," replied Annie quietly.

Terry looked up and met Annie's steady gaze and remembered that moment in the hall at her debut and the look she had seen on Annie's face as she took leave of Hugh Deming. Embarrassed at having said the wrong thing, she averted her gaze and laughed self-consciously. "Well, goodness, there's no need to worry about *that*. He hasn't proposed yet, or even said he—cares for me. And all he's ever done is—is to hold my hand in the cab last night."

And then Hal was bringing the boys back to Annie and the motor launch was waiting to take the yachting party aboard the *Kelpie*, and Hal took Terry's arm and hurried her up the pier. Annie watched the girl's tall, slender figure, striking in the white duck skirt, tailored shirtwaist, and navy blue box coat, with a rakish white yachting cap crowning her magnificent head of hair, swinging along with Hal Forrester's hand on her arm. Just before she stepped into the launch, Terry turned and waved to Annie, and Annie, returning the wave, whispered, "Poor kiddie, I hope everything turns out all right for you."

There had been a time when, though she adored her boys, Annie had wished for a girl, but now she was glad she didn't have one. Life was so much more difficult and uncertain for girls, but boys could always make their own way. They didn't have to sit at home, waiting and hoping, while other people decided their fate.

She'd promised Hugh and Joseph that after they'd seen the boats she'd take them to the Old Curiosity Shop at the end of Colman Dock, where she'd spent so many happy hours as a child, dreaming over the treasures from all over the world. As they entered the musty old curio shop, the same bent, myopic, gentle old man in his black alpaca coat and skullcap peered out, nodded to them, and then went back to his cubbyhole, like a prairie dog popping into his burrow.

Annie was as fascinated as the boys at the masks of Alaskan Indian medicine men, the feather capes of Siwash chieftains, the totems, shells, sea horses. Nostalgia for the wild little freckle-faced kid she'd been swept over her and it seemed that there were two Annies bending over the dusty cases: one, the handsomely gowned woman with a husband and two fine children and a house on the First Hill; the other, Kit Jordan's "waterfront rat" dreaming of far places and a future that was to hold thin china cups with gold bands, a fine house, and a handsome young gentleman with ironic gray eyes and a soft voice who would carry her away with him to be his true love. And all the dream came true, she thought ruefully, except the best part, which somehow went wrong.

All at once the curio shop was oppressive with ghosts and she tore the boys away from its treasures, promising ice cream for tea. Hugh and Joseph burst ahead of her out the door, whooping, and ran smack into a passer-by, who laughed and caught them, held them a moment against her skirts, smiling over their heads at their mother.

"Boys!" cried Annie. "Say you're sorry for running into the lady." But they had already torn themselves away and were chasing a gull that had settled down on the pier. "Excuse them, please," she apologized. "They're just like wild Indians."

"Oh, that's all right," said the woman, smiling. "I like kids. Yours are real cute, too, in those sailor suits."

Something about her teased at Annie's memory. She was tall and well built, strikingly dressed in a flared red twill skirt, with a black bolero jacket trimmed in red braid, and she wore a large black Gainsborough hat with a sweeping black ostrich plume. At first glance her face seemed beautiful, with transparently white skin, brilliant gray eyes and delicate features, but a second glance revealed the sharpness of the cheekbones, the bruiselike shadows under the lovely eyes, the droop of the skillfully rouged mouth. It was on second glance that Annie recognized her.

"Maizie!" she cried, and held out her hand. "Don't you remember me—Annie Jordan?"

The woman's smile faded and she tensed, staring sharply and defensively at the younger woman. Then she put out her black-gloved hand awkwardly and clasped Annie's, recognition brightening her face. "Good heavens! It *is* Annie. I'd never of known you."

"Well, it's been a long time," laughed Annie. "But it's good to see you again, Maizie."

The woman smiled wryly, drew her hand away. "Is it?"

"Of course it is. I wouldn't say so if I didn't mean it."

Maizie La Tour suddenly laughed. "That's right, Annie, you always were an honest youngster. Full of the old Nick, but honest. I guess you do mean it. My, how fine you look."

"Thanks, Maizie. You're looking very nice, too. What a beautiful hat!"

"D'ye like it? I shouldn't wear it down here on the waterfront, but I was feeling blue and there's nothing like a becoming hat to set a woman to rights."

The little boys rushed up to their mother, demanding to go home and have the ice cream she'd promised. Annie turned to her old friend. "Maizie, come home with me to tea. We haven't seen each other in so long and there's so much to talk about. Please do."

Maizie drew back. Her voice was low and she didn't meet Annie's eyes. "I better not, Annie. Thanks just the same."

"Please, Maizie. Or—if you have an appointment——"

Maizie shook her head, gave Annie an odd look. "No. I'm free till evening. I'd like to come, honest. But it wouldn't look right for you. What if some of your First Hill friends was to see me going into your house with you?" She smiled dryly. "I'm fairly well known about town."

"I may live on the First Hill," cried Annie warmly, "but I still do as I please, and I don't give a fig what people say. So come along. Here's a cab now." And without waiting for her answer, she took Maizie's arm and, shooing the boys before her, hailed the cab and got them all in.

As they bowled along Front Street, Annie said, "Did you see the yacht that sailed out of the harbor a little while ago, Maizie?"

"The *Kelpie?* Sure, I was in Jake's Place and I watched from the window. Nice crowd of young folks went out on her, all spick and span in their white ducks."

"They're off on a cruise up the Sound." Annie looked at her guest. "Did you notice that tall, stunning girl in a blue coat and a yachting cap?"

"The one that fed the gull out of her hand? Sure, I noticed her more than the rest. She had more class than any of them. Why? Is she a friend of yours?" Maizie looked at Annie questioningly.

Annie put her hand over Maizie's and said gently, "A very special friend. That was Terry Compton. Your daughter."

For a moment Maizie sat staring at Annie, her gray eyes enormous in her white face, and then a soft, proud smile sweetened her tired mouth and a mist of tears blurred her eyes. "So that was Terry. My little girl. Why, bless her heart!" Suddenly she squeezed Annie's hand hard and whispered, her eyes blazing, "It's true, Annie, I *did* notice her and I thought she was the best of the lot—the finest-looking, the classiest. And I didn't even know who she was!"

When the cab stopped at the white-pillared mansion on Boren Avenue, Maizie stared in disbelief. "Honest, Annie, is this where you live?"

"Yes," smiled Annie. "I finally made it. Remember how I used to say I'd live in a fine house on the First Hill and drink out of thin china cups?"

"You were a crazy kid, but I always had a hunch you'd get what you wanted, and I guess you did."

"Not everything I wanted, Maizie." Annie pressed her hand. "I guess nobody ever does." The little boys had tumbled out of the cab and were chasing the striped cat up onto the porch. "Come along, Maizie, we'll go up to my sitting room and I'll have Nora bring us a nice tea and keep my wild Indians outside so we can really talk."

Annie's sitting room was as feminine and friendly as the rest of the house was formal and forbidding. The afternoon sun streamed through the sheer white lace curtains; the carpet was pale blue with pink, tiny roses, the furniture light and graceful. Magazines were tossed carelessly on the tea table before the pale blue sofa, a sewing basket overflowing with darning had been left on the floor beside the rocker, and a child's red ball had rolled under the armchair. A gray kitten lay curled up on the window seat.

Maizie sat down stiffly in the big chair while Annie took off her hat and jacket. Just as she was about to light a cigarette, she caught herself and started to put the cigarettes back in her bag. But Annie, turning from the dresser, saw her and cried, "Go ahead and smoke, for goodness sakes!"

"Well, I wouldn't want to get you in bad with your help, Annie." But she lit the cigarette, drew on it gratefully.

"Nora's not that kind," said Annie, sitting on the sofa and clearing the tea table of magazines. "The first maid I hired was so prim and proper she gave me the willies. So I let her go and then I found Nora. She's grand."

There was a discreet tap on the door and Nora came in with the tea tray. "There's naught but the pound cake left from supper, ma'am," she murmured apologetically. "Did I know ye'd be havin' comp'ny, I'd've baked some scones and laid in a cucumber fer san'widges. But I fixed some cinnamon toasts and I used the China tea the master imported special from Frisco, ma'am."

"That's just fine, Nora, thanks. Oh, by the way, I promised the boys ice cream for their tea. One scoop apiece and then outside to play till suppertime."

Nora winked at her mistress, chuckled, and went out. Annie poured a cup of the China tea for Maizie, who sipped it, nibbled at cinnamon toast.

The kitten got down from the window seat, stretched fore and aft, yawned pinkly, and jumped up on Annie's lap.

"So that was my Terry," Maizie said softly with a faint smile. "I'd never of known her, Annie." She shook her head in wonderment. "All grown up and a lady and all. But no wonder, since I haven't seen her since she was ten years old, the day she went off with her father——"

"You can be proud of her, Maizie," said Annie. "She's a lovely girl and just as good as she is good-looking. We're great friends, Terry and I."

"I'm real glad of that, Annie. I didn't know, when I wrote and told you about Compton wanting to take her and bring her up and all, if you'd want to bother looking out for her. You being up here on the First Hill and maybe wanting to forget the waterfront——"

"I'll never forget the waterfront, Maizie," cried Annie hotly. "Nor how good you were to me when I was a kid and you, the star of the Variety Theater, took time to be kind to me. I'm proud you asked me to look out for Terry. If I had a daughter, I'd want her to be just like her."

Maizie took another sip of her tea, and her face, though it was sad, had somehow grown younger and softer. "It was a hard thing to do, Annie, sending her away from me. Just ten years old, and such a sweet kiddie. Awful hard, knowing I'd never see or talk to her again, or know if she was okay or lonesome, or sick, or if her father and his wife would be good to her." She shook her head slowly and her face tightened at the memory. "The hardest thing I ever had to do, so help me God."

Annie's eyes were misty and her voice shook. "It must have been terrible, Maizie. It must have broken your heart."

"It nearly killed me," said Maizie in a strange, lost voice. "I swear, Annie, I was like a dead woman for days. I'll say this for Bess Fuller, she sure treated me white. Bought me a ticket on one of those excursion boats that go up the Sound to Victoria, B.C., put me on it, and told me to take the whole week off."

She lit a cigarette and drew the smoke in deeply. "You know I didn't speak to a soul that whole week, except to order meals and the like? I just walked up and down the deck and looked at the water and the islands and let the spray blow over my face. When we got to Victoria, I got off the boat and walked all over the town, up and down the streets, and I swear, Annie, I couldn't tell you what that town looks like. All I could see was that poor little kid's big eyes looking at me when I said good-by to her. She didn't cry or take on, she never did, she was the best kid you ever saw, not a bit of trouble to anyone. She just looked at me as if I'd hit her for no reason. She couldn't understand why I was sending her away with a strange man. It didn't mean a thing to her when I told her Compton was her father. Why should it? She'd never laid eyes on him before. She just picked up the doll I'd given her that Christmas and her little satchel full of her clothes and—went out of my life."

"It was the bravest, most unselfish thing I've ever heard of,

Maizie," whispered Annie, the tears falling unashamedly down her cheeks.

"No, it wasn't, honey. It was just the only thing I could do." She looked at Annie earnestly. "What kind of a mother would I have been to stand in my girl's way when she had a chance to be brought up in a fine home and be looked after proper and get a good schooling and all?"

She stared at the end of her cigarette and went on as if talking to herself, in a quiet, sad voice, as though she'd already gone over and over every point many times.

"What kind of home could I give her? As long as she was a baby and I had my job at Considine's and my little flat over the theater and old Ma Bellows to look after her when I was working, it was okay. It wasn't the best, but it was okay. Then the Variety closed up and all I could get was one-night stands in tank towns and I had to leave the kid with boardinghouse keepers. It wasn't good, and I knew it, but I kept hoping something'd break."

She snubbed out her cigarette in her saucer and lit another. "The last show I was in went broke in Portland." She glanced up at Annie over her cigarette and smiled. "Oh, that was a sour-puss town if there ever was one! Don't ever go broke in Portland, Oregon, dear." She drew in a long drag of the cigarette. "All I had was my fare home and I owed two months' board bill, with the landlady threatening to put Terry and me on the street. I was really up against it."

"Why didn't you let Merritt Compton know about your trouble, Maizie?" said Annie hotly.

"Maybe I should have, but honey, that was all over and done with." She suddenly smiled and her whole countenance took on a graciousness that quite transformed it. "Merritt and I had a wonderful time while it lasted. We parted the best of friends, even if his old man did make him divorce me. I guess I didn't want to spoil that. And besides, by that time he was already married again to a socialite from Pennsylvania. He was way out of my class, anyhow, Annie."

"He was your child's father, Maizie," insisted Annie. "Didn't he know?"

"Not then, and I don't think he'd ever have known—not from me. I think it was Bess Fuller who told him."

"I remember Bess Fuller," said Annie with a reminiscent smile. "She and Ma were bitter enemies. They were always trying to run each other out of business. Ma swore that Bess started up her dance hall just to draw customers away from Ma's Nugget Saloon. A big, fat woman with frizzy pink hair and two gold front teeth?"

"That's Bess, and a kinder woman never drew breath, Annie, so help me!" cried Maizie. "She was a famous vaudeville singer in her day, and a beauty, too, the toast of Frisco's Barbary Coast. But she's smarter than I ever was. She saved her money, and when her voice went and she put on weight, she had a nest egg to start her own business. But she never forgets her own bad times, and she always has a helping hand for an actress down on her luck."

Maizie stared off into space, her face sharpened with memories. "I'll never forget what she did for Terry and me. There I was, thrown out of my boardinghouse with a little tyke to worry about, and along comes Bess. She paid my board bill, got our clothes out of hock, and says the kiddie and I can sleep in the spare room in her apartment over the dance hall. Then she offers me a job as hostess in the joint."

"Bess ran a decent place, too, Maizie," said Annie. "I remember when some of the holier-than-thou First Hill ladies tried to have it closed down, Jim Petley at the *Argus* wrote a fine editorial, praising Bess for giving the waterfront a place for clean entertainment."

"Well, the First Hill crowd finally got their way. About five years after I went to work for Bess she had to close down the dance hall and open a boardinghouse."

"What did you do then, Maizie?" Annie asked.

Maizie gave a short laugh. "Oh, I starved for a bit, then I got a job in a cheap stock company, playing second leads, and left town. Wound up in Frisco, broke again, and landed in a honky-tonk on the Embarcadero, singing ragtime, six turns a night. I'd be there yet, but I got sick and had to quit. I only got back in town a couple weeks ago."

Annie reached out a hand for her cup, but Maizie shook her head. "No, thanks, dearie. Tea isn't exactly my favorite drink." She laughed. "Know what I'm doing now? Slinging hash at Jake's Place, six till twelve. This is my day off. Quite a comedown, eh, for Maizie La Tour, star of Considine's Variety Theater?"

"You've had a lot of bad luck, Maizie, but let's hope things will be better for you now." Annie put her hand on Maizie's arm and gave it a squeeze.

"Thanks, Annie." Terry's mother gave a wry smile. "Who knows? While there's life, they say, there's hope. I'm doing okay. Got a place to sleep. Bess saw to that, put me up at her boardinghouse. I get three squares a day at the café. Jake's a good guy to work for. I still got a cough from when I was sick in Frisco, but I don't worry about that."

She leaned forward and gave Annie a long, intent look. "Is Terry really happy? Is Compton good to the girl, Annie?"

"I'm sure she's very happy, Maizie. Her father seems to think the world of her. I was at her debut a few weeks ago and she was just like a young queen. And when I talked to her today before she went off on the cruise, she was bubbling over with excitement. She has lots of beaux and is a great success in society. I even think she's in love."

"Poor kid!" cried Maizie, shaking her head. "I hope she has more sense than I did and doesn't fall for the first good-looking guy that bats his eyes at her and promises her the sun and the moon for just one little kiss! You think this fella means business? He'll marry her?"

56

"Right now I think Terry could marry almost any eligible young man on the First Hill," replied Annie, realizing that respectable marriage meant more to Terry's mother than all the beaux, debuts, social triumphs; that if she'd ever kept it, her life might have been very different. Yet at the same time Annie knew that Maizie was one of these people who wouldn't have been able to make a success of marriage anyhow; not, perhaps, from any flaw in her character, but from an innate restlessness that, had she been a more gifted actress, might have brought her a triumphant career. "Terry can pick and choose, Maizie, and I feel pretty sure she'll make a right choice."

Maizie, never taking her eyes from Annie's face, nodded in satisfaction. "She's got class, that girl. Not just looks. Lord, I had plenty of that and what did it ever get me, except trouble. But Terry's not like me. Oh, she looks some like me, but she's different. She's got some of that high-toned Compton blood in her, and that's okay."

She sighed and put out her cigarette in her teacup. "All I want is for Terry to get married to a good man and have a real home of her own. That's the only reason I let Compton take her, Annie. The only reason in God's world. I used to lie awake nights, wondering what was going to happen to the poor kid when she grew up. Well——"

She got up, went to the mirror to adjust her hat, repaint her scarlet mouth. "My old man used to larrup me with his razor strop for curling my hair and painting my mouth with raspberry juice. That's why I ran away with the carnival when I was fourteen. Wonder what he'd think of me now, if he's still alive?" She shrugged. "He always said I'd come to a bad end."

Annie went downstairs with her, and at the door Maizie turned and shook her hand. "It was mighty nice of you to have me up here, Annie. You know one reason why I didn't feel like coming?" She laughed. "I didn't know but what you'd start preaching to me about 'the error of my ways.' But, honest, it was just like old times."

"It was, Maizie, and I hope you'll come again."

"Well, I don't know about that, but I'd like to hear how my girl's making out once in a while. Just drop me a line. You know the address."

"Maizie, if you'd like to see Terry, I could arrange to have her here sometime. She often talks about you, and I know she'd like to see you."

Maizie shook her head. "Thanks, Annie, but I gave my word to Compton not to see her or get in touch with her. God knows I'd like to, but I gave my word." A look of conscious pride touched her face. "One thing about me, I never broke a promise yet."

From the hall window, Annie watched as Maizie walked down the drive to the street to take the cable car that stopped at the corner. There were the same grace and pride in her bearing that made people turn to look at her daughter. As Annie stood watching, a hansom cab came along, slowed down beside Maizie. A man leaned out, tipping his hat, smiling, and evidently speaking to her. Maizie neither slowed her brisk, swinging pace nor turned her head, though it seemed to Annie that she held herself more erect and seemed to gather a mantle of dignity about her.

The cab continued to follow her at a snail's pace, with its passenger's silly, grinning face hanging out like a child's painted balloon. How lonely and unprotected Maizie looked, stepping along in her sad, proud dignity, her head high, the brave plume sweeping her hat, Annie thought, her heart hot with rage at the predatory male. How stupid of me not to have sent her home in our carriage, she berated herself.

At the corner, Maizie stopped to wait for the cable car, and the cab stopped, too. Annie would have given a lot to know who the man was who was so bent on persecuting her. Perhaps some sportive young devil who'd been drinking, or even, quite possibly, some respectable family man, whose wife was out of town, determined to make the most of his brief freedom.

Whoever he was, Annie hated him, wished she herself were a man and could dash out, pull him out of the cab, and thrash him.

The cable car suddenly appeared, rocketing along its tracks. Maizie stepped out into the street and hailed it. It screeched to a stop and she got on and was carried away down the hill. Annie let the curtain fall with a sense of relief that Maizie had, this time, escaped. But she knew, of course, that there was no escape for Terry's tragic mother.

Four

"COME where my love lies dreaming . . . so sweetly dreaming the happy hours away . . ." harmonized the clear young voices to the sentimental tinkle of Bob Brinker's mandolin and the accompaniment of lapping waves against the boat's sides, the languid flap of a sail touched by a breeze too light to fill canvas.

The moon was high in the cloudless light sky. Radiance streamed from its round white fullness in a sequined path across the Sound, making the dark waters quiver and glitter as if they held a net full of small, struggling, silver fishes.

Moonlight touched the hair, the lips of the girls with magic, shone in the dark eyes of the young man sitting beside Terry Compton, watching her as she sang. Moonlight had laid a spell on the *Kelpie*, which lay just outside the harbor of Elliot Bay, and upon the voyagers, who sat on boat cushions or deck chairs, grouped about the mandolin player in the stern.

The wooded islands and the long dark bulk of the Olympic Peninsula were sharply etched against the pale night sky. Far down the harbor, the red and green of ships' lanterns bobbed with the faint swells, and the lights of Seattle glimmered like a far-off city in a dream.

It was the last night out and they had celebrated the end of the cruise with Dungeness crabs bought in Port Angeles the day before. A brisk, steady breeze had carried them past Port Townsend and the lower end of Whidby Island that afternoon and then, by suppertime, had deserted them and left them becalmed above Richmond Beach, enmeshed in the silver net of moonlight, an enchantment no one regretted but Dr. Condon, who had appointments the next day, and Genevieve Lansing, whose beau, Ralph Greene, had succumbed to a squall the third day out and was only now beginning to feel like a human being.

Genevieve had consoled herself with Kate Condon's amusing Canadian nephew, Cleve Morrison, but, having been unable to charm Hal Forrester away from Terry, was eager for the cruise to end before proximity and moonlight delivered him irrevocably out of her reach.

She sat now on a cushion, clasping her knees, the moonlight making a nimbus of her fair hair, gazing soulfully out over the water, but jealously aware that Terry and Hal were holding hands. She had a beau on each side, whispering sweet nothings into her ears, and she had let Ralph slip his arm about her waist for a few minutes.

Ralph was trying to make up for time lost while he was seasick, by an excess of devotion. All day he had waited on her hand and foot, had engaged in a wrestling match with Cleve, had done a swan dive off the bowsprit when the boys went swimming, all for her approval. She had only smiled lazily and said, "Oh, Ralph, you're such a fool." Which had encouraged him so much that he'd snatched off her straw sailor, put it on his own head, and proceeded to do an imitation of Eddie Foy doing an imitation of Chauncey Olcott.

Cleve Morrison had told her she was the prettiest girl in the States and had begged her to go driving with him the next afternoon to show him the sights of Seattle. She was pleased by all these attentions, had teased and flirted with her two admirers, but never for a moment did she lose sight of what Terry and Hal were up to. There was a hard little core of anger in her breast that she was aware of even when Cleve was smiling into her eyes and paying her compliments or Ralph showing off for her benefit. She wanted Hal Forrester.

She had wanted him since the night of Terry's coming-out party. The fact that he was rushing Terry only intensified her interest in him. She knew all about the flowers he sent her, the number of times he called, for her friend confided everything in her. Terry, of course, was quite silly about him. When Gen had tried to tell her she was using the wrong tactics, that no girl in her right mind ever let a man know how she felt about him until she was sure of him, Terry had given her one of her stupid, wide glances and cried, "But, Gen, how can I help showing that I like him?"

That was what rankled deepest. If she'd lost him to a superior adversary who played the game by the accepted rules, Gen wouldn't have minded half as much. But to lose him to a big, dumb girl who wore her heart on her sleeve was too much. The only comfort she took at all was in her mother's remark that Hal was obviously a young man who knew on which side his bread was buttered.

"It isn't fair," she told herself fiercely. "She has *everything* I want. Papa is quite rich and important, but Mr. Compton is twice as rich and twice as important. Terry gets a debut and a dress from Marshall Field and pearls and a dog collar. She even got the lead in the senior play at school that I tried out for. And now she's going to get Hal Forrester!"

Suddenly she couldn't stand the thought that even now, sitting across from her in the shadow of the loosely flapping mainsail, he might be proposing to Terry. They had stopped singing now, and Bob was idly picking out chords on his mandolin, while Milly Fox, his fiancée, leaned dreamily against his shoulder with the blissful privilege of an engaged girl.

As if possessed, Genevieve jumped up, laughing crazily, ran

lightly over the deck in her sneakers, and climbed out onto the end of the bowsprit. At that moment, a gust of wind appeared from nowhere, the sails flapped wildly, and the boat came about. She clung desperately to the bowlines, still laughing as the men rushed to the bow to rescue her.

"Gen! Get back. What's got into you?" cried Ralph, reaching out a hand for her. "Come down. We're getting under way."

But she shook her head. "Don't touch me. Don't you dare touch me."

"Let me get her," said Cleve, pushing past Ralph. "Don't be an idiot, Gen. You might fall off. Are you moon-struck?"

She laughed. "Yes. Moon-struck. Bewitched. Keep away. I warn you."

Hal stood watching her with both hands in his pockets and an odd smile on his mouth. "You make a very pretty figure-head, Miss Lansing," he said in an amused, casual tone. "I think you broke the spell and brought us a wind. Can I give you a hand down now?"

Without a word, she put one hand out; he clasped it and, as she let go the rope, caught her about the waist and lifted her down to the deck. For just a second, she clung to him, drooped her head against his chest. Then he let her go, made a little bow, and laughed. "Your servant, ma'am," he said mockingly, and realizing that he saw through her, she laughed, too, and whispered, "Meet me up here later, when they've gone below."

Dr. Condon came up with a stern face. "Don't ever do a fool thing like that again, young lady, or you'll never set foot on this yacht again."

Terry, who had watched the whole performance from the stern where she and Hal had been sitting, was the only one who hadn't rushed forward in dismay. She was still sitting on the deck chair where he had left her when Hal came back and sat down beside her again.

"I must say," he smiled, "you look remarkably unperturbed. Isn't Miss Lansing your friend?"

"Oh yes," she replied. "One of my best friends. But you see, I know her very well. We went to boarding school together." She smiled at him calmly. "I remember when I got the lead in the senior play, she was so wild that she rushed out in the rain, caught a terrible cold, and was in the infirmary until the play was over. I think she's mad because you've been paying me so much attention."

Hal gave her a penetrating look. "She asked me to meet her later, when everyone has gone below."

Terry met his eyes gravely. "You oughtn't to have told me that, Hal. It isn't fair to Gen."

"It *was* rather caddish, wasn't it?" He took her hand and twined his fingers in hers. "I only told you in hopes of making you jealous. Are you?"

"I might be, I guess, if you do meet her," she answered candidly. "Though I haven't any right to be."

"I assure you that I have no intention nor desire to have a rendezvous with your schoolmate," he protested, pressing her hand. "And you do have every right to be jealous if I did."

"Why?" She withdrew her hand and sat staring at the shimmering water, her heart beating fast. "I have no claim on you."

"The first night we met, my darling, you claimed me as your own," he whispered, recapturing her hand and bending toward her. "Since that moment, I've dreamed of nothing but the hope of someday claiming you as my wife."

She turned her face to his and in the moonlight her eyes were dark and troubled. "Tell me right out what you mean, Hal. I'm not clever about men. I don't understand pretty speeches."

"I'm not making a pretty speech, Terry." His voice was low and for once the words didn't come so glibly. "I mean—what I'm trying to say is—I love you. I want to marry you."

She sat quite still, trying to read the dark, handsome mask

64

of his face as the pale moonlight revealed it. Her heart, which had been beating so fast, was suddenly slow and heavy in her breast. This was what she had longed for and dreamed about. This was what she knew Isobel and her father wanted for her —a proposal of marriage from a suitable young man. It was the goal of all her friends. Yet now that it had come, she was frightened and uncertain. She remembered what Annie Jordan had said to her on the dock only a few days ago.

"Terry!" he cried softly. "Was I mistaken? Don't you care for me? Or have I spoken too soon?"

There was such a real note of concern in his voice that she squeezed his hand in sudden sympathy. "It's not that, Hal. I do care for you. At least, I think I do. But love is so terribly important. And marriage is forever."

He put her hand to his lips, kissed it reverently, and as he bent his dark, smooth head she had a wild impulse to press her cheek upon it, to hold it against her breast. Oh, surely, she thought, I must love him.

"Bless you for saying that, Terry," he murmured. "I know I'm not good enough for you. I'm not rich or important, but someday I may be."

"Hal, I've got to be honest with you." She took her hand away and drew slightly apart from him. "I don't care about marrying a rich, important man. I just want to be happy. But I don't think I could be happy unless my father approved of my husband. I can't give you my answer until you talk to him."

He laughed. "Now I must be honest with you, dearest. I know I shouldn't have spoken to you without your father's permission. But he is a very formidable person, Terry. Frankly, I'm a bit in awe of him. He's one of the biggest men in the Northwest and who am I? My family is good, but we haven't much money any more. I have a mediocre job as a law clerk in Mr. Deming's office. My aunt Erica has backed me socially. But actually, I'm not much of a catch for the daughter of Merritt Compton, the lumber baron."

She made a deprecating little gesture, but he went on. "It's true, darling. But I've got good prospects, I've made the right contacts, and out here there's unlimited opportunity for a smart man. But if I couldn't go to your father and say, 'Your daughter cares for me and is willing to take a chance with me,' he'd probably show me the door the moment I opened my mouth."

"No," said Terry. "Father isn't like that. I'm a bit awed by him sometimes, myself. But he's very fair, Hal, and really awfully kind."

With a good wind in her sails, the *Kelpie* seemed to fly down the bay. The water hissed past her prow, slapped against her sides. The air had turned cold and the moon was no longer bright. Dr. Condon proposed that they go below where Kate was making hot chocolate in the galley. Terry and Hal stayed for a few minutes after the others left, watching the moon sinking into the Sound. It had turned a strange orange now and looked as if it were on fire.

Standing at the rail, Terry shivered and Hal put his arm around her and she felt the warmth of his body against hers. She felt very strange and weak and yet as if there were fire in her veins. But when he, sensing her emotion, drew her closer and bent his lips to hers, she was suddenly panicky and turned away. His lips touched her cool cheek for a moment and then he let her go.

"Forgive me," he whispered. "Are you angry?"

She shook her head. She struggled to find words to explain, but could not. She only half understood her own feelings, yet she knew that it would be wrong to let that weakness and fire overrule her instinct to wait. Was it because she wasn't sure of herself, or was it the rigid social code of her training that forbade the slightest liberty until the contract had been sealed?

"We'd better go below with the others," she said, and wondered if the tumult in her heart and mind would show on her face to her friends.

But they were all laughing and drinking hot chocolate, with

66

the long-horned gramophone grinding out ragtime, and no one but Gen Lansing noticed the flush on her cheeks and the brilliance of her eyes. Gen took one look at the two of them; angry color swept her face and she turned her back and began to flirt with Cleve Morrison.

For the rest of the trip she ignored them both. She knew it would be useless to go on deck in hopes that Hal would follow her, for she felt sure that something had been resolved between them while they were up there alone. It was the instinct of a jealous woman, for she was sick with jealousy and disappointment, yet she refused to accept her defeat as final. After all, she thought bitterly, even if they're engaged, there's still a chance. Anything can happen until they're actually married. I wonder what Mr. Halloway Putnam Forrester, the Third, would think if he knew that rich, pampered Miss Compton's mother was a cheap Variety Theater actress?

It was nearly three in the morning when they finally docked and trailed down Front Street looking for a cab. At that hour cabs were few and far between, but the old waffle man came clopping along in his wagon with his weary white horse, and they hailed him gleefully. Like the hot-tamale man, he was a familiar Seattle character, the mainstay of late revelers in need of sustenance before going home, and he served his waffles hot and buttery, dusted with powdered sugar.

In their crumpled white ducks, the yachting party sat on the steps of Jake's Saloon, long ago shut up for the night, and ate waffles with their fingers until a lone, night-prowling cab hove in sight. Since the driver refused to take them all, the Condons and Cleve Morrison agreed to wait for another, which the cabbie promised would be along soon, and the engaged couple, Bob and Milly, in order to have a few more minutes together, elected to wait with them.

Even in the cab, Genevieve ignored Terry and Hal, kept up a lively banter with Ralph, who was too sleepy to respond in his best form. Hal was aware of Gen's coldness and found it amusing, but Terry, realizing how late it was, could think of nothing but facing her father when she got home. She was sure he'd still be up, waiting for her. Hal was right, he was a formidable person, and while indulgent in many ways, was also oddly stricter than her friends' fathers. She was afraid, not so much for herself, as for how he would act toward Hal.

Merritt Compton was still up and was at the door before Hal could open it for Terry. For two hours he had been pacing the floor in his study, smoking furiously until the air was blue with cigar smoke.

"Come in," he said in the carefully restrained voice which Terry knew indicated he was in a cold fury. "Terry, my dear, please go straight to your room to bed. And you, young man, come into my study for a very few minutes. Tell the cab to wait. You'll have trouble finding another *at this hour.*"

"Father," said Terry quickly, "it wasn't Hal's fault we were so late getting in——"

"I'll explain to your father," interrupted Hal quietly. "Good night, Terry, and thanks for a wonderful week." He gave her hand a faint squeeze and she knew he wanted her out of the way before her father's wrath descended on him.

"Good night, Hal. It *was* a wonderful week—for me, too." She turned to Compton and lifted her face for his kiss, like a child. "Good night, Father. I'm sorry if I caused you worry."

He touched her forehead briefly with his lips and gave her a steady look. "Yes, I think you are, my dear. Good night. I'll talk to you in the morning."

She went upstairs, undressed quickly, and got into bed, and though she was anxious for poor Hal in the study with her father's deep-set, unrelenting eyes on him, almost as soon as her head touched the pillow she was asleep and didn't hear the cab drive away half an hour later.

Five

SHE could easily have slept the clock round, but at seven-thirty Isobel woke her to come down for breakfast. There was no use in protesting, for no matter how late members of his household got to bed, Compton expected everyone to be at the long fumed-oak table in the stately dining room by eight o'clock, properly dressed. He considered it a slovenly habit to appear at breakfast in even the prettiest peignoir or dressing gown, which was a source of intense irritation to his wife, who hated having to struggle into a corset and dress so early in the day and had no appetite for anything but coffee and toast at that hour. Her husband never knew that as soon as he was out the front door Isobel went back upstairs, undressed, and returned to bed for another two hours' sleep, after which Hannah brought her a proper breakfast on a tray.

When Terry came down, Isobel and her father were already seated and Hannah was bringing in the eggs scrambled with chicken livers, Merritt's favorite dish, and Sadie was handing round the smoking hot popovers in their nest of a crisp white napkin.

"I'm sorry to be late, Father," Terry murmured as she took her place. It had been agony to wake up, but once she had washed in cold water and dressed in a fresh white batiste blouse and her pleated navy-blue poplin skirt, she felt as wide awake and refreshed as if she'd had eight hours' sleep. Her eyes were bright, with a soft, secret shine to them that made Isobel glance at her sharply, and her transparent skin glowed.

"Staying up all night seems to agree with you, kiddie," said Merritt, throwing back his head and looking keenly at her through narrowed eyes, an odd trick he had which some people found disconcerting, but which Terry was used to.

"Oh, I feel perfectly wonderful," she cried, smiling, "now that I'm up. But it was a struggle to get out of bed." She helped herself generously to the eggs and livers, took two pop-overs, and whispered to Sadie that she'd love some of Hannah's gooseberry jam. "I'm starved," she said to Isobel.

"How you people can eat like that so early in the day!" sighed Isobel. "No, thank you, Hannah. Nothing but black coffee and a piece of buttered toast, as usual."

"Breakfast is the most important meal of the day," Compton pronounced dogmatically. "If you'd eat a good breakfast, Isobel, and not fill up at lunch and dinner, as well as at teatime, you wouldn't have such a problem getting into your corsets."

Isobel colored and shot him an angry glance. It enraged her to be reminded of her weight, though she was always lamenting it herself. She turned to Terry. "My goodness, child, what time did you get home? Your father was nearly out of his mind with worry."

"We were becalmed just outside the harbor," replied Terry, glancing quickly at her father and wondering what had happened in the study after she'd gone to bed. "It was no one's fault we were so late."

"Mr. Forrester explained that to me quite satisfactorily," said Compton. "I'm sorry if I was abrupt with you both this morning. But as Isobel says, I was concerned." He put down his fork and leaned back in his chair, once more throwing back his head to look at his daughter. "I want to know what you think about this young man, Hal Forrester, Terry."

Color washed over the girl's face, stained her throat, and for a moment she couldn't meet his eyes or answer him.

Isobel laughed. "Why, Terry Compton, you're blushing! There's your answer, Merritt."

"Terry will tell me what I want to know, Isobel," said Compton quietly, not taking his eyes from his daughter's face.

She met his gaze. "I like him very much, Father."

"Are you in love with him?" he demanded sharply. Then he smiled coldly. "Or, I should say, do you *fancy* yourself in love with him?"

Her eyes darkened and color came and went in her cheeks, but her gaze did not falter. "I—I think so, Father."

"Last night, or rather this morning, he told me that he had proposed marriage to you and that you had accepted him." There was a hostile note in his voice that made Terry's heart sink. He doesn't like Hal, she thought, he's refused his consent.

"I told him that I cared for him, Father, but that I couldn't marry without your approval." Her eyes, meeting his, were clear and honest, and her voice had a depth and dignity that struck him to the heart.

Impulsively he reached out his hand and put it over hers, which lay, slim and defenseless, by her plate. "You told him that, did you, kiddie? Good. You did exactly right. I'm very touched that you feel that way, Terry."

"It's only what any properly brought up girl would do, Merritt," observed Isobel dryly, annoyed at his display of emotion. "But hurry up and tell us what you said to him, for pity's sake. Can't you see we're on tenterhooks?"

"All in good time, my dear," he replied. "I wanted to find out first what Terry's feelings are." He deliberately buttered another popover, while the two women exchanged exasperated glances. "I'd like more coffee, please." So they must wait until Sadie was summoned and had refilled his cup and had re-

71

turned to the kitchen before he said, "I told Mr. Forrester that three-forty in the morning was hardly the time to discuss so grave a subject. I gave him permission to wait upon me in my study this afternoon at five. An hour, I believe, when you, Terry, will be attending a tea in your honor given by Mrs. Struther at the Firlock Club."

"Oh, Father!" cried Terry desperately. "At least you can tell me what you think of him. If—if you approve or not."

"He seems to be a personable, well-bred young fellow. I don't know yet what his prospects are or how soon he will be in a position to support a wife."

"He's considered one of the most eligible bachelors in town!" cried Isobel, and Terry gave her a grateful glance. "He comes from a fine old Plymouth family. He's a graduate of Harvard, he's Erica Crawford's only nephew, and, since she hasn't any children, will probably be her heir."

"Erica Crawford is in her middle forties and in excellent health," remarked her husband dryly. "He will have a long wait for his inheritance, and at the rate his gay aunt is spending her money, it may not amount to a row of beans when he comes into it."

"Now, Merritt, I hope you're not going to be pigheaded about this," insisted his wife. "I've heard you say time and again that money wasn't half as important as initiative and brains, and from all I've heard, Hal Forrester has both."

"That remains to be seen, my dear," he replied evenly. "There is also one other quality which is necessary in any young man who comes courting my daughter, and that is character."

"I think you'd be a fool to stand in Terry's way if she wants to marry the boy, Merritt," argued Isobel, as if the girl weren't there at all. "I think you're forgetting one important thing in his favor. He's a stranger to Seattle and probably knows very little about certain events in the past."

"I think you've said quite enough, Isobel." Merritt's voice was low, controlled, but his eyes were snapping.

She was not to be silenced, however. "No, I haven't! The best thing in the world for Terry and for us would be for her to make a suitable marriage as soon as possible. And you know it!" Her face was hot with angry color.

Terry sat, staring at her plate, wishing she could excuse herself and disappear, but no one left the table until her father did, and besides, a certain dogged courage made her feel that she must stay at all costs.

Merritt Compton folded his napkin with elaborate care and inserted it into the heavily carved silver napkin ring with his initials engraved on it. Then he pushed back his chair and stood up. "No matter what my decision may be about Mr. Forrester, Isobel, the fact remains that Terry is only eighteen years old. She is too young for marriage, and if I consent to an engagement with this young man, I will not agree to having it announced for six months, nor to a wedding under a year."

Without another glance at either of them, he strode out of the room, got his hat and coat from the hall closet, and slammed out of the house.

The moment the door shut behind him, Isobel turned to Terry, her eyes sparkling. "Oh, Terry dear, I'm so excited!" she cried, clasping the girl's hand. "Don't worry about Merritt. He'll give his consent, I'm sure." Her voice, her eyes, her hand-clasp were warm and eager and Terry's embarrassment and hurt gave way before this sudden kindness.

"You know your father," Isobel laughed. "He likes to bluster and huff and puff, but he'll come round. And you won't have to wait a year for the wedding, either, I promise you that!"

"But Isobel, maybe he's right. Maybe I *am* too young to get married now."

"Nonsense! I was just nineteen when I was married and my

73

mother was sixteen. I believe in early marriages. Look at Marguerite Brookes! She had a beau when she was eighteen who was crazy to marry her, but her mother was a widow and couldn't bear to let her go, so Marguerite put her young man off and what happened? He went to San Francisco, met another girl and married her. And poor Marguerite is still a spinster, and at her age she'll probably never marry." Isobel's voice indicated that Marguerite might just as well be dead as husbandless.

"But if he'd really loved her, Isobel, wouldn't he have waited?" cried Terry, thinking that the independent woman she'd met at her debut didn't seem to be pining away for her faithless lover.

Isobel laughed shortly. "My dear girl, never make a man wait too long. Women can wait, but not men. It's out of sight, out of mind with them. And remember, there's always some other girl just as pretty as you around the next corner." She tapped Terry's arm with her forefinger. "If you take my advice, you'll marry Hal Forrester as soon as possible."

She rang for Hannah. "Hannah," she said briskly, "I'm not going back to bed today. I'll have my breakfast now. Popovers, ham and eggs, another pot of coffee." She turned to Terry, who was folding her napkin, about to excuse herself from the table. "Now, Terry, we'll start planning. First of all, the engagement party. I don't care what Merritt said this morning, the sooner you announce your engagement the better. I think I know how to get around your father. If I drop a hint to Marguerite Brookes, she'll mention it in her society column and then he'll have to announce it officially. I'll have Miss Florian come next week and start sewing for you. I'll need a few new things, too."

But it was never announced officially.

Hal gave a good account of himself that afternoon and Merritt Compton gave his consent to the engagement with the stipulations he'd outlined to his wife and daughter. Isobel

74

dropped her hint to Marguerite, who ran a sly paragraph in her "Town Topics," suggesting that a certain beautiful young belle who was being escorted everywhere by a dashing Easterner might soon be ordering orange blossoms from California. Hal and Terry were seen looking at diamond solitaires in Simon Burnett's new jewelry store and the leading florist had a standing order to deliver a dozen American Beauty roses each week to Miss Compton. Isobel and Miss Florian were deep in trousseau plans and Compton had grudgingly consented to announce the engagement at his traditional eggnog party New Year's Day.

Terry was caught up in the excitement, in the dream, and each morning she wakened feeling that it must, indeed, be a dream, and that soon she would really wake up and find that it wasn't true. All the events of the past months had taken on the quality of unreality. First the debut and her unexpected success. Then Hal Forrester's ardent courting, culminating in his proposal. Her father's capitulation, Isobel's unusual kindness, warmth, and interest in her. Her times with Hal, when she felt sure that her feeling for him matched his devotion to her and the thrill of being seen with him by her friends, who accepted their unannounced betrothal as a *fait accompli*. All but Gen Lansing, who always gave her a sharp little smile, as if she didn't believe in it for a moment. She and Gen weren't so close as they had been. Not since the yachting party had Terry confided in her, sensing an antagonism in her friend that made her uneasy.

The day it all ended was the first one that Terry had wakened with a sense of certainty that all this was really happening to her. It was just before Christmas and the weather, which had been dreary and dark, cleared overnight, turned so warm that several people reported crocuses and tulips in bloom. She lay for a few minutes, smelling the fresh, cool morning air and watching the sunlight dancing on the ceiling, and all at once the feeling of unreality left her. It wasn't a dream after all; it

75

was true. She was engaged to marry Hal Forrester. She was wearing his ring on a ribbon around her neck; soon she would be able to wear it openly on her finger for all the world to see, and she was going to be so very, very happy.

Six

OLD Charley Compton, Merritt's father, founded the Compton Lumber Company on a lumber grab in the '70s. Honest in his personal dealings with people, reasonably if not scrupulously honest in business, he, like the other enterprising men of his day, saw nothing reprehensible in cheating the government if he could get away with it.

Under the Homestead Act of 1862, he was able to acquire several thousand acres of virgin timber lands in Washington Territory for a song, was reputed to have hired dummy entrymen to enter claims for tracts which they immediately turned over to him for small fees. He saw nothing wrong with this, when big lumber companies in the East had grabbed off timber tracts in Michigan, Minnesota, and Wisconsin by filing names taken from the St. Paul and Chicago city directories. Far from considering himself an exploiter of the Western lands, he felt he was a benefactor, whose capital and energy brought money and enterprise to "develop" the country.

Charley had served his time in the logging camps because that was how he had to learn what he needed to know about lumbering. But once his company was well established he never went near the camps. He sat in his office in the Pioneer

Building overlooking Pioneer Square and the totem pole stolen from the Alaskan Indians, hired capable foremen, and left the logging to them. He didn't care how they did it, just so long as they kept the logs rolling down to the mills. He might as well have been on Wall Street, New York City, for all he cared about the woods. The lumber meant only one thing to him; it was a commodity which he could and did trade in shrewdly and through it he built up the business and fortune which his son inherited at twenty-five when old Charley died of a stroke.

Merritt was an altogether different breed of man from Charley. Born in Seattle, he was a true Westerner with a fierce pride in the fine, rich country. He loved the Northwest and pitied anyone who had to live anywhere else. His father had sent him out as a youngster, summers, to the camps, to toughen him up, teach him to sweat, and Merritt had loved it. He liked working with the rough, bull-strong, independent loggers from sunup to dusk. He never lost his feeling for the tall trees and, after he took over the company, watched the timber with a jealous eye. Every year, in early summer and fall, he made the rounds of the camps, from the Skagit River to Grays Harbor.

Terry started going with her father to the camps the second summer she came to live with him. Isobel was called to Pennsylvania by her mother's illness, and Merritt, not knowing what to do with the child, since Hannah, the cook-house-keeper, was on vacation, took her along with him up the Skagit.

He outfitted her like a boy, with levis, flannel shirt, and sneakers. Except for the two thick brown braids hanging halfway down her back, she looked like a boy in the getup, tall, straight, long-legged. Like a boy, too, she took to the woods, trudged along the skid road behind her father, followed the crews, made friends with the loggers and cook, climbed trees, learned to fish in the brook.

Up to then, Terry had been shy and uncertain with him and he hadn't known how to go about making friends with her.

But on the trip up the Sound in the island steamer, her shyness disappeared and she chattered away, asking questions, noticing everything, eager and excited. To his surprise and delight, he discovered that she was bright, frank, and responsive, a real little person. In camp she was never a bit of trouble, obeyed rules, ate what was put before her, never fussed. She hadn't even shed a tear the time she fell out of a young spruce and broke her arm.

She was acting just as bravely now, Merritt observed, over what had happened between her and Hal Forrester. Not a whimper, not, so far as he knew, a tear.

The whole matter of the broken engagement baffled him. The announcement party had been planned for New Year's Day, when the Comptons always gave their traditional eggnog party. Two weeks before New Year's, just before Christmas, not Terry, but Isobel, her face sharp with outrage and disappointment, had come to him and told him it was all off. Terry had returned Hal's ring and without making any explanation had announced that the engagement was broken.

"And Miss Florian just finished making her the loveliest gown for the announcement party, and I've sent to Marshall Field for swatches for the wedding dress," wailed Isobel, looking ready to cry. "The invitations are already printed, too. Thank goodness I haven't had time to address them and send them out!"

He had waited for Terry to tell him the whole story, but she had not. She'd had a relapse of a bad cold she'd caught before Christmas and the doctor had put her to bed for a few days. Other young men had squired her to holiday parties and she had danced till dawn on New Year's Eve. She gave a gay box party for the young crowd at the Moore Theater, where Maude Adams was playing in *The Little Minister*; a luncheon at the Firlock Club on Lake Washington for Mrs. Struther, who had sponsored her debut and had entertained handsomely for her; a small supper with auction bridge, the new card rage, afterward, for Dr. and Mrs. Condon, and another for Bob Brinker and Milly Fox, at whose wedding next fall she was to be a bridesmaid.

The only cue he had was once when he asked her why he never saw Gen Lansing at the house any more. Terry had gone white, had stared at him blankly. "We're not friends any more, Father," she'd replied quietly, and he had left it at that. If he had not loved her so much he might have been bold enough to come right out and ask her why she had returned Hal's ring.

But he hadn't really worried about her until after the winter's social whirl was over and he gradually became aware that the procession of young men and young women in and out of the house had dwindled to a very few. She was nearly always home now when he got back from the office. When she did go out it was usually with Ned Deming or with her women friends. She saw a great deal of her dowdy, loyal friend, Mable Fisher, and often lunched downtown and went to matinees with Mrs. Ed Bauer. But the glow, the secret shine had gone out of her eyes and there was a listlessness about her that bothered him.

"What's the matter with Terry?" he asked Isobel one night after the girl had complained of a headache and gone to bed soon after dinner, leaving them playing double Canfield in the study.

"She's eating her heart out for Hal Forrester, if you really want to know," Isobel answered crossly.

"But why? Didn't she return his ring and break off the engagement herself?" he cried.

Isobel shrugged and put a queen on his king. "Who knows? She gave him back his ring, but whether it was her idea or his—she didn't say."

"What are you driving at, Isobel?" He gave her a hard look.

"All I know is that when Terry came down with that beastly cold, the first time, remember, two weeks before Christmas, she canceled all her dates with Hal for a week. Quite rightly, since she felt miserable and looked a sight. In the **meantime**, hostesses who had planned for Hal to escort Terry to their parties paired him off with Gen Lansing. Maybe Gen finagled it herself, I wouldn't put it past her. I used to like that girl, but I strongly suspect that she had something to do with the break between Hal and Terry. Ever since Terry returned his ring, he's been seen everywhere with Gen."

Merritt brought the flat of his hand down sharply on the card table. "I never did trust that little cat!" he cried. "I should have warned Terry against her. And I'd like to get my hands on that Forrester fellow if it's his fault they broke up!"

"If you hadn't insisted on waiting till New Year's to announce the engagement, he couldn't have got out of it," snapped his wife. "As it was, even though he'd given her a ring, it wasn't official, though of course the whole town knew about it. But still, technically, he wasn't committed."

"A man of honor would have considered himself committed the moment he asked my girl to marry him, announcement or no announcement," stormed Compton, cutting off the end of a cigar savagely.

"Well, actually, Terry has no one to blame but herself. She's got too much pride. Pride is a good thing, of course, but sometimes it's foolish." Isobel shuffled the cards, sighing. "In this case, I think it was foolish. No matter what happened, if she'd held him to it, Hal couldn't have got out of the engagement and continue to be received by our friends. She was a fool to let him go."

"But what *did* happen!" he roared. "That's what I want to know. All this side-stepping and secrecy. It's not like Terry at all. Why doesn't she come to me and tell me all about it?"

"If you want to know what I think, Merritt," said his wife with a smug little smile, "I think somehow Gen Lansing found out the whole story about Terry's mother and told Hal. He's a New Englander, very proper, very family-conscious, and he's new to the West. Can't you just see his blue blood curdle at the revelation that he was engaged to marry a girl whose mother was a cheap Variety actress and a divorcee!"

"That's enough!" With a violent sweep of his big hand he scattered the cards, pushed back his chair, flung his cigar into the fireplace. Leaning both palms on the table, he fixed her with a glare so terrible, so burning, that she drew back in alarm. "Never say that about Terry again. Let her mother alone, too. No matter what she is, she gave me the only child I'll ever have. Don't forget that, Isobel Vandergrift."

Isobel flushed, her lips trembled, and tears clouded her china-blue eyes. "You're a cruel, unfeeling man, Merritt Compton," she choked. "You know how I tried to give you a child. I've cried myself to sleep night after night because I couldn't have a baby of my own to love. When you brought Terry to me I accepted her. I tried to be a mother to her—I did my best——"

"You've never been a real mother to the girl, Isobel. You never could forget that she was Maizie's daughter. You never loved her and you tried your best to marry her off to this Forrester boy to get her out of your way."

Compton was in one of his rare, blind rages. His voice boomed without thought for the servants or the girl upstairs in her bedroom. "Maybe I can't blame you too much. I suppose you can't help being jealous. But I blame that slick, smooth-talking Easterner for breaking my girl's heart. So help me, I'll make it hot for him. If Beauchamp Deming wants to keep on getting his retaining fee as my lawyer, he'll fire Forrester tomorrow. I have *some* influence in this town. Very well, I'll use it to make sure Mr. Halloway Putnam Forrester, Third, can't get a decent job in Seattle and has to hightail it back to Massachusetts where nobody will upset his delicate sensibilities——"

"If you do that, Father, you'll make me even more unhappy than I am now," said Terry quietly.

Neither Merritt nor Isobel had heard the study door open,

nor did they know how long she had been standing there in the sprigged pink and blue foulard peignoir Isobel had given her for Christmas, her heavy chestnut hair unbound and falling almost to her waist, her face luminous in its pallor, her gray eyes enormous.

"Terry!" cried her father, wheeling. "I thought you were in bed."

"I was, Father. In bed, but not asleep." She gave him a swift, odd look and then glided across the room to Isobel, who was staring at her as if she were a revenant. Terry bent and laid her cheek against her stepmother's and said softly, "It's not your fault if you couldn't love me, Isobel. You did try and you've been good to me. I'm terribly sorry you couldn't have a daughter of your own to love and had to have me, instead."

Isobel sat stiffly, supported by her corsets, pressing her handkerchief to her swimming eyes, and her plump chin quivered uncontrollably. She opened her mouth to speak, but could not, reached up and patted Terry's cheek instead, then hid her face in her hands.

Terry looked at her father with dry, clear, steady eyes. "None of this is her fault, Father," she said. "It really isn't Hal's, either. So please don't take it out on them. If you're worried about me, don't be. I'll be all right." She gave him a faint smile. "My heart isn't quite broken, you see, just chipped a little."

She moved toward the door, but Compton barred the way. His hard hands came down on her slender, straight shoulders, appealingly soft under the thin negligee. His deep-set, burning eyes met hers and she did not flinch under his gaze. "Terry," he said, pressing his fingers into her flesh, in his urgency unaware that he was hurting her, "I don't know how much you heard just now. This, you must always remember, you are *my* daughter, you are a Compton. I'm proud of you and I love you. Don't forget that."

"I won't, Father," she whispered. "I'm proud to be your

daughter and a Compton. But I am my mother's daughter, too, and I'll never forget that, or her."

They stood for a moment staring at each other, and suddenly Terry leaned her head against him and wept. She made no sound and only the heaving of her body indicated that she was weeping. For the first time since she was a child, he held her and caressed her hair with his heavy, clumsily tender hand. For the first time since she had returned Hal's ring, Terry let herself give way to the anguish she had kept proudly to herself.

Oh, my beloved, he was thinking as his heart and his flesh took comfort from the surrender of her sorrow to him, can you ever forgive me for what I have done to you, my innocent? Isobel is not to blame, nor that stuffed shirt you wanted to marry. I, and I alone, am to blame. Is that what you are trying to tell me, my daughter, my beloved? Is that why you are weeping when I never saw you cry before? I promised myself that I'd protect you, keep you from all hurt, and here I am, powerless to stop your tears.

"Terry girl," he whispered, "I'm going up to the Skagit River Camp in a few weeks. Would you like to come with me, the way you used to when you were little, before you went away to school?"

A long shudder went through her; for a moment she clung to him, then she lifted her head, tears still bright in her eyes. "Oh, yes, Father, may I? I'd like it better than anything."

Isobel didn't approve, since it would mean that Terry would miss the June cotillions, which were probably the most important social events of the year. Also, she considered a logging camp a most unsuitable place for a young lady of quality to spend her vacation.

But ever since Terry had come to her defense that night in the study, Isobel had felt differently toward the girl. She was still jealous of her and she knew that Merritt, in some ways, was more devoted to her than to his wife, though since Terry had championed her, he had been gentler and more understanding. She now found herself hoping that the girl would find a good husband, not so much to get her out of the way, as for Terry herself to find happiness. Several times she'd lain awake nights wondering if things would have been different if she could have taken the child to her heart when she first came to them.

So when Terry told her she was planning to make the trip to the Skagit River Camp with Compton, Isobel stewed a bit; then, since both Terry and her father had made up their minds to it, busied herself seeing that Miss Florian turned out a beautifully tailored covert cloth divided riding skirt for Terry.

"Though why I should bother, I don't know," she'd sighed, "since no one will see you but a lot of rough lumberjacks!"

Seven

THEY made the first part of the trip by steamer up the Sound to Anacortes on one of Hugh Deming's fast new passenger boats, *Potlach*. It was the same route the *Kelpie* had taken the fall before. Terry, recognizing the course, pointed out places where they'd put in for supplies, or where they had anchored so the boys could fish or swim. Compton was relieved to see no sign in her face or voice that the memories hurt.

Terry herself was surprised and grateful that she felt no pangs at retracing that romantic cruise. Until the night she'd wept in her father's arms, she had nursed in secret the pain and shock of the awful day that Hal had come to the house, tight-lipped and withdrawn, and asked her to go walking with him in the park. But once she had given way to her misery, it had seemed to vanish. For a few days she'd felt lost without it, empty and exhausted. Then she had wakened one morning with a sense of well-being and energy surging over her. It was as if she'd been very ill for a while and was now, suddenly, well again.

Standing by her father in the bow of the steamer, with the green water cutting cleanly away from the plunging prow, the salt, stinging spray cold on her cheeks and lips, the long, low shape of Whidby Island pushing away the early morning fog on their right, she wondered how she could have been so miserable simply because a silly young man had felt he couldn't marry the daughter of a "notorious woman." Even the shock of learning what a false friend Gen Lansing had proven was gone. In the freshness of the morning, the figures of Hal Forrester and Gen seemed to dwindle until they became no bigger than dolls, with no more importance or meaning for her than the dolls she'd adored as a child but, having outgrown, had pushed into a closet and forgotten.

The ship's rail vibrated under her hand. The hissing prow turned a neat, green furrow, edged with boiling foam. Gulls rode the swells like serene little boats or rose with dangling red legs to veer and bank against the wind, one minute standing still in mid-air as if painted against the sky, and then, with a powerful upbeat of shining wings, climbing above the ship, crying hysterically, their shrill, wild voices sending a shiver of delight through the girl's body.

She breathed deeply the wet, bracing air, pungent with that mingling of rank sea smell and resinous-woods smell that makes Puget Sound air so exhilarating and haunting. The biting, tonic aroma of floating islands of dark-brown, shining kelp and seaweed dotting the channel; the boat smell of tarred ropes and paint and coal smoke blowing every which way from the red funnels of the steamer. From the island they were passing, the sharply sweet breath of the fog-damp forests of fir and spruce, cedar and hemlock hidden by the mists. She felt wonderfully alive, expectant, and best of all, *free*.

A white-coated steward emerged from the companionway, struck three low notes on a gong, and popped down again. Her father turned with a smile. "First call for breakfast, kiddie. Hungry?"

"Ravenous!" She thought she had never been so hungry in her life. In the dining salon, the round tables gleamed with crisp white linen and silver. The starched white tents of the napkins looked like an encampment. Terry had never got over her childhood delight in eating on a boat, looking out at the water.

The dining steward seated them at the side with portholes to look out, presented them with elaborate menus decorated with violently tinted photographs of Mount Rainier and various North Star steamships. They breakfasted on tender, pink-fleshed salmon trout, which, like Olympia oysters and Dungeness crabs, are the jealous pride of the Pacific Northwest and can never rightly be enjoyed anywhere else in the world, since they must be cooked with the cold freshness of the Sound still on them.

They each drank a pot of strong, black coffee, and as Merritt cut off the end of his after-breakfast cigar, he threw back his head, narrowed his eyes, and gave his daughter his long, appraising look. "Well, Terry? I guess you're all right now, eh?"

She smiled across the table at him, her color fresh and glowing from the wind, her eyes bright. "I'm fine, Father."

"Not still hankering after that young——"

She shook her head quickly, not wanting him to bring even the ghost of Hal Forrester to mind. "All over. Honest Injun. What I'm hankering for now is to get a horse under me and start up the trail to the Skagit Camp." She leaned forward, smiling reminiscently. "Is Ole Olssen still cook and does he still wear a derby hat in the kitchen?"

"You bet." Merritt chuckled. "One of the swampers pinched the derby last summer and Ole went after him with a meat cleaver. When Ole sees you, he's going to bust a gut. Ever since you went away to school and stopped coming to camp with me, he's been asking about you."

"It'll be like coming home, Father," she said. "How I hated the summers when Isobel made me stay in town and go to ladylike parties and picnics and dancing school."

He laughed. "I hated them too, kiddie. But Isobel was right.

You had to learn to be a proper young lady, you know. I couldn't teach you that, taking you off to the camps."

"If I'd been a boy, it'd have been different," she cried. "I've often wished I was, and I'll bet you have, too."

He shook his head and smiled. "I've never wished for you to be any different from what you are, Terry. Remember that."

Merritt went up on the bridge to talk to the captain, an old friend of his, and Terry went out on deck again and watched the fog lifting over the Sound and the sun striking the green water. Just as on that first trip with her father, the shyness and uncertainties that had built up between them in town melted away when they were headed for the woods and they felt natural and at ease with each other. I like my father, she thought, leaning on the rail. He treats me like a person and when I'm with him I can be myself, not somebody I think others expect me to be. Maybe, she thought, that's the real reason why Hal wouldn't marry me, because he had thought I was somebody I wasn't and he couldn't adjust himself to the person I really am.

Before the steamer docked at Anacortes, Terry changed from her fashionable traveling suit to the divided riding skirt, flannel shirt, and high laced boots. The freedom of the short skirt and comfortable, loose, man-tailored shirt was exhilarating, made her wish she could always dress that way. The boots, while sturdy enough for tramping the woods, were of a fine, light, soft calfskin, very supple and easy to walk in. Merritt had had them made specially for her by an old Mexican bootmaker.

Compton, waiting for her on deck as the steamer jockeyed into the slip, looked burly and rugged in his heavy plaid lumberjack shirt, levis stuffed into high-tops, with two waterproof ponchos slung over his shoulder in case of rain. Yet even dressed like any logger off for the woods, he looked commanding. A swift rush of pride and affection for him shone in

Terry's eyes as he turned, smiling, to take her grip. How puny and ineffectual Hal Forrester seemed in contrast, how conventional and overelegant, how *Eastern!* I'll never marry, she thought in quick decision, until I can find a man who measures up to Merritt Compton and to the West!

At Anacortes, they took the stage to Sedro-Woolley, where the old half-breed, Joe Samish, dark as an old saddle, wrinkled as the last winter apple on the bough, was waiting for them with the pack mule for their luggage and the Indian ponies to take them up the trail to the Skagit River Camp.

At school, the young ladies had worn long-skirted cumbersome riding habits and had sat sidesaddle. In the short divided skirt, Terry could sit her horse like a man. The big Western saddle felt solid and secure and she liked the feel of the pony's compact little body under her thighs.

They were good, wiry Indian ponies, small, knowledgeable, sure-footed, clever as goats on the trails. Terry dug her heels into the long stirrups, patted her pony's narrow buckskin neck, and clucked to him. He twitched one ear back and broke into a sweet canter. She let him run for a quarter of a mile, his long white mane streaming, then headed him back to the little caravan and took her place behind Compton on his stocky pinto. She knew that the pace had to be set by the slower, more heavily laden mule, which, in addition to their luggage, carried supplies for the camp: kippered salmon, corned beef in big tins, cans of butter and fruit, treats that Compton never failed to bring to the men on his visits.

Her father grinned at her as she swung into line. "Both of you feeling your oats, eh?"

"I couldn't resist letting him out to see what he could do," she laughed, patting the buckskin's neck. "He's a nice animal."

Presently the sawmills, busy and dusty, noisy with the whine and scream of saws, and the sprawling ranch houses, where white, long-legged chickens were scattered like bits of torn paper over the ragged fields, were behind them. They left the

90

highway and turned off onto the river trail that for a while was enclosed on both sides by second-growth spruce and hemlock and heavy, close-packed underbrush: lush, shiny salal, salmonberry bright with orange-pink blossoms, Oregon grape, dark green and spiny-leaved with tiny clusters of pale yellow flowers, low, thick huckleberry bushes, and wild roses adrift in pink and white.

Then one green wall fell away and the river, whose rush and roar had been muted by the heavy growth, leaped into sight, flashing like a silver sword in the sun, its voice dark and thunderous. The rich, close, earthy scents of trees and shrubs gave way to the fresh cold wet river smell, a wild, wilderness fragrance that had the breath of the mountains and snow and pure, cold winds in it. They stopped to drink and to water the animals, and though they'd had lunch in Sedro-Woolley, Joe Samish brought out a packet of thick ham sandwiches he'd had his wife put up for them and they squatted on the riverbank and ate them hungrily.

That night they made camp on the riverbank, deep in the forest, with towering Douglas firs sighing above them, the first stars very far away, pricking through the dark interlocking branches, a lonely night wind troubling the treetops. The Siwash unpacked supplies and blankets, built a small, careful squaw fire in the clearing, cut fir boughs for their beds, while Terry and her father went fishing up and down the bank.

Between them they caught enough cutthroat trout for a fine supper, which Compton cooked himself in the big iron skillet over a bed of coals. No food ever tasted as wonderful, Terry thought, as fresh-caught river trout, crisp bacon, and steaming, black coffee cooked out of doors with the smell of fir boughs, wood smoke, and running water to give it flavor.

She was bone-weary from long hours in the saddle, the blessed tiredness that makes you aware of every muscle in your body and asks for nothing better than to roll up in a blanket, stretch out on a bed of springy fir boughs, breathe one deep heart-satisfying breath of wild, sweet air, and know no more until the clang of a spoon on a frying pan wakes you for breakfast before the sun is up.

Next day the going was slower, for the trail veered away from the riverbank and began to climb. Chipmunks chattered at them from the trees, flicking their saucy tails; jays scolded and flashed, blue and white, across the path. Once a black bear lumbered through the brush and, smelling the horses, plunged down the steep side with a crackling of twigs and branches. Once they saw an eagle poised dead-still above them in the high, blue sky.

At one place they entered a dead forest of bare, silvery spires, where wild blackberry vines in vivid green growth were busily trying to cover the ravages of some terrible holocaust. Compton pulled up his pony and pointed to the ghostly silver forest and his voice was stern and biting. "Look at that, Terry. Once that was a fine stand of Douglas fir. Look at it now. It's enough to break your heart."

"What happened, Father?" she cried. "A forest fire?"

"Yes. A forest fire, caused by careless loggers burning slashings." He brought his fist down viciously on his pommel and the pinto danced in pretended alarm. "Forest fires are the curse of the Northwest. Some of them can't be helped, those that are set by lightning. But most of them are the result of foolishness." He sounded like a prophet excoriating wickedness. "Some people think the timber will last forever—there's so much of it, it'll never run out. But it takes a good thirty years to grow a fir big enough to market, and a stupid fool can destroy a whole forest in a few hours. If I had my way, any man proven guilty of starting a forest fire, whether by design or accident, would be treated as a murderer and strung up. And any logging company that lets its men burn slashings carelessly ought to be put out of business!"

They reached the Skagit River Camp at dusk that same day.

For several miles they had been following the abandoned skid road which suddenly led into a vast clearing, amid tree stumps, piles of sawdust and yellow chips. The air was dry and dusty and smelled of freshly cut timber, of resin, and in the slanting rays of the setting sun, a shimmering golden haze hung over the camp. Mules and horses were grazing in a wild pasture fenced off from the camp, and they raised their ears, gazed at the new arrivals, and whickered. Smoke rose in thin blue streamers from the cookhouse. But there was not a soul in sight.

Compton turned in his saddle and said to Terry, "Must all be in the cookhouse at chow." He swung off his pony, helped Terry to dismount, and left the Siwash to unload the pack mule and pasture the ponies.

As they rounded the corner of the cookhouse, they came upon a curious sight. A silent, tense ring of lumberjacks was standing or squatting, watching two men fighting. There was no sound but the grunts and heavy breathing of the antagonists and the sudden sharp intake of breath or a sympathetic grunt from the onlookers when a particularly telling blow landed. So intent were they on the battle that the newcomers walked over unnoticed to the outer fringe of the circle. Terry caught hold of her father's arm and held it tightly.

The two fighters were giants. Stripped to the waist, barefoot, wearing nothing but faded blue levis, they looked like savages. Sweat and blood were shiny on their naked bodies. They followed no rules, fought like animals; now entwined in a passionate embrace, now panting and snorting when one of them broke loose, then coming together with lowered heads like rutting stags. They slugged each other viciously, murderously.

One of the giants was blond, almost an albino, with a thatch of tow-white hair, a white torso now pink from his opponent's blows and striped with blood. The other had black, curly hair and his body was burned to a rich mahogany. Suddenly the albino kneed the other man below the belt and he doubled up, fell to his knees, while a rumble of anger and disapproval went up from the crowd.

"Fight fair, Swede!" roared a hoarse, angry voice. "Let him get up. On your feet, Matt!"

But the Swede had already thrown himself on his adversary's back and was slowly grinding him to the earth. Terry's fingers dug into her father's arm and she had to grit her teeth to keep from crying out in protest. With a sudden twist of his powerful back, the black-haired fighter threw off his assailant, leaped to his feet, breathing hard, while the other man picked himself up.

"Come and get it, Swede!" he cried, a slow, relentless grin pulling back his bleeding lips.

He danced gracefully just out of reach as the Swede lunged forward, bellowing like a bull, and met the carefully aimed, shattering uppercut on the jaw. With a sigh he dropped to the ground on his back, his arms spread wide, and lay still. A shout went up from the spectators, and Terry hid her face against her father, feeling sick.

The victor stood a moment, tense and ready for attack, and then, seeing that the big albino was not going to get up, bent over him. The Swede's eyes were closed and a thin trickle of blood oozed out of his loose mouth. The tense circle of onlookers broke. Two of the men ran out and picked up the limp body of the fallen gladiator. The others converged on the winner, laughing, shouting, clapping him on the back. Somebody tossed him his shirt, which he used to wipe the blood and sweat off his face before putting on.

Jack Dobie, the foreman, turned and saw Terry and her father. "Merritt! What the devil!" he cried, grinning and hurrying up to them. "I didn't see you come into camp. Some fight, eh?"

Compton gripped his hand. "Bully fight, Jack. Who's the black-haired guy who knocked out that low-hitting Swede?"

"That's Matt Regan, the high-climber from Michigan. The fellow who talked you into trying 'high-lead' logging last fall."

"I should have recognized him." Merritt laughed. "He's a fighter, all right. Thought he was going to slug me in my office when I didn't cotton to his scheme right off. How's it going?"

"Darn well, Merritt. We haven't got it licked yet and Matt's the only skilled topper in camp, but I can see it revolutionizing logging in the Northwest," cried the foreman.

"You don't say?" Compton smiled. "Well, we'll have a chance to talk about it later."

The triumphal party surged past, too excited to notice the newcomers, but as the Irishman, still panting from his fight, came abreast of the girl, he lifted his head and saw her. Their eyes met for an instant and he smiled jauntily. But Terry, shaken by the brutality of the fight, which was the first time she had seen two human beings maul and batter each other with such savagery, could not return his smile. She gave him a sober, frightened look and turned away, her face pale.

As Dobie led the way to the cabin which had been prepared for them, her father took her arm and, feeling it tremble, looked at her in concern. "What's the matter, Terry?"

"Nothing. I guess I'm just tired," she murmured, evading his gaze.

"Yes," he said, frowning at her look of whiteness and exhaustion, "you're tired and you're upset. I had no business letting you see that fight, kiddie. It wasn't a pretty sight for a young girl. I'm sorry." He gave her arm a squeeze. "I'll have Ole send you some supper on a tray. No need for you to come to the cookhouse tonight."

But she moved away from his arm, erect and independent. "I'm all right now, Father. I'll eat my supper with you at the cookhouse."

Eight

THE men were subdued at supper. They had clomped in their heavy, calked boots into the cookhouse, laughing, cutting capers, shouting good-natured cracks, full of the vicarious stimulation of the good fight they'd just seen, which had ended in victory for the Irishman they liked and defeat for the Swede who was a sorehead and a "boomer." Someone had started up a rowdy lumberjack song and they'd roared it out, beating time with their forks, intermittently yelling for "cookee" and "grub."

Then someone passed the word that the Boss and his daughter were in camp and on their way to supper, and like a wind blowing over a wheat field, the news had rippled through the cookhouse, silencing the loud voices and the exuberance. When Compton and the tall, pale girl in the tan riding skirt and tailored flannel shirt, which she'd brightened for supper with a blue scarf, entered the mess hall, the place was as quiet as a schoolroom when the principal comes to visit.

Jack Dobie, a slight, wiry, middle-aged man with thinning hair, pale blue, heavy-lidded eyes, and a lean, weather-beaten face deeply grooved by the disappointments and sorrows of a life in which luck had consistently been against him, got up from his seat at the smaller of the two long tables and motioned to the latecomers.

All eyes were on the girl as her father pulled out her chair and seated her, but the moment she lifted her head and looked up, every man was studiously regarding his plate. Except one. As if drawn by a magnet, the girl slowly turned her head and met the intense blue gaze of the black Irishman. There was a faint, arrogant smile on his bruised and swollen lips and he continued to stare at her until the color washed over her pale cheeks and she looked away.

Then the cook and his helper trotted in with trays piled high with great platters of steaming stew, tureens of boiled potatoes, huge bowls of mashed turnips, mountains of home-baked, soggy bread, and hunger took the place of curiosity as the men dived into the food. Long arms reached out and speared potatoes and bread; platters were emptied as soon as they were put down and the cook's helper went running back to the kitchen to fill them up again.

Ole Olssen, wearing his famous black derby, paused at Dobie's table, wiped his palms down his long white apron, and shook hands with Compton and Terry, who was delighted to see a familiar face. Except for Ole and the foreman, there was no one in camp now who had been there when she was a child.

"By golly, it ain't liddle Terry, all grown up so big and fine!" chuckled the cook, beaming at her. "You bane yoong lady now, kiddie! I bet you don't climb trees no more, hey?"

All through the meal Terry was conscious both of the shyness of the other men who, if she looked up suddenly and caught their eyes on her, instantly bent again to their plates, and of the boldness of Matt Regan's gaze. He ate with as much gusto as the others, but he scarcely took his eyes off her, except to help himself to more stew or to grab the arm of the sweating boy waiting table and ask for more coffee.

The men galloped through the meal as if they were catching

a train, stampeded out the door as soon as the last scrap of apple pie was gone. Matt Regan was the last to go, filling his pipe from a cloth sack of tobacco as he went. At the door he paused, stuffed the sack into his shirt pocket, leaned against the wall as he got his pipe going, looking across the room at Terry. She knew his eyes were on her and the color bloomed in her cheeks, but she was determined not to look up. When she did, he was gone and she was both relieved and disappointed.

After supper Terry, her father, and Dobie took a stroll around camp in the water-fresh coolness of river dusk. There were still some logs waiting to be skidded down the steep bank into the river, for when the bull cook clanged the triangle for chow, the men dropped everything and ran. Compton inspected the logs carefully for soundness and size.

"You're cutting them smaller this year, Jack," he observed. "These look like second-growth trees to me."

Dobie nodded. "Most of the big stuff is gone from this stand, Merritt. We're still getting Number One Sitka spruce and hemlock, but the big Douglas are pretty well logged out. I figure it's about time to move camp farther up the slopes."

Compton puffed on a cigar, one foot resting on a log. "I don't like to take the smaller stuff," he said thoughtfully. "Figured I wouldn't have to touch it in my lifetime, leave it for the next generation. I thought it'd be years yet before the big fellows ran out on this chance."

"It would have been, Merritt, the careful way you log. But that fire three years ago that started over the divide on Steiner's tract took some of our best timber." Dobie's voice was bitter and he shook his head. "That's the hell of it. Steiner's crews are careless, burning slashings, a fire gets going, a wind blows it our way, and before we can control it, a hundred acres of Compton timber have gone up in smoke!"

"I know, Jack. Nineteen hundred and two was a terrible year

for forest fires in the Northwest. From Coos Bay to Bellingham and from Enumclaw to the ocean, they raged like tornadoes. Why, down in Seattle, we didn't see the sun for three weeks because of the smoke."

Compton laid his arm affectionately across Dobie's shoulder, moved away from the logs. He was fond of the wiry, little man who was so able and dependable and so dogged by bad luck; lost his own timber through fire and hadn't capital to start over; lost his wife and only child in a diphtheria epidemic. Dobie had never remarried and if he occasionally solaced himself with the company of a certain black-eyed half-breed waitress down in Sedro-Woolley, no one blamed him, least of all Merritt.

"Fact is," said Compton confidentially, "I've been thinking of acquiring more land. Wanted to do it a year or so ago, but money was pretty tight and I decided to wait till after the elections. Now that Teddy Roosevelt is in the White House again, things are settling down. Looks as if he's going to do something about conservation, too."

"Darn well better," rumbled Dobie. "About time somebody did. The way they're taking the timber out here it won't be long before the Northwest is logged off like Minnesota and Michigan. Wish you could get Steiner to sell. He's too close for comfort, and in spite of the fire, he's still got a lot of good timber over there."

"That's exactly what I had in mind, Jack. We'll go over it all tomorrow. Now, what about this high-flying scheme of that wild Irishman's—this high-lead logging? What d'ye think of it?"

"By golly, Merritt, I'm all for it," said the foreman eagerly. "You told me to go slow, so I haven't changed over completely. Couldn't if I wanted to—haven't enough skilled men who understand it. Regan's the only professional topper I've got. But he's been training Red and Tommy, a couple of

99

fallers, and with just the three of them handling the spars, we've got out more logs so far than the whole camp working with the donkeys alone."

"According to what Regan told me last fall when he put it up to me, they've been doing it in Michigan for years," said Merritt thoughtfully.

"That's right, Merritt. A fella named Butters, Horace Butters, started it in his Michigan camp about 1886 or '7. Regan worked for his son back there before he drifted West. That's where he learned it."

Terry, who had been quietly listening to their talk as she used to when she was a child, at mention of the Irishman was curious enough to venture a question. "What do you mean by high-lead logging, Mr. Dobie? And why is it better than the old way?"

They all sat down on a fallen log while the foreman explained. "It's faster this way, Terry, and better for the logs. They don't get scratched up and gouged as they do when they're hauled through the brush, and it saves the small stuff from getting knocked down and broken.

"You know how we used to log—how everyone does it out here. The fallers take down the trees, the buckers saw 'em into logs. Then they're attached by chokers to a cable, hauled by donkey engines to the skids, and shot down into the river or loaded onto lumber trains if there's no water handy. Before the donkeys came along, we used bull teams or mules to haul them down the skid road."

Terry nodded, remembering her father's stories of the bull teams and how, in the old days when he was a boy, they greased the skid roads with tallow, axle grease, dogfish oil, and once, with rancid butter thrown out by a restaurant.

"This way, we take 'em through the air." Dobie smiled at her look of incredulity. "That's a fact, Terry. Regan, the topper, goes up a spar tree, a two-hundred-foot Douglas, say, chopping and sawing off all the branches on his way up. Then he saws off the top. Red goes up with a cable and shiv and rigs the spar. Regan tops another tree in line with the first one; Red goes up and attaches another cable to it, and so on. A long wire rope attached to the cable is chokered onto your log. We start the donkey engine, which operates the shiv or pulley, and the log is carried through the air from spar tree to spar tree, till we get it where we want to skid it into the river."

"Isn't it awfully dangerous?" cried Terry.

"It takes a good man to be a topper, all right," replied the foreman soberly. "Matt says in the old days when Butters first began his high-lead operations, they used what they called 'springboards'—small platforms just wide enough for a man to stand on. They'd make their way up by chopping notches in the bark, insert the springboard, saw off all the branches they could reach, then set another springboard a few feet higher. It was slow and dangerous, as you can imagine. Wait till you see the kickback on a big Douglas just after it's been topped and imagine trying to keep your balance on a narrow board stuck into the side way up in the air."

"How does Regan get up the trees?" asked Compton, knocking the ashes off his cigar and carefully grinding them into the dirt with his toe. "I know he requisitioned a lot of fancy equipment from the Roebling people."

"Well, by the time Matt started high-climbing, they were using iron spurs, like telephone linemen, and a climbing rope. It's still no game for an amateur. I don't see how he does it, myself. Matt tried to show me, but I couldn't get the hang of it. Too old, I guess." Dobie laughed ruefully, took out papers and a sack of Bull Durham to roll a cigarette in his thin, freckled fingers.

"If it's so good, I wonder why it hasn't been tried out here before?" mused Compton. "I mentioned it to a couple of lumbermen at a Whoo-Whoo lodge meeting this winter and they'd never heard of it."

"Takes a while for us to get the new things out West, Merritt. Maybe there aren't enough skilled high-climbers, and most of 'em stay East or die young." Dobie grinned and shrugged. "What the devil, anyhow. Sooner or later, it'll catch on out here, but no need for us to spread the word, eh? Let 'em wonder how come we can get the logs out so much faster."

"You've got something there, Jack," laughed Compton.

Terry left them still talking high-lead, and wandered away in the green evening coolness which was full of the sleepy, querulous, settling-down noises of innumerable small birds in the bushes and branches, and came to the tinkling little brook that divided the camp, where she'd spent long, golden summer hours wading in its icy water till her feet were red and numb, catching minnows with her hands. The spruce she'd fallen out of when she broke her arm was still there, its dark green, heavy boughs sweeping down to the stream. She smiled up at it and murmured, "Ole doesn't think I can climb trees any more now that I bane yoong lady. But I yoost bet I can."

With a quick glance to see that her father and Dobie were deep in conversation and heading back toward the cabin, she caught one of the lower branches and swung herself up. It wasn't as easy in her riding skirt and boots as it used to be in her boy's jeans and sneakers, but she managed to climb to a higher, stouter bough where, hidden in the prickly thick branches, she could peek out at the camp, feeling again the delicious sense of surveying the world from on high, knowing that no one could see her.

She watched the bull cook come out of the cookhouse and throw a basin of dishwater off the porch, whistling, and pausing a moment to stretch his tired back and take a deep breath of the woodsy air. A group of loggers were pitching horseshoes behind the bunkhouse and she heard the sharp ring of metal and the shouts of the players. Her father and Dobie disappeared into the cabin and shut the door. Someone was splitting firewood by the shed. One of the ponies, pastured with the camp horses, lifted his head and whinnied softly. Three men emerged from the bunkhouse, arm in arm, with the tall, black-haired one in the middle, and came stumbling toward the brook, singing "In the Shade of the Old Apple Tree," in close harmony.

By the time Terry realized they were headed in her direction, it was too late to climb down from her tree without being seen. This wouldn't have bothered "liddle Terry" in her levis, but it would certainly embarrass the "yoong lady" in her smartly tailored riding skirt, especially since she'd recognized the dark man in the middle as Matt Regan. She was trapped and the only thing she could do was to stay hidden in the spruce and hope they'd move on soon.

But when they reached the brook they squatted down on the bank under the spruce, talking and laughing and evidently passing a bottle around. Terry knew that drinking in camp was strictly forbidden.

One of the men evidently remembered it and said, "Better not let Dobie or the Big Boss see that bottle, Matt."

"And since when have I been afraid o' bosses, Red, me boyo? And am I not as good or better, better, I say, than the two o' them?" cried a strong, humorous, uninhibited voice. "I'd like to see Dobie or Mr. Merritt Compton, Esquire, lay out Swede Peterson cold, I would."

"You're right, Matt," agreed a younger voice eagerly. "Compton's a fine, big man, but I'll bet he's not the fighter you are. Boy, that was lovely, the way you caught ole Swede on the chin."

The first man laughed. "The squarehead never knew what hit him."

"Let's have a drink on it, Matt," cried the younger man. "To Swede, who never knew what hit him, and to Matt Regan, the best logger, topper, and fighter in Skagit County."

"Skagit County, is it?" cried Matt Regan. "'Tis hardly worth passing the bottle for, Tommy."

"I wasn't through, Matt, best logger and fighter in Skagit County and the whole Pacific Northwest!"

"Thank ye, lad. I might add the Michigan woods, too, but being a modest man, I'll let it pass."

The bottle was handed round and there ensued a tranquil, reflective silence. Terry, cramped in the tree, wished they'd finish the bottle and move on. But they showed no signs of budging.

"Well, now," said the first man. "Let's drink to Boss Compton and to Miss Terry, his strapping daughter. By golly, there's a handsome wench, eh, Matt?"

"Watch yer tongue, Red," muttered the Irishman.

"Whatsa matter, Matt? I didn't say nothin'."

"Watch it, that's all."

"Since when did you get elected president of the Watch and Ward Society, Irish? I seen you eyin' her at supper. Seen her givin' you the eye, too," drawled Red, sniggering.

There was a quick scuffle, and peeping through the branches, her face scarlet but her eyes curious, Terry saw the big Irishman grab the brawny, red-headed logger by the shirt. "So help me, if ye don't shut up that kind o' talk, Red, I'll bust yer face wide open."

The third man, a blond, downy-faced youngster not more than twenty, pulled them apart, laughing tipsily. "Aw, knock it off, boys. Don't spoil our lil' party by fightin'."

Regan shoved Red away from him angrily and they both sat down on the bank and drank from the bottle again, moodily.

"Aw, Matt," complained Red in a hurt voice, "you got no call getting tough with me. How'd I know you was sweet on Compton's daughter?"

"Who says I'm sweet on her?" roared the Irishman. "She's nothing to me. I never saw her until t'night. But she's a lady, ye lunk-head. Ye don't talk about her kind like she was one o' them gals down in Sedro-Woolley."

"Okay. Okay. I apologize to Miss Compton. And to you,

Matt. But speaking of Sedro-Woolley, wasn't it on account of Rita at the Gem Café you and Axel tried to ruin each other t'day?"

Matt took another swallow from the bottle, wiped his mouth with his sleeve, and sighed deeply. "She had something to do with it, I'll grant ye. But the Swede and I have hated each other's guts ever since I came to this camp."

"I thought Rita was Dobie's girl, Matt," said the youngster.

"She's anyone's girl, Tommy. Only poor old Dobie don't know it and keeps on footing her bills. Axel got sore on account of he couldn't make time with her and I did. He was gonna tell Dobie I'd cut him out with Rita. That's why I fought him."

Red snickered. "She must be quite a gal to make you and Swede tear into each other the way you did."

"It wasn't on her account, Red!" cried Regan hotly. "Ye think I'd fight over her? I like Dobie and he's had a lot o' bad luck. If he wants to think Rita's his girl, no white-headed louse of a Swede is gonna bust holes in his balloon."

"Terry. . . . Ter-ry!" From the cabin Merritt Compton stood cupping his hands and calling.

"Come on, fellas, we better high-tail it back to the bunk-house before the Big Boss starts nosin' around," said Tommy in a whisper. The three men got to their feet and catfooted it across the clearing toward the camp buildings.

Terry dropped quickly down from the tree, her legs and feet cramped and tingling from her long vigil. Her face was still burning with shame when she met her father in front of their cabin, but fortunately it was too dark by then for him to see her embarrassment.

"Oh, there you are, kiddie," he cried in relief. "I'm sorry the way we left you, but Dobie and I got talking."

"That's all right, Father. I took a walk by myself. But I think I'm ready to turn in now."

"You must be dead tired, Terry. It's been quite a day for you."

In the darkness she smiled. "Oh yes, quite a day, Father."

But tired as she was and grateful for the bed, made up with clean cotton blankets in lieu of sheets, she found it hard to get to sleep. She continued to burn with shame and a kind of horrible excitement every time she thought of the crude man-talk she'd overheard. How awful to know that men talked like that about women—not just bad women, like that Rita the fight had been over, but about nice women, like herself. Did all men talk that way when they were together, or only just rough lumberjacks?

But she remembered how angry the Irishman had been at what Red had said about her, and she sat up in bed and looked at the bar of moonlight striping the floor and heard an owl hoo-hooing off in the woods, and thought, *He* isn't like the others. He wouldn't let them talk that way about me. And yet, remembering how his eyes had held hers at supper, his smile when he looked up and saw her after the fight, she shivered and put her hands up to her hot cheeks.

Nine

THAT night, Matt Regan had his Irish up. He and Red and Tommy had done too much celebrating, but Matt had been known to finish off a bottle alone and unassisted and still stay on his feet.

Whether it was the fight and the intoxication of his triumph over Swede, or the fact that there was a desirable and inaccessible woman in camp, or the resentment Matt always felt when the Big Boss was around, an old resentment not directed at Merritt Compton personally but at him as a symbol of the Boss, against whom the Irishman's whole nature was in rebellion—at any rate, Matt was belligerent.

The boys in the bunkhouse started talking about the Boss's daughter, first with admiration and speculation, then with more imagination. "By golly, she's a fine big girl!" cried Jake, a bucker. "I could really go for her."

"Aw, she ain't my type," retorted one of the fallers. "Too big and lanky. I like 'em little and snuggly."

Regan got up and, without warning, grabbed both men off their bunks and, holding each one by the shirt, shook them till their teeth rattled. "The Boss's daughter is a lady," he roared. "An' she's the most beautiful creature God ever made.

107

She's Helen of Troy and Deirdre, the Irish Queen and Lillian Russell all rolled into one. Don't ye dare foul her name by speakin' it with yer dirty mouths!"

"I don't know who them other dames are, Matt, but I'll take Lillian Russell, m'self," yelled someone, and the men howled with laughter.

Matt threw the two men back onto their bunks as if they'd been bundles of dirty rags, strode out into the middle of the floor, a black, angry giant with doubled fists swinging. "The next one to make a crack about Miss Compton gets a taste o' what I gave the Swede t'day."

Silence fell upon the bunkhouse and then Tommy's high, tipsy young voice rang out. "Fer Pete's sake, fellas, lay off the Boss's daughter. Can't ye see she's Matt Regan's lady?"

Matt whirled, his face crimson, but the boy ducked out the door and when he sneaked in again later, Matt was stretched out on his bunk, snoring.

In the morning Dobie himself had to rout Matt out of bed. When he didn't appear at breakfast, Red and Tommy, bleary-eyed, but on deck, said he was sick. It was Axel Peterson, now recovered from the beating the Irishman had given him, who went up to the foreman after breakfast and said, "Regan ain't sick. He's sleepin' it off."

Jack Dobie didn't like the Swede and he'd been glad Matt had licked him the day before. He knew nothing of the cause of the fight, other than that in his experience in logging camps the Irish and the Swedes usually hated each other on sight. It had been a clean fight, except for the once that Peterson had fouled Regan, and it had been out in the open with bare fists, not a knifing in the dark. Since Compton hadn't objected to it, he had let it ride. But drinking in camp was something else again. The rules about it were rigid and all the men knew and respected them. Dobie was disappointed that Regan, the ablest and most intelligent man in camp, should have flouted them.

"All right, Matt," he said, shaking his shoulder. "On your feet. Where did you get the brew?"

Matt shook his head and pawed at his face, wiping away invisible cobwebs.

"The fairies brought it to me, Jacko, bless their black hearts."

"You know darn well it's against the rules to bring beer into camp."

"Then 'tis the wee people, the small, green folks, ye'd better be scoldin', not honest Matt Regan, Jacko."

Dobie pulled off the blanket and threw it on the floor. "Look, Regan, don't give me that Irish blarney of yours. You know Compton is here on an inspection tour and he wants to see the high-lead stuff in operation. You're the only topper in camp and if you can't work, we lose a day."

"Did I ever make you lose a day yet, Jack Dobic?" asked Matt reproachfully, swinging himself off the bunk and blinking at the cruel sunlight coming in the open door. "Who says I can't work?"

"I say so. You're in no shape to go aloft. Between the bruises you got fighting the Swede and your little party last night, you're in great condition! Look at yourself. You can't even open your eyes!"

"I can climb trees with me eyes shut, lad. Jist give me a chance to wash the cobwebs off me face and a half dozen eggs and·a pot o' coffee into me belly and I'll be nimble as a monkey."

Half an hour later, Matt came swaggering up to Dobie, who was standing with Compton and his daughter outside the foreman's shack. His eyes were still bloodshot, but his black curls were wet and his rugged face glowing from the bucket of cold spring water Tommy had sloshed over him as he stood, raw as a bird, dancing up and down behind the bunkhouse. He met Compton's deepset gaze, but avoided glancing at the girl.

He needn't have worried, she was as intent on avoiding him.

"Mr. Compton doesn't think you should go aloft today, Matt," said Dobie. "We can't take the responsibility."

"Sure, that's kind of Mr. Compton, indeed," replied Matt scornfully, speaking directly to the foreman. "But I'll take the responsibility, thanks. It's aloft I'm going, Jack."

Dobie glanced at Compton, who gave no sign, studied the end of his cigar. Merritt never gave orders to the men, always left his foremen free to handle their own problems. He was annoyed at Dobie for having told Regan it was his decision. Actually, when Jack had asked his opinion, he'd said it was up to the foreman, that he himself had made it clear to Regan from the beginning that his high-lead stunt was on his own and that if he got hurt it was his own lookout.

"Okay, Matt," said Dobie reluctantly. "It's up to you if you want to take the chance. But whether you work today or not, you still get fined a week's pay for your celebration last night. That's the rule and you know it."

"I do, indeed, Jack," replied the Irishman easily, as if the money were too slight an issue to mention. "I accept the fine and I accept the responsibility for breaking me neck, which I won't do." With a nod in Compton's direction, he strode off and joined the men getting ready to go into the woods.

"He accepts the fine and the responsibility, he says!" growled Dobie. "That impudent Irish fool! I'd hope he'd break his cocky neck except that he's the best man I've got, and besides, I like the black devil."

"Did he tell you where he got the beer?" asked Merritt, a smile twitching his hard mouth.

"He said the fairies brought it to him, the wee, green folk!"

Compton exploded in laughter and Terry couldn't keep her face straight, either. The moment she'd seen Matt Regan swagger toward them, she'd stiffened with embarrassment. If he'd once looked her way, she was sure he'd have known from her blushes that she'd been up the tree listening to him and his pals last night.

"I want to watch this fellow work," said Merritt. "I'd like to see if his wee, green folk can keep him from falling out of a tree."

"If they don't, you may be sure St. Patrick will," laughed Dobie ruefully. "He's got the luck of the Irish, all right. Never saw a man less concerned about his life and limbs. Wait till you see him top a 150-foot Douglas. And you should have watched him fighting Steiner's forest fire. Two of our men were knocked out by smoke and Regan brought them in. He was stripped to the waist, his pants half burned off, and he was black as the pit. You'd have thought he was ready to quit. But Tommy comes running, yelling that the fire has jumped the divide and is into our best stand of firs, so off he goes with shovel and ax and a pack of weary men at his back. By golly, Merritt, if it hadn't been for Regan, we might not have this camp here today."

"That wasn't luck!" cried Compton. "That was just plain, old-fashioned guts. Come along, Terry, don't you want to see this Northwestern Paul Bunyan in action?"

By the time they caught up with the men who were cutting Sitka spruce half a mile up the river, Regan was sixty feet up a giant Douglas that Dobie estimated at between 150 and 160 feet tall. Supported only by a leather safety belt, with his climbing rope cinched around the trunk, spurs dug into the stout bark, the topper was hacking at the first small branches with his ax, which, like the saw, when not in use dangled from a rope at his belt. The feathery branches floated lazily down through the morning sunshine with a soft swish, crackling as they hit the underbrush below.

Having disposed of all the branches within reach, the Irishman flipped loose his climbing rope, and with a movement as swift and subtle as an intricate ballet step, kicked his spurs free as he threw the rope higher up the tree. The rope arced in the air, encircled the tree, and was instantly jerked tight again to the safety belt, which, in a movement too swift for the watchers below to catch, had been pushed farther up the trunk, too. For a moment the climber dangled in thin air before his spurs bit into the bark again. Terry held her breath and felt her heart pound, until the spurs caught and clung.

"It's like rubbing your head and patting your stomach at the same time," said Compton in open admiration. "Only at 150 feet in the air. By golly, that takes more than guts, Jack. That takes perfect co-ordination, timing, and balance, as well as muscles of steel!"

"As I said, it's no job for an amateur," smiled Dobie, who had his watch open in his hand. "That's why, I think, nobody else out here has gone in for high-lead logging. There are lots of men with guts and brawn, but this takes brains, too."

Now the branches were thick enough so that the topper had to use his saw, and when they flew off the tree and crashed to earth, they were as big as young logs.

"For a man with a hangover, Jack, your Irishman seems to be making out all right," observed Compton.

Dobie nodded. "So far, so good. He hasn't reached the top yet. I hope he can judge the undercut right."

"Is the hardest part the topping of the tree, Mr. Dobie?" Terry's throat was dry and her eyes glittered with excitement and strain. In her imagination, every time the topper threw the climbing rope and moved farther up the tree, she saw him hurtling to earth like the branches. Sweat prickled under her arms as it had the night of her debut, and she didn't know if she could bear to watch that casual, debonair figure go much higher, yet she knew she couldn't take her eyes off him.

"It's chancy, Terry," replied the foreman grimly. "A lot of things can go wrong. If the undercut is placed right, if the tree doesn't split or the top twist as it falls, everything will be fine.

Matt's best friend back in Michigan was killed when a tree he was topping split."

Compton glanced at the girl and saw her go white. He was beginning to feel nervous himself. The jaunty figure of the man now nearly 150 feet in the air seemed lonely and vulnerable. All the lower branches were gone; there remained only the narrow, pointed top and as they watched, craning their necks, Matt reached behind him for the saw.

The other loggers who had been working in the spruce had gradually ceased their sawing and chopping and gathered around the base of the great tree. Red and Tommy had been watching tensely for some time. But now it was as though the whole forest paused and held its breath.

"He's going to place the undercut now," murmured Dobie. No one else spoke. There was a curious sense of awe and tension among the loggers. In silence they watched, with sober faces, every eye on the small, unprotected figure of the man clinging to the naked, towering spar.

He was so far above them that the sound of the saw was only a faint, high keening. Then there was the sudden cra-a-ck! of breaking timber. Terry shivered and there was a queer rushing in her ears, and as she watched, the tall, spirelike top began to tilt, eased over slowly, slowly, as if in a dream, then, suddenly free of the tree, with a strange, whistling sound plummeted through the air and crashed to earth, splintering the young growth in its path.

As the top broke away, the great tree rocked wildly back and forth, whipping the tiny figure of the man clinging to it angrily, as if he were a parasite the giant was trying to dislodge. Oh, dear Lord, thought Terry, he can't hold on. The safety belt is sure to snap! But the parasite held fast, and after what seemed hours the tree righted itself and was still, and from the loggers there rose a great shout. They clapped each other's backs, danced, swore, cheered. Far above, the topper looked down and waved in triumph. Terry wanted to shout with the men, too; instead, she grabbed her father's arm and hugged it, crying, "Oh, wasn't it wonderful, Father? I was so scared I feel all shaky inside."

"A good clean job," replied her father, smiling at her. "I feel a bit weak, myself."

Dobie let out a great sigh, and Terry, seeing the look of relief on his sober face, knew that he'd been scared, too. "That blasted Irishman. He's never topped a bad tree, yet. But I thought he'd pushed his luck too far, today. Thank God I was wrong."

The loggers waited till Regan had descended, which took much less time than getting to the top, and when he kicked his spurs loose and dropped to his feet, they were all over him, thumping his back and making much of him.

The foreman turned to Compton with a wry smile. "See what makes him so cocky? He's a king to the rest of the loggers."

Matt broke away from his admirers, who went back to work, and swaggered up to Dobie with an arrogant smile. "Well, Jack, me lad, didn't I tell ye I could climb with me eyes shut?"

"One day you'll push that Irish luck of yours too far, Matt," said Dobie soberly.

Compton extended his hand. "Good work, Regan. You really gave us a thrill."

Merritt and the Irishman were nearly of a height, with Regan maybe half an inch taller. Both were powerfully built, but Compton was rangier, a little finer made, as if two blocks of stone had been hewed by the same sculptor, but he had finished off the one man's figure with more care and had left the other with rougher edges. Compton had his head back, regarding the younger man with his steady look of appraisal.

"Thank you, sir," said Matt calmly, meeting his look evenly, unbothered by it. "But I'm afraid I was a bit on the slow side today."

114

"Ten minutes slower than your usual time," the foreman observed, snapping shut his watch.

"My apologies, Jacko. But at least I didn't break me neck." He gave a short laugh and suddenly glanced at Terry. He met her eyes squarely and gave her a courtly bow.

Her face was flushed but she held her head high, moved away from her father, and put out her hand. "You were wonderful," she cried, "and you scared me to death. But I'm awfully glad you didn't break your neck."

His hard hand gripped hers for an instant and then let it go. Color burned quickly under his eyes, but his gaze didn't falter. He laughed softly. "Now, there, ma'am, we've something in common. I'm glad I didn't, too. And thanks for your good will."

There had been a softness, a deference in his voice that belied the way he'd looked at her in the cookhouse, and in his eyes that one swift moment that they met hers, there had been a sort of homage. She was glad she'd shaken his hand and spoken to him, though her father, after the topper had followed Red and Tommy to the next spar tree, had given her a strange, frowning look.

The next day, being Sunday, the logging operations stopped. A few of the men had quit early on Saturday to ride into town, but since they were paid by the number of feet of timber cut, most of them, not wanting to lose money, hung around camp, washing their clothes, pitching horseshoes, or playing poker in the mess hall.

Terry, knowing that her father and Dobie were going over the books and planning next year's operations in the foreman's shack, decided to go riding. After breakfast she went down to the corral and found Matt Regan waiting for her, her buckskin and one of the camp horses already saddled.

"Good morning, ma'am," he smiled. "Dobie said I was to go along with you. We killed a cougar last week on the trail."

"Thanks very much for saddling my pony, but I'm not at all afraid of cougars," she replied.

"I'm sure ye're not, Miss Compton, but 'twould give me great pleasure to escort ye." He didn't smile now and his voice was soft as a dove.

"I really prefer riding alone, but since you've had orders to accompany me, I won't upset things." Her voice was cheerfully aloof. "I'd like to ride over the divide and see the view."

He made as if to help her mount, but she was too quick for him and sprang easily into the saddle, a rebuff that made his face redden. He was clumsy mounting the big, heavy-footed bay, not much better than a plow horse, but actually the only kind he knew how to handle. The Indian ponies looked too smart and mischievous for him, pricking their ears, stamping their narrow feet, rolling their eyes at him. He felt awkward on a horse and only the powerful urge to be with this haughty, gray-eyed girl could have made him submit to the indignity of attempting something at which he did not excel.

Terry saw at once that he was uncomfortable, out of his element, and was amused, though she was careful not to show it. But it made up for the way he'd stared at her in the mess hall and for her secret ordeal in the tree, and gave her the sense of having the advantage over him.

They rode in silence through camp and took the old pack trail through the woods, Terry in the lead. It had rained in the night, and bright, cold drops shook down on them from low-hanging branches. The air smelled washed and new, with the clean, white smell of cut wood. The forest cascaded with fluty, bubbling bird song that showered down on them like the bright drops.

The happy morning sunlight struck through the dark evergreens, warmed the backs of their necks, drew out the scents of bark and needles and rich earth. Chipmunks flew from branch to branch, "tut-tut-tutting" at them, nibbled fir cones and dropped bits on the path before them. Once there was a sudden rustle in the brush, the red gleam of a shining flank, and Matt cried out, "There goes a deer!"

Terry swung round in her saddle to smile at him, oddly pleased that he'd seen the swift beautiful flash, too. "I saw him! A buck, wasn't it? Isn't it wonderful, how full of life the woods are? Deer, chipmunks, birds——"

"Ah, yes, indeed, and mice in their wee holes, peeping out at us, no doubt, and moles digging tunnels in the earth. And down in the river, the trout snapping at flies and flicking their silvery tails. Ah, 'tis wonderful, the wildlife going on all the time and paying no heed to us at all!" The words burst out of him in an eager rush, as if they'd been growing and growing while he rode behind her, keeping silence till the right time to speak.

"And even the cougars, you know, lying in the sun on a rock above us, meaning no harm unless we bother them!" she cried.

"Even the cougars," he replied, his eyes shining. "They're part of the plan, too. All God's good creatures."

His face was open and childish in his pleasure, and in the soft lilt of his gentle voice there was no trace of the coarseness, the male harshness that had both shocked and fascinated her when she was hidden in the tree. She was amazed and touched that this big, strong, reckless man, who could be so deadly in a fight and so audacious climbing a great tree, could hold such a depth of tenderness in his voice.

She drew rein and let him bring up his horse so that they could ride together on the trail. They smiled at each other and all at once the tension that had been between them was gone and they rode on together, knee to knee, bending their heads when a hemlock bough swept too low, talking easily about the woods, identifying the birdcalls.

"Hark! There's a brown thrush. Ah, he has a fine song, that one!"

"I thought it sounded like a meadowlark."

"No, ma'am. The larks like the valleys where they can nest in the grass."

"Of course. You're right. Oh, listen to the chickadees! There's no mistaking them."

"A good, homely, cheerful little song, too. Puts you in mind of nest-building and the missus sitting on a clutch of eggs, while the old man brings home the bacon."

They laughed together over the domestic life of the chickadee and their eyes lingered on each other's face, she discovering that for all his virility, his mouth was kind and young; he, that her aloof, gray eyes sometimes held dancing, golden lights. A silence fell between them and he bent to adjust a stirrup and Terry leaned to pat her pony's neck. It was an easy, a thoughtful silence, without strain, as if what they had just seen in each other's face needed to be considered quietly. Then they smiled at each other and rode to the top of the divide.

Here she let him help her dismount, holding out her hands and leaning strongly into his. But the touch of each other's flesh destroyed the easiness of their silence. Her hands were strong and narrow, but they were the smooth, subtle hands of a woman; his, hard, muscular, masculine. They were made instantly aware again of each other. The flame that had made her shiver in bed, remembering it, leaped into his eyes, though they drew quickly apart, Terry turning to throw the reins over the pony's head, which was all he needed by way of tethering, he to see to his own horse. But before she had turned, before she had resumed the mask of breeding or training or perhaps instinctive reserve again, he had seen an answering flame in her eyes.

His hands shook as he looped the bay's reins over a stump, and he stayed there, fumbling with his pipe and tobacco until he had the pipe filled and going. He was glad that she had walked away from him to the edge of the divide, where the land dropped down to a deep gully, where whitened spires of a great forest gave testimony of the fire that three years ago had roared over from Steiner's camp.

Presently he joined her and they sat on the needle-strewn ground, hot from the sun, and talked about the forest fire, gazed out over the distant green sea of timber. Their voices were wary and aloof, as if they did not dare to let any warmth or humor lead them astray. They avoided each other's face. The silence that fell between them now was a heavy, uncomfortable thing, not like that warm, gentle quietness on the trail.

Matt was angry at himself for not having taken her in his arms that moment of their hands meeting, when he was certain she felt as he did, and angry at her, too, for being who and what she was and so preventing what was natural and therefore right and meant to happen.

Terry sensed his anger, as she had sensed her danger the moment their hands touched. The man beside her oppressed her with his big, handsome body, the masculine smell of tobacco and leather that hung about him. Even the sight of his tanned, powerful hands as they cradled his pipe offended her and made her long to escape him. The memory of their warmth and strength clasping hers made her throat tighten and a weakness lay hold of her body. In that weakness, which was like a soft, enervating fire loosening her limbs, she could imagine herself turning to him, soft-eyed, and with one glance summoning him to her.

She had felt this weakness and fire before, on the yacht when she longed to hold Hal Forrester's sleek head against her breast, and she hated and feared it. She knew it for what it was, now—not love, as she had thought, but the dark, unworthy, indiscriminating urge of physical attraction. Something else she suddenly knew, as she sat clasping her knees and resisting the silent pull of the man who ignored her as she did him—she had never been in love with Hal at all. She hadn't even been as drawn to him as she was to this rough, arrogant Irish logger.

"We'd better be getting back," she said, self-conscious and stiff, and got to her feet. "It must be lunch time. I'm hungry, aren't you?"

"Yes," he said, giving her an odd, measuring glance. "I'm hungry, too."

She smiled coldly and turned away, caught her pony, and before he could offer to help her was in the saddle. Without waiting for him to mount she started off down the trail. She heard him lumbering after her, the big bay heavy-footed on the trail, and a cruel smile curved her mouth. He rode like a plowboy and she knew all about his discomfort on a horse. There was a way to punish him for all her grievances against him, particularly for that moment of weakness on the divide. She waited till he came up to her, hot-faced and disgruntled, and flinging him a cool, challenging look over her shoulder, cried, "Race you into camp!"

It was a devilish thing to suggest on the narrow, rocky trail which was barely wide enough for the two of them at a careful gait, and unfair, since her pony was as sure-footed as a mountain goat and she a fine horsewoman, while Matt, who could climb a 200-foot tree as easily as a flight of stairs, was uneasy even on a clod like the big bay.

He knew exactly what she was doing and why, and he had no choice but to accept her challenge. His eyes were ice-blue with rage and he gave her the same arrogant smile he'd given Dobie when he'd tried to stop him from climbing the day before. "You're on, me girl!" he cried, and kicked the bay's heavy flanks.

She laughed, touched the pony lightly, and he took off down the trail with his ears back, as if he knew the devil that had prompted her and was in complete accord.

It wasn't the pony's fault, but her own crazy pride, her reckless disregard of the hazards of the trail. The hemlock branch which they'd ducked on the way up seemed to appear out of nowhere. They were going too fast for her to turn out for it and she forgot to duck. It hit her squarely on the chest, knocked her out of the saddle. Instinctively, she kicked herself free of the stirrups when she felt herself going, but there was no way to avoid the edge of shale she hit as she landed on the ground.

Matt, pounding down the trail after her, was hard put to rein in his horse when he saw the slim inert body tossed halfway into the brush. He dismounted with terror and pain in his heart, all anger dissipated by the sight of the lovely chestnut hair shaken down over the still, white face, and went down on his knees beside her.

The sight of blood on her white cheek made his hand tremble as he brushed away the dirt and leaves from her hair and face. He was a man turned to jelly, a whimpering, supplicating idiot as he lifted her in his arms and called upon the blessed saints to save her. She was in his arms as he'd imagined since he first laid eyes on her, but as he held her against the rock of his breast, there was no fire in his veins, only a holy weakness of pity and fear, and tears smarting in his throat.

Presently she moaned, stirred, and her eyes opened, dark, opaque, without recognition. "Darlin'," he whispered in agony. "Ah, poor darlin'. Ye're not dead, then, praise be."

As he held her, crooning and whispering like a mother to a hurt child, the darkness left her eyes, met his clearly, and then, as if in a dream, she raised her arms and put them around his neck. He bent his head and his lips met hers, tenderly and humbly.

But it was all quite different when she was on her feet, shaken, but independent and aloof again. He wanted to bring her into camp on his horse, but she'd have none of it. She still had a fey look about her, half in this world and half out of it, but she insisted upon getting back onto the pony. He himself was not quite right in the head, what with his terror, and then with holding her in his arms and their kiss, which she seemed to have forgotten.

121

She rode the pony into the corral and dismounted before Matt could get to her. When he came toward her, grave-faced and worried, she turned and smiled distantly, as if they'd had nothing but a pleasant ride together. "Are ye all right, for sure?" he cried, anguish and tenderness in his voice, his eyes dark, looking down at her.

"Oh, quite all right, thanks!" she replied, with an embarrassed laugh. "Thanks so much for helping me when I took that tumble." A little color came into her face and she added, glancing away, "I'd be grateful if you didn't mention the—the spill to anyone."

"I'll mention nothing," he said curtly, hurt by what he knew she meant.

"Thanks." And that was all. He was dismissed as if he'd been nothing but a groom, as if there'd never been that moment of oneness on the trail nor the sweet, pure meeting of their lips when she returned from the dead.

He watched her walk away from him, tall and proud, with the sweet, silken cascade of hair that had brushed his cheeks as he bent to her all neatly coiled again at her neck, and the dark bud of anger burst into hot bloom in his heart. "You Terry Compton," he whispered with tight lips. "You lovely, long-legged, sweet-mouthed creature! You think you can put your arms around me, give me your lips, and then walk away as if nothing had happened? You think you can do that to Matt Regan? You think that's to be the end of it?"

And then all the rage and wildness and scorn went out of him and he turned to the patient, heavy-footed plow horse and stroked his long face. "It's the end, if that's how she wants it, Jim. Who am I to the likes of her? And the thorn in me heart is that I could have had her up there on the mountain if I'd not been so blasted noble!"

He tended to the horses, carried the saddles to the barn, and, though the bull cook was clanging the triangle for noon dinner, turned his back on camp and strode off through the pasture into the woods on the far side of the trail they'd taken that morning.

His heart was like a wineskin filled to bursting with anger and despair. Once again his strong pride in himself, his knowledge of his strength and power and the drive that was in him to bring the world to terms, tangled with the old, dark melancholy that mocked him, that asked him, Who is Matt Regan that he should be so set up about himself? Why should Matt Regan, born of ignorant, downtrodden Irish peasants, shanty Irish, challenge fate and strike out against the world and lay plans to master it and come into glory?

"Who is Matt Regan?" he cried bitterly, lying on his stomach, with his face on one arm in the hot sweet redolent needles under the hemlocks, banging his great fist into the ground. "Who is he that this queen, this rose of the world, this haughty, cool-eyed flirt should look at him in kindness? Why should she not treat me like a groom, a handyman, like the scum of Irish scum that I am? Why must I raise me eyes to her, instead of being content with the Ritas, the Daisys that think I'm a god?"

He wept. He laid his black, tight-curled head on his arms and shook like a mountain under God's wrathful thunderbolt. But the storm passed and he sprang up, scorning the melancholy and the submission, and raised both clenched fists to the sky, the anger searing him again, restoring him, giving him back his power and manhood.

"But I want her!" he raged, his face dark with fury. "She's my woman. I knew it the minute I laid eyes on her, all bloody and bruised as I was and looking up to see that face, that face out of all the world that I knew in a flash was for me, and no other. She knows it, too. She knew it today on the trail. She wants me the way I want her, and if she denies it, she lies. I felt her wanting me on the divide, when we sat there, tongue-tied, afraid to look at each other for the flame burning between us. It was all lies she was saying just now, with her cool glance and her lady-of-the-manor voice. The truth was in her arms reaching up to me and her mouth kissing me, before she'd come back to herself and remembered who she was, Miss Terry Compton, the Boss's daughter!"

Suddenly he laughed, threw his arms wide, and felt all the great aliveness of his muscles, his fine, alert body that had served him so well. "Who is this Matt Regan, indeed! He's nobody's groom, he's nobody's man but his own. Oh, ye'll hear from Matt Regan yet, my sweet girl, my gray-eyed queen. Ye'll find out soon enough who this Matt Regan is!"

Ten

TERRY walked away from the corral, holding herself very stiff and erect, and Matt Regan watched her with angry eyes. He had no way of knowing that when she dismissed him so summarily she was fighting the dizziness that made her concentrate on keeping her balance, on not giving way to the sickness that swept over her.

She heard the bull cook clanging the triangle and the harsh, metallic sound echoed in her head, as if he were beating on it instead of the piece of iron swinging from a hook just outside the mess hall. For a moment she closed her eyes against the bright sunlight, which was like a brass band in her brain.

Opening them again, she saw her father and Dobie emerge from the office and start across the clearing to the cookhouse, saw loggers high-tailing it up from the brook where they'd been washing clothes, and they were like the jerky, out-of-focus figures she'd once seen at a lantern show.

"It's only a few more feet to the cabin," she told herself, "and if I concentrate on that and nothing else, I can make it."

So she kept her eyes fixed on the cabin, ignored her father's arm raised in greeting, ignored the brass band crashing in her head and the waves of blackness rushing up from the ground,

125

and by putting one foot before the other was able to close the space between her and the cabin, was able to push open the door and grope her way to the bed before she collapsed.

She didn't go completely out, or if she did, came to in a few minutes, for when the skinny, freckle-faced boy who waited tables, tapped on the cabin door, sent by her father to see why she hadn't come to noon dinner, she answered and told him that she had a headache and didn't feel like eating.

When she wakened again, the sun was gone and the cabin was dusky and cool. Her father bent over her anxiously. "Terry," he whispered, in the bewildered, awed voice of a man confronted by a woman's indisposition. "Are you sick?"

She stared at him a moment before answering. It took a while for his face to come into focus. The faintness was gone, but there was a cruel hammering in her head. "I have a headache, Father." She looked at his sober, worried face with its expression of helplessness, and thought that the best and strongest of men are inadequate at such times. All at once, she longed for Isobel, who would know what to do and would do it, without love, perhaps, but with efficiency.

"But you were fine this morning!" he insisted, almost as if angry at her for causing him the helplessness and the worry. "You've been sleeping ever since noon. Was it something you ate, perhaps?"

She smiled faintly. "I don't think so, Father. I may as well tell you, I guess. I took a tumble out riding this morning. It was my own fault. I was racing the pony down the trail and forgot to dodge an overhanging branch."

"Wasn't Regan with you?" cried Compton, suddenly presented with someone to lash out at, since he couldn't very well scold a sick girl. "Why didn't he tell me you'd fallen?"

"I made him promise not to. Besides, I was all right until I started to walk from the corral to the cabin."

"Are you sure you didn't break any bones? How bad is the headache?"

"No bones broken, Father, and I think maybe my head is a wee bit better."

"I'll have Ole fix you supper on a tray and I'll bring it over to you myself."

"I really don't want any supper." Then, because he was so obviously anxious to do something for her, she agreed to try to eat a bowl of soup, and after standing looking down at her, jingling keys nervously in his pants pockets, he went off to the cookhouse.

A girl at school had fallen off her horse during a riding lesson and the doctor had said she'd suffered a concussion. There had been a great to-do and she'd been taken to the hospital. But Terry decided to say nothing about that to her father. It would only upset him and there was nothing to be done off here in the woods, and she didn't want him to cut short his visit because of her. Besides, it was quite possible that the headache would be gone in the morning.

She drank the soup Merritt brought her and did feel better; the blinding headache had now settled down to a steady throb. Next morning she dressed and went to the cookhouse for breakfast, feeling that to stay in bed was to give in to the pain and that maybe by acting as if it didn't exist she could conquer it. On the way back to the cabin she fainted and Dobie helped Compton carry her inside and put her on the bed. He shook his head and looked grave. "I'm afraid it's a concussion, Merritt. I think you'd better get her to a doctor."

"But she can't ride the trail in this condition!" cried Merritt angrily. He didn't know whom or what he was angry at, he only knew that he was confronted with a situation in which he felt inadequate and that someone should pay for it. "That blasted Regan!"

Dobie looked up at him, frowning. "What did Matt have to do with it?"

"He was riding with her. He was supposed to look out for her, wasn't he?" Merritt wasn't making sense in his desperate concern for Terry. He knew it but refused to admit it. "He knew she'd taken a tumble and didn't report it to me."

"I don't think you can blame Regan because Terry fell off her horse, Merritt," said Dobie quietly. "And if I know Terry, she probably told him to keep quiet about it, afraid you'd make a fuss."

"All right, it wasn't Regan's fault. It was Terry's fault, as she admitted to me. Showing off, racing the pony. But that doesn't help any, does it?" He paced up and down the room where Terry lay on the bed, conscious now, but limp and white, her eyes closed. "We've got to get her to Seattle. There's a hospital at Anacortes, but I wouldn't take a dog there. She can't ride for two days with a concussion. And how else can we get her down?"

"There's the river, Merritt," said Dobie thoughtfully.

Merritt snorted. "The river! Are you suggesting we take her down by log boom?"

Dobie, having had his share of suffering and knowing the blind rage a man gets into when he cannot help those he loves, was patient and understanding with his boss.

"Not by log boom, Merritt. But Matt Regan has a big Indian canoe. He's fixed it up so that it's tight and safe. That's how he gets to town for a spree. With two good men at the paddles, the trip to Sedro-Woolley can be made in less than twelve hours."

"Fine. But what about the rapids?" Merritt paused in his pacing to shoot a sharp glance at his foreman. "There are a few bad spots on the Skagit."

"Bad for a boom of logs, but not too bad for a canoe handled by an expert."

"Regan is an expert?"

"He can handle his canoe."

"What I want to know is whether he can get my girl safely down the river so that I can put her on the next boat for Seattle."

128

"You can paddle a canoe, Merritt." Dobie's voice was quiet, reasonable.

Merritt wheeled, tight-lipped. "Yes, I can paddle a canoe. You know blamed well I can, Jack. You and I have fished together in Canada, haven't we?"

Dobie gave him a steady, calm look. "I'm talking now, Merritt, about whether you can forget you're the Big Boss, and paddle a canoe with Matt Regan, taking orders from him?"

"Taking orders——!" Compton glared at him. Then Terry moaned faintly and he darted to her side. "Terry girl. You all right?"

She opened her eyes and murmured something, then was lost again, not unconscious, but not quite able to bridge the gap between unconsciousness and full awareness and too tired to try. She heard the men's voices as a low, urgent murmur which didn't concern her greatly. She heard Dobie speak of the river and of Matt Regan's canoe, and soon, in her mind, she was floating down the river, floating, floating—and the black Irishman's blue eyes were smiling into hers.

The steady, cadenced plash of paddles chopping away the miles, the deep undertone of the river, the whisper of the canoe as it skimmed over the water were all about her as she woke. The wind from their swift passage fanned her face with coolness and the smell of the river was in her nostrils. She was lying on a pallet on the floor of the canoe and for a while she was content to lie with closed eyes, letting the dream go on.

But the sounds and smells were too clear for a dream. She opened her eyes, looking up first at the narrow sky, piercingly blue, far above her, then slowly, lest she waken the pain which was still asleep, let her gaze move to the trees growing down to the riverbank, to the sides of the canoe, to the flash a paddle made as it rose, dripping silver, and plunged again.

She lay for some time, fascinated by the paddle. Presently she noticed the hand implementing its action and she stared at it for a while. It was brown and powerful, but not clumsy, on the contrary, very deft with the paddle. She recognized the hand and tried to remember where she had seen it before.

Then she had the feeling that someone was looking at her and she turned her head very slowly, raised her eyes, and met those of the Irishman, not smiling, as in the dream, but dark and troubled. She was going to smile at him, but he quickly shifted his gaze to the river ahead and his face became an Indian's mask of impassiveness, his lips stern, his brow calm.

He sat in the stern of the canoe, facing her, and she lay, with half-closed eyes, watching the swing of his shoulders as he paddled. His faded blue shirt was open at the neck, the sleeves rolled above his elbows. She put one arm across her forehead to shut out the sun, and from under it she observed the strong brown column of his throat, the hardness of his bare forearms. He looked younger, more boyish, with his throat and arms exposed.

Once he glanced at her again and she pretended to be asleep, but she saw the strange look of yearning and anxiety on his face, and quickly shut her eyes lest he catch her spying on him. Her heart burned within her and she kept her eyes closed a long time, letting herself sink back into a half dream. And now she let herself remember what the pain and the fainting had covered over in her mind.

She remembered that she had been in his arms and he was looking down at her with just that same look of tenderness and fear. She had reached up to him, drawing his face down to hers, and their mouths had touched softly, with such sweetness that the memory of it brought tears smarting under her closed eyelids.

She lay quite still, aware of such happiness as she had never known before. She knew that she had been cruel to him afterward, because first she had been afraid, then the dizziness had swept over her, blotting out everything but the need to get to the cabin. But now for a time she let herself be happy, and part of the happiness was that, in spite of how she had treated him, he was with her now, so close that she could put out a hand and touch him, and that when he thought himself unobserved that same look came back into his face.

She thought she could be content to float down the river with him forever.

"Rapids ahead!" sang out her father's voice, and instantly the dream of happiness was dashed away, her eyes flew open, and she realized that she and Matt Regan weren't alone on the river. Compton was in the bow.

"I see them, sir," replied Matt, darting a glance at Terry, who had raised herself to a sitting position. "Lie down flat and hold tight to the sides. This will be rough," he said to her quickly.

"Is Terry awake?" Compton half turned and paused in his paddling.

"She's awake, but don't turn or stop paddling," commanded Matt sharply. "The rocks are in the middle, but there's a channel on the right. When I say 'Go!' paddle as hard and fast as you can on the left."

Suddenly the roar of the rapids was in their ears, the sun was bright on tossed spray, and the slight craft was flung wildly about as the current caught it and spun it toward the rocks. Terry had one glimpse of Matt bent over the paddle, the muscles in his neck standing out like cords, and then she hid her face on the pallet, gripping the canoe's sides desperately.

Spray was flung over her, the canoe shot up into the air and hit again with a terrific smack and she waited for it to break apart. Then, all at once, the thunder of the rapids was behind them and the boat was floating gently on calm water. Matt had his paddle across his knees and was wiping the sweat off his forehead with his arm.

"We made it!" shouted Compton. Then he turned and looked anxiously at the girl. "You all right, kiddie?"

"Yes, Father. I'm all right." She sat up and smiled at him.

131

"How's your head?"

"Much better. The pain is gone for the moment." She was almost breathless from excitement. "But, golly, I'm hungry!"

A little farther on at a bend in the river there was a narrow shingle of beach, where they pulled up the canoe, made a fire to boil coffee, and ate the sandwiches and cold ham Ole had put up for them. The men rested for half an hour after lunch and then they went on, changing places, with Compton in the stern, facing Terry, and Matt in the bow.

For a while Terry talked to her father, then she slept again. She was relieved not to have Matt in the stern, for now she was angry at herself for having remembered their kiss and for giving way to that ridiculous feeling of happiness. Ever since they shot the rapids, he had carefully avoided looking at her. She wondered if what she had seen on his face had been merely the hallucination of her concussion. As she watched her father paddle and met his smile, a feeling of safety and security warmed her. She felt as if she had been on the edge of a precipice and his hand had pulled her back just in time.

Night was coming down through the trees when they reached the landing, just above a sawmill near Sedro-Woolley, where Matt kept his canoe when he went into town. Merritt left Terry with the Irishman, while he went up the trail to rout out a rancher who lived nearby to hire his buggy and team to take them to town.

Terry sat on a log and tried to make herself presentable while Matt busied himself pulling up the canoe and securing it in the bushes. Then he filled and lighted his pipe and sat down on the landing, watching her as she took down her long hair, combed it, and coiled it neatly again at her neck.

She was aware of his scrutiny, but she kept her face averted and, when she was finished with her toilet, sat with hands clasped about her knees, staring at the dark river and wishing for her father's return. There was nothing she could say to this man. Small talk was impossible, after what had happened between them.

Suddenly he spoke, not looking at her. "This may be the last chance I'll get to talk to you. I want you to know who I am. My parents were poor Irish immigrants and my father was killed in a coal mine in Pennsylvania when I was twelve. My mother died soon after, giving birth to her seventh child. Thank God, the child died with her. They put us kids in a home, but I ran away after a year and got a job as bull cook in a logging camp in Michigan. That's where I learned high-lead logging and got to be a topper."

Why are you telling me all this? she wanted to ask. What is it to me who you are, or where you came from? But she listened to every word.

"My parents had a miserable life and they died young because they were poor. I made up my mind that wouldn't happen to me. I'm strong and I'm smart and I'm not afraid to take chances. Another thing, I'm my own man. No boss will ever own me. One day, I'll be boss."

He stopped for a moment, got up and walked up and down, talking, it seemed, as much to himself or to some unseen listener as to her. "When they found gold in Alaska, I quit the lumber camp and hit for the Klondike. I was only twenty, but I survived where lots of good men died. I struck a rich claim and I got out with a good grubstake. It's cached away in a Seattle bank and I won't touch it till I'm ready to start out for myself. I'm going to have my own lumber company and I'm going to have money and power. I'm going to be somebody."

He sat down again and was silent, pulling on his pipe and staring into the gathering darkness.

"Why did you tell me all this?" she asked, after a bit.

He turned and looked toward her, but in the dusk her face was shadowy. He couldn't see what she was thinking.

"I wanted you to know," he said simply. "I wanted you to know who Matt Regan really is."

A lantern shone down the trail and Merritt Compton called, "Ahoy, there! I've got a wagon, Terry. And the *Potlach* doesn't sail till midnight. I'll have you in Seattle by morning."

There was something she wanted to say, something Matt Regan was waiting for her to say, but there was no time, now. Perhaps there would never be a time to say it. She stood up and looked toward him, but it was too dark to see his face clearly, and then her father had his arm around her and was helping her up the trail.

Eleven

AT the Kermiss given for charity at the Firlock Club in late June, Genevieve Lansing led off the ball as Queen, with Hal Forrester as her King. Mrs. Struther, who ran the affair, had been extremely put out when Terry Compton declined the committee's nomination for the honor, on her physician's advice.

"I'm disappointed in Terry," she told her husband, after the committee meeting where Mrs. Ainsworth had successfully carried the day for her niece, Genevieve, after the note of regrets from Terry had been read. "First she gets herself unofficially engaged to this Forrester boy, who is attractive, I'll grant you, but he hasn't a bean. Then, according to gossip, he wants to break it off just before the Comptons had planned a huge announcement party, and Terry, meek as a lamb, gives him back his ring."

"What else could she do, my dear?" her husband protested mildly.

"Any girl with gumption or spirit would have held him to it, and he could like it or lump it!" cried Theodora, with a glance that indicated what would have happened to him in similar circumstances.

"Perhaps it's because she *is* a girl of spirit that she let him go," he suggested, smiling. "She didn't seem to me like the kind who would want a man if he didn't want her."

"Manley, don't be a sentimentalist!" snapped his wife. "What she should have done was to refuse to return his ring, go through with the announcement party, and then, a few months later, break off the engagement herself. That way, it would look as if he'd been the jilted party. As it is, she's lost face, let herself in for a lot of unpleasant gossip, and all but ruined her chances of a brilliant marriage."

"You should prepare a booklet, Theo, my pet, on how to get a man to propose, how to hang on to him, and how to lose him gracefully. You could present it to each sweet young thing on the night of her debut." He laughed and patted her hand. "What else has Terry done to displease you, dear?"

"Turned down a chance to be Queen of the Kermiss, after the way I worked to get her nominated!" She sniffed crossly. "Says she isn't well enough to go through with it."

"If the child isn't well, my dear——"

"Rubbish! She could have recouped all her losses, had all the young men flocking around her again, and scotched the rumor that she's pining away for that Forrester fellow."

Even Mable Fisher urged Terry not to turn down the honor of being Queen of the Kermiss. "Gen Lansing is telling it all over town that you've had a nervous breakdown because Hal Forrester jilted you, Terry." Mable's honest face was pink with indignation. "I know that's not true. You broke it off yourself. But if you were Queen it would show everyone that you don't care a fig for Hal!"

Terry laughed affectionately. "Dear Mable, you're so loyal. But I don't see how my being Kermiss Queen would prove I don't care for Hal. And I have nothing so romantic as a nervous breakdown, just a crack on the head from falling off a horse."

"Then you do still care for Hal!" moaned Mable in distress.

136

Terry looked thoughtful. "I don't think so, Mable. It still hurts to know that what I thought was love, wasn't. But mostly it's hurt pride, and being ashamed that people are talking about me, I guess. I do have pride, you know. Isobel says it's my worst fault."

"I'm glad you're proud!" cried Mable staunchly. "That's why I want you to be Queen. Oh, I can just see you sweeping into the ball in a beautiful gown and a tiara, snubbing all the people who've gossiped about you, and looking every inch a queen!"

"Thanks, dear. But can you see me leading off the ball with Hal? He's to be King, you know."

Mable suddenly burst into tears and flung herself at Terry, embracing her. "Oh, I just HATE Hal Forrester! I really do. He's spoiled everything, Terry. He isn't worth your little finger, and everything was going so well for you—your lovely debut and all the parties and beaux and now——"

"Now—what, Mable?" asked Terry quietly, gently disengaging herself from Mable's damp embrace.

"Now, Gen Lansing says your social career is ruined. She —she, oh Terry! She says you'll probably end up marrying someone like Ned Deming!"

"And what's the matter with Ned?" Terry's voice was amused, but her eyes glittered with anger. "He's one of the nicest, sweetest boys I know. The only one of my so-called beaux who's called on me every week since I've been sick."

"Oh, Terry, you wouldn't *marry* Ned, would you?" Mable gasped, dabbing at her eyes.

"Why not? My family will be crushed if I turn out an old maid."

"Oh, because you're so beautiful and—and romantic, and he's so unexciting and dull. You're not in *love* with him, are you?" Mable looked so horrified that Terry was impatient with her.

"I'm not 'in love' with anyone and I wonder if that's so important," replied Terry coldly. "Being in love seems to bring people nothing but grief and pain. Ned is a very fine person and we're the best of friends. I can't think of a better basis for marriage."

Somewhere in the back of her mind she heard someone say that love was terribly important and that marriage was forever. She'd been terribly impressed when she first heard that, but that was when she was a callow girl, before she had suffered and grown up. It was before she'd discovered it was possible to fancy yourself in love with a man who didn't even belong to your world and with whom marriage was quite out of the question.

It had now been nearly a month since Matt Regan brought her down from camp in his canoe. Nearly a month since they sat by the river and he told her who he was and what he wanted out of life. She had taken the boat to Seattle and he had, she supposed, gone back to camp. While she was lying in bed as the doctor had ordered, she had been so sure that she would hear from him. There had been something unfinished between them, and she felt that Matt was not the man to leave things unfinished. At first she had been afraid to hear from him, then she had longed for some word, finally she had retreated into anger at him for ignoring her, and anger at herself for having thought about him.

Mable was looking at her oddly. "You mean, he's proposed, Terry, and you've accepted him?"

"Who? Oh—Ned. Heavens, no, he's much too bashful. All I meant was that I could, I think, marry him if I want, and it may be that sometime I'll want to. Right now, I'm not at all interested in getting engaged to anyone."

But when Ned asked her to go to the Kermiss Ball with him, she accepted.

Isobel, who had been quite as disappointed as Theodora Struther when Dr. Sharpless was firm about insisting that the excitement of the pre-ball parties, the costume fittings, and rehearsals attendant upon being Queen might bring back the headaches which had disappeared after two weeks in bed, was pleased that, at least, Terry was going to the ball, even if she wasn't to be Queen. She immediately started planning a new dress for her.

Terry could see the wheels beginning to turn in her head. After all, Ned Deming wasn't too bad a catch, there was plenty of money and family background, his grandfather had been old Judge Deming from Virginia. Isobel, Terry knew, still hoped to marry her off before she became passée, and after a few years of being "out," the bloom was quickly gone from a debutante who remained too long an unclaimed treasure.

"There isn't much time, but if Miss Florian works night and day, she can have your dress ready for the ball."

"But Isobel," protested Terry, "I have at least three ball gowns I've worn only a few times."

"Nonsense, my dear. You can't wear those things to the Kermiss, where everyone else will have something new. Why, you haven't had a new gown since the one Florrie made for your announcement party." Isobel sighed heavily and Terry looked away, coloring. "The latest thing," her stepmother went on quickly, "is embroidered voile or appliquéd chiffon. Double skirts are all the rage in the East and gray is the prevailing color this season. I know just the style for you. Gray voile, trimmed with a deeper shade of ribbon, half an inch wide. The vest will be embroidered in a Dresden pattern, the sleeves trimmed with ribbon. The skirt will be composed of three large ruffles, the lowest being very full, sweeping the floor, with ribbon shirred in rows of tiny ruffles on each large one. The gray will complement your eyes and bring out the pearly tones of your skin, and with it you must wear my amethyst necklace and eardrops."

"Oh, Isobel, you sound just like a fashion book!" laughed Terry.

Isobel smiled. "Naturally. I'm quoting from one which just

arrived from New York. Florrie let me see it before anyone else."

The gray voile was created by the indefatigable Miss Florian, who seemed to have no life beyond dressing young ladies of society in the latest fashion. She was down on her knees doing something to the hem of the voile when Terry said, "Do you realize what an important person you are, Florrie?"

The odd little woman with the bright black eyes, wispy gray hair, and nimble hands nearly swallowed her mouthful of pins. Dropping back on her heels, she peered at the girl over her steel-rimmed spectacles. "Now, Miss Terry, don't you go to joshing me!" she mumbled.

"I mean it. I'll bet you're responsible for at least half the First Hill marriages in the last ten years. Any girl wearing a dress you've made feels beautiful, whether she is or not."

Miss Florian took the pins out of her mouth and smiled, her face very pink and soft. An odd thought came to Terry—Miss Florian might have been a very pretty girl when she was young. Why had she turned into such a drab little wisp of a woman? Was it because she hadn't married? Did a woman shrink and dwindle and wither up without love?

"Why, thank you, dearie. That's a sweet thing to say. I do take pride in my work. And it's a joy to make something for anyone that wears clothes with your style, Miss Terry. Which I can't say as much for all my customers!" Her bright black eyes sparkled like tiny bits of jet. "The day I'm looking forward to is the one I cut out your wedding gown."

Terry found herself blushing, but she laughed. "You may have quite a wait for that, Florrie. I'm fancy free at the moment."

"See that you don't make me wait too long, dearie," she warned, "or you'll wind up like me, a spinster, with no one in the world but a cat and a fat old spaniel."

"Why didn't you ever marry?" asked Terry. "You must have had lots of chances."

The dressmaker bridled and her eyes snapped. "Oh, I did. I had plenty of chances. You'd not believe it now, but when I was a girl I was pretty as a picture, but too independent, too choosy. None of my suitors was good enough for me, I thought. I was waiting for Mr. Right." She snorted. "Well, Mr. Right never showed up and here I am. Now, turn around and let me pin up the back."

The gray voile was a great success and Terry received many compliments at the Kermiss Ball. Even Mrs. Struther, who was still huffy about her refusing the Queenship, told her she looked stunning. Her dance card was quickly filled and when Ned brought it back to her, just before the Grand March started, he looked uncomfortable and pinker than ever.

"I hope you won't mind, Terry, but Hal Forrester put himself down for the fourth, a waltz. I couldn't very well get out of it."

A little color came into her cheeks, but she smiled and shrugged. "Why should I mind? Mr. Forrester is an excellent dancer, as I remember."

Ned swallowed and jingled a pocketful of coins. "Well, I—I d-didn't know. I m-mean. Good Lord, Terry, I wouldn't want to embarrass you."

"I'm not embarrassed, Ned," she replied calmly, and put her hand on his arm, as the music for the Grand March started with a rousing rendition of "Columbia, the Gem of the Ocean."

But when Hal came toward her to claim his dance, she trembled inwardly for a moment and her hands were suddenly like ice. It had not bothered her at all to see him lead off the Grand March with Gen Lansing or to watch them being crowned King and Queen with mock solemnity by the mayor. But it was strange to see him coming across the floor, looking for her with that eager half smile that she knew so well, now that they meant nothing to each other.

His shoulders, under the well-cut tail coat, were as graceful, he was as handsome and poised as ever, though he seemed smaller than she remembered. He's very attractive, she thought. Poor Ned does seem rather a clod beside him. But I'm glad it's all over. I'm sure that I'm not in love with him, thank goodness. Yet I *do* feel strange.

He bowed over her hand and when he lifted his head, she met his questioning gaze with directness. "This *is* our dance, isn't it?" he murmured, smiling.

"I believe it is, Mr. Forrester." Her voice was neither warm nor cold, but completely devoid of emotion.

As they glided away over the floor to the same haunting music the orchestra had played at her debut, a curious thought came to her. I wonder what it would be like to dance with Matt Regan.

"You're looking very lovely," said Hal softly. "Your gown is exquisite."

"Thank you. My dressmaker will be pleased."

"I was distressed to hear you'd been ill. I trust you are quite recovered now?"

"Oh, yes. It was really nothing much—a slight concussion from a fall when I was horseback riding in the country." There, she thought, that will take care of Gen's talk about a nervous breakdown.

"Really? What rotten luck. A concussion can be dangerous. You must take care of yourself."

"Awfully kind of you to be so solicitous!" she replied with a mocking smile.

He met her eyes gravely, said in an odd, brusk voice, "I shall always be concerned over your health and safety."

There was no mistaking his sincerity. Good heavens, she thought, is it possible that he still cares? Is he sorry for what he did to me? Well, it's a little late now, Mr. Forrester. "You *are* kind," she answered lightly, and began to talk about the round of parties beginning for Bob Brinker and Milly Fox, who were to be married in September.

When the waltz ended he held her arm for a moment, looking down at her as if he didn't want to let her go. "Thank you for the dance, Terry," he said quietly. "I wasn't sure if you'd dance with me."

She laughed and turned away to shake out the ruffles of her short train which she'd caught up through one of her bracelets while they were waltzing. "Why shouldn't I? I've always found you a good dancing partner." Smiling, she put her hand out to Ned, who had come up with a glass of punch.

Ned was such a dear, as good as bread, and without question devoted to her. He had been a stocky, rosy-cheeked little boy, with a habit of blushing easily and of stammering when excited. He had grown up into a stocky, pink young man, clumsy but kind, and he still had difficulty with words under stress.

The night of the Kermiss Ball he came very close to proposing in the cab taking Terry home. With the sixth sense women have about such things as imminent proposals or kisses, she could see it coming and kept talking gaily about the Kermiss, laughing a great deal, until the ride was over. He gave her a languishing look as she pressed his hand at her door and thanked him for the evening, and could only stammer, "It was s-swell of you to c-come with me, Terry."

In her room, as she stood at the dressing table stripping off her long white evening gloves and removing Isobel's amethysts, she wondered if she had made a mistake in not encouraging Ned. She wondered if it was dancing with Hal and recognizing his attraction, which, superficial as she now knew it to be, could still make her heart beat faster, that had made her forget all Ned's fine qualities and remember only that physically he didn't appeal to her. Or that moment when she was dancing with Hal and suddenly thought about Matt Regan.

"Am I going to be like poor Miss Florian?" she asked herself. "Waiting for Mr. Right till it's too late?" Weren't character and kindness and devotion worth more in a husband than physical attraction, which she had already learned could be so treacherous? Twice now she'd been drawn to men who excited her and each time she'd been made unhappy and ashamed. Now that she was back in her proper milieu she found it inconceivable that she had kissed Matt Regan. The very thought of what had happened between them that morning on the trail made her cheeks flame with humiliation.

"Am I going to turn out like my mother? Make a mess of my marriage and be looked down on?" she whispered, and was instantly ashamed of the disloyalty. But though she tried to put the thought out of her mind, it kept coming back. At just what point she had begun to feel this guilty shame about her mother, she did not know. Perhaps it had started when she first came to live with her father and Isobel and was not encouraged to speak of her mother nor of her life with her. She could not remember that either Isobel or her father had spoken unkindly to her about Maizie; it had been more an atmosphere, a silence that she was quick to sense held both a mystery and a disapproval. She did remember just once that Isobel, her face very pink, had brought up the matter. It was shortly before she left for her first term at Wolfe Hall and her stepmother had been schooling her on her manners and deportment.

"It would be better," she had said stiffly, "not to mention that you haven't always lived here on the First Hill with us, Terry. The girls you will meet at boarding school come from the very best families, and you must take your place as one of them. It will not help you if they know that your mother was an—actress and you once lived on the waterfront."

There had been a little edge of hurt in Terry's mind when she thought about her mother after that, but in the excitement of going away to school and making new friends, it had been, if not forgotten, hidden and pushed down by new experiences, then by the process of growing up. Yet the hurt, the queer, unexplained sense of shame had not disappeared. It had been there all the time, though she had refused to face it until Hal Forrester put his finger on it, and even then, in her pain and anger she had run away from it. But tonight, for the first time, she let herself look honestly at the fact that she loved her mother but was ashamed of her.

The knowledge that her mother had been divorced, that she was a "notorious woman," and that it was a disgrace for her to have been a Variety actress and a dance-hall hostess had not come all at once at the time Hal broke their engagement, yet Terry could not tell when or how she had known. Perhaps the knowledge had come to her as a child and, because she did not know what the implications were, had simply stored it away in her mind, where it had lain dim and forgotten until Gen Lansing's jealousy had suddenly turned the light of awareness on it and Terry had seen it in all its ugly reality.

She sat down on the bed and took off her smart new gun-metal pumps with the cut-steel buckles and thought about Gen, with whom she'd had one brief encounter that evening at the ball.

It was during the supper intermission when she was sitting with Marguerite Brookes, waiting for Ned to bring them creamed chicken and aspic salad. Gen, on Hal's arm, paused to speak to Marguerite, then suddenly seemed aware of Terry.

"Why, Terry!" she cried effusively, "I didn't know you were here. I thought you were bedridden."

"You make her sound like old Mrs. Kittinger with her broken hip," remarked Marguerite dryly.

"Oh, I didn't mean that! I only thought you were under the doctor's orders, darling," gushed Gen, holding on possessively to Hal, who, having bowed to both ladies, held himself aloof.

"Only to the extent that he refused to let me accept the honor of being Queen of the Kermiss," replied Terry calmly.

Gen reddened and her eyes were sharp as points of ice. "What a disappointment for you, dear. I do hope you didn't have to come to the ball alone."

"No, I have a most satisfactory escort. At present he is foraging for food for us."

"How nice. *So* good to see you, dear, though I *could* wish you didn't look so wan and tired," and Gen swept on, the aigrette in her tiara nodding.

"Bravo, Terry!" Marguerite exclaimed after they'd gone. "You put her very neatly in her place. Nasty little chit. I'll give her short shrift in my column, believe me."

"It was mean of me to say that about being asked to be Queen, but I couldn't resist it. I don't like being patronized."

I suppose, Terry thought with a funny little thrust of pride, that Gen will marry Hal, but at least he asked me first and she'll be second choice, just as she was tonight for Kermiss Queen.

She got into bed and lay staring at the dark shapes of the furniture, ghostly in the early morning light, unable to sleep. Too many things churning in her head; too many emotions troubling her heart. She longed to be back in the woods, lying on a fir-bough bed under the stars, or in the cabin at camp, where she had been able to forget Gen, Hal, the curious network of social duties, poses, intrigues that made up her life in town.

Matt Regan came into her thoughts of the camp, but she resolutely shut out the memory of their ride together, the canoe trip, their last, strange, unfinished conversation, and concentrated on the thrilling sight of him clinging to the great fir the morning she watched him top the spar.

Yet when she finally slept she dreamed of waltzing with Hal, all alone on the dance floor of a great hall. Everyone else was standing around, watching them and applauding, and suddenly Hal turned into Matt in his faded blue shirt and levis and the music went faster and faster until it ended with a crash and all the people burst into mocking laughter and Matt let her go and turned to the crowd and shouted, "I want you to know who I am. I'm Matt Regan and I'm going to be some-

146

body," and the people, the hall, Matt dissolved into a mist and she was floating on the river, lying in the bottom of a canoe and her father was leaning over her saying, "You're a Compton. Remember that . . ."

Twelve

THE day after the Kermiss Ball Terry decided to go to see Annie Jordan. She wakened that morning with a feeling of absolute necessity to talk to someone about her mother, about Ned, about her sense of confusion and uncertainty over the way her life was turning out. There was no one but Annie she could talk to.

Mable was a brick and she loved her dearly, but she couldn't talk to her. Once, when Terry had confided in her that she was sick of "society" and wished there were something else she could do other than marry "suitably," Mable had urged her to give it all up and become a missionary.

Mable had just come from a meeting of the Baptist Ladies' Mission Circle, where an ardent young minister, who, according to her, looked like a saint, had talked to them about mission work among the Alaskan Indians. Her eyes had shone and her face was so transfigured she looked almost pretty. "Think of how wonderful it would be! To give up everything, all your selfish hopes and desires, to serve those poor people who have never heard about Jesus!"

There had been quite a religious revival all over the country that year and even the society butterflies had gone to evangelical meetings, had put on bazaars to raise money for the conversion of the heathen, and sewed Mother Hubbards to cover pagan nakedness in the South Seas. Several young women had been so carried away that they had gone out to teach in mission schools.

Listening to Mable, Terry had seriously considered the peace, the sense of doing something worth while that such a life would bring, but she said, "It would be wonderful, Mable, if one did it out of conviction. You could do it sincerely, I know. I'm afraid for me it would be merely an escape and that would be selfish and not good at all. I don't want to escape. I just want to know where I'm going."

The day following the ball was the one for the ladies of Queen Anne Hill to be "at home," and Isobel asked Terry at lunch to accompany her on her calls. It was the custom then for the homes on each of Seattle's many hills to be open to receive callers on certain days in the week. Ladies from the other sections of town, elegantly attired, white-gloved, and carrying little embroidered silk cardcases, spent the afternoon dropping in on their friends to sip tea, nibble cucumber or watercress sandwiches, check up on the latest gossip, and leave cards.

It was, to Terry, one of the most tiresome and pointless of the many social rituals imposed on her and for once she demurred. Since she knew that Isobel didn't quite approve of Annie, she didn't tell her what she planned to do, but pleaded fatigue from the excitement of the ball. Isobel, who had been afraid that the girl's concussion might develop into "brain fever," an affliction no one quite understood but which sounded dreadful, didn't press the point, only urged her to rest after lunch.

As soon as her stepmother had been whisked away in the carriage, Terry left on foot for the big house on Boren Avenue. Nora answered her ring and told her regretfully that Mrs. Bauer had gone walking in Volunteer Park and wouldn't be back till teatime. Terry hadn't been in the park since the day in December she'd walked there with Hal Forrester. But she was so intent on seeing Annie *today* that she decided to take the trolley to the park and try to find her.

She had always loved Volunteer Park and the fact that she had been so miserable the last time she was there couldn't spoil her pleasure in it now. The quiet, graveled walks leading through wide green sunny stretches of lawn, with neatly bordered, sedate flower beds on each side, madroña, maple, and hazelnut trees casting their lacy shadows, sprinklers twinkling away, showering the grass with rainbow drops, the scent of warm, cut grass, the sweetness of the purple heliotrope in the sunken garden had a kind of enchantment that filled the heart with peace.

There was something quite wonderful in stepping off the busy city street—where trolley cars clanged and jangled their bells, and cabs, carriages, delivery wagons clattered and jolted over the pavements—and being engulfed in this green silence, as if you had shut a door. The street noises began to sound fainter almost as soon as you went through the entrance and up the main walk, and by the time you reached the sunken garden they were gone.

After half an hour of wandering about, looking for Annie, Terry found a bench near the sunken garden shaded by a great gnarled madroña whose red bark was peeling in thin ribbons. She took off her hat, running the hatpin through the crown, leaned back and closed her eyes. How simple life could be, she thought, if instead of the clangor and clamor of the world and the turbulence of one's emotions and the proddings of other people, one could let go and be a part of sunlight and air and flowering earth. Or even if one could carry away a bit of this serenity and order and take it out, in times of stress, like a talisman.

Presently she became aware of low voices on her left, where a high rhododendron hedge hid both her and whoever was on the other side. She tried to close her ears to the voices, but instead, found herself straining to catch the words.

A man's low, passionate voice was pleading, "Why not? Why is it wrong to divorce a woman you don't love and never did love so that you can marry the woman who can make you happy?"

The woman's voice was too low for Terry to hear, but she couldn't shut out the man's reply, "Would she rather have me leave her?"

Terry, feeling uncomfortably like an eavesdropper, was afraid to get up and leave for fear they would see her and be embarrassed. She sat very still, with her hands over her ears, thinking, Why even here in this peaceful park there is no peace because there are human beings in it. She wondered who had been listening when she and Hal had their painful conversation.

At last she took her hands from her ears, hoping the people on the other side of the hedge might have walked on, and heard the man say, "Then what are we to do?" There was a long pause, and Terry was waiting for the answer, too. Then for the first time she heard the woman's voice clearly.

"We mustn't see each other again, Hugh. We must go back to those who love us and try to make them happy."

I know that voice! thought the girl. A picture flashed into her mind of a beautiful woman in a black net dress with a silver gauze scarf over her flaming red hair, standing in the hall, looking up with love and sadness into a man's face.

Even as Terry recognized Annie's voice, the woman herself, in a white linen tailored suit, her unmistakable red hair hatless, suddenly appeared on the graveled walk, and without a backward glance hurried away toward the gate. Terry shrank against the bench, grateful that Annie hadn't seen her, and after a bit the man emerged from behind the hedge, stood staring down the path along which Annie had disappeared. It was Hugh Deming. He stood for a moment, pressing his hand to his forehead, then turned without glancing at the bench, and walked in the opposite direction from that Annie had taken.

As soon as they had both gone, Terry, in a panic to get out of the park without meeting either of them, hurried down a side path, hoping it might lead eventually to the street. But it turned out to be a short cut to the main walk and as she came to the junction, there was Annie, walking slowly, with her head down. She looked up just as Terry, in confusion, stopped and tried to shrink back into the shrubbery. For a moment Annie's eyes were blank, as if she hadn't seen her, then recognition came into her face and she smiled and said, "Why, hello, Terry. Where did you come from?"

The girl blushed and stammered. "I—I took a short cut. I didn't know it would come out here." Then, realizing that Nora would tell Annie she'd been to see her, she admitted that she'd been looking for her.

"I'm sorry I wasn't home when you came to see me," said Annie. "I'm glad you found me, after all."

"Yes. I'm glad, too. I wanted to talk to you."

Something in Terry's voice, in her eyes that couldn't quite meet Annie's as frankly as usual, must have given away her uneasiness.

Annie put her hand on Terry's arm, looked into her face, and said quietly, "You saw me with Hugh Deming just now, didn't you?"

Terry thought of denying it, but could not. She wasn't a good liar, and with Annie's great dark eyes on hers, she had to be honest. "I'm terribly sorry, Annie. I was sitting on a bench by the rhododendron hedge. I didn't mean to listen, and when I found out who it was, I took the short cut to avoid meeting you."

"I'm sorry, too, Terry," said Annie regretfully. She looked off across the lawns where children were playing with a ball. The line of her white cheek was poignant.

"I *promise* not to tell anyone, Annie. You know you can trust me," cried the girl unhappily.

"I know that, dear." Annie squeezed her arm gently, and they began to walk slowly down the path together. "That isn't why I'm sorry. It's because I'm so fond of you and I know you're fond of me, and it hurts me to have you discover something—well, like this about me."

"But it doesn't make me any less fond of you, Annie! I think I've known about it—I mean about you and Hugh Deming being in love—ever since my coming-out party."

Annie gave her a startled look. "You *knew*, Terry? But how could you? I danced with him just once and hardly spoke to him the rest of the evening."

Terry colored. "Oh, Annie, it looks as if I'd been spying on you, but truly I haven't. I just seem to be in the wrong places at the wrong times. I saw you saying good-by at the door and from the look on your face I knew you loved him and were sad about it."

Annie closed her eyes and stood in silence for a moment. Then she turned and smiled wryly at Terry. "I didn't know it showed so plainly. I've never been good at hiding my feelings."

"You thought you were alone. No one else saw you but me, and I thought it was beautiful. I remember wishing that someday I'd care enough for a man to look at him that way."

Annie sighed. "I don't know whether to say I hope you do, or to hope you don't, and be spared the suffering. Maybe you're enough like me to think the suffering worth the few moments——" She broke off, drew a long breath. "I guess I'd rather have loved Hugh, in spite of everything, than never to have known what love could really be."

"What hurts most, I think," murmured the girl shyly, "is to find out that what you thought was love was just a—a counterfeit. It makes you feel so cheap. It makes you wonder if you'd know true love if it came along."

"I think *you* will, Terry dear," said Annie gently, looking at her downcast face. "I just hope and pray that when your true love comes, nothing will keep you apart."

When they reached the street, she put her hand on Terry's arm and said, "There's a little confectionery shop on the corner, Mrs. Schmidt's. She serves tea in the afternoon at tables in the back. There's seldom anyone there at this time of day. Let's go in and have tea. You said you wanted to talk to me. I'd take you home with me, only I—I'm not quite ready to go home yet."

The shop was deserted except for two schoolboys in knickers and turtle-necked jerseys eating huge scoops of strawberry ice cream at the counter in front. Terry and Annie sat at a little round, marble-topped table in the back, on "ice cream" chairs with twisted wire backs and legs, ordered tea and almond macaroons from the smiling, plump German woman.

"I think I should explain to you about Hugh and me," said Annie, after Mrs. Schmidt had bustled off to make their tea. "We fell in love years ago, when I was only seventeen, before either of us was married. Today was the first time we've been alone together since we parted so long ago."

Terry said, "You don't have to explain anything to me, Annie. I'm sure you wouldn't ever do anything wrong."

Annie smiled at her youthful solemnity. "Don't be too sure, dear. Is there anyone who wouldn't, or mightn't, or who hasn't? It's mighty hard not to do wrong. Sometimes it's even hard to know which *are* the wrong things."

She clasped her large, strong, well-kept hands, with the wide gold wedding ring on the left and a handsome diamond, encircled with small rubies, on the right, on the table top and seemed to be contemplating them. "Was it wrong of me to love Hugh or wrong to marry Ed, not loving him? One thing seems wrong to the people who make the rules, but maybe God thinks the other was wrong."

"It was wrong of my mother to have given me away to strangers. My father was a stranger when he took me. Isobel

154

still is. I could never desert a child of mine!" whispered Terry in a low, bitter voice.

Annie glanced at her, but the girl's face was averted.

"Your mother didn't desert you, Terry!" cried Annie. "It nearly killed her to let you go. She loved you better than anything in the world, and she still loves you. She did a brave thing when she let your father take you so you could be brought up as a lady and have all the advantages he could give you."

Terry's face was still averted, but when Annie put her hand on the girl's, Terry clasped it hard.

Mrs. Schmidt arrived with tea and a plate of newly baked, tender macaroons and for a while they were silent and Annie poured out their tea. The German woman took her stand at the counter in front, the boys clomped out noisily, and late afternoon quiet descended on the little shop.

Terry sipped her tea and crumbled a macaroon, looking thoughtful. "I'm glad you told me that about my mother, Annie. I've never stopped loving her, but lately I've felt ashamed of her. I—I've been afraid I'd turn out like her— do the wrong things and end up badly. I mean, spoil my life, lose people's respect."

"I don't think you'll turn out like Maizie. She never had your chances," said Annie.

Terry gave a short laugh. "I haven't done so well, so far, with my chances."

"You've done very well, Terry. You're a fine, lovely girl. As for Hal Forrester, if he was that much of a stuffed shirt you're well rid of him. Unless"—Annie looked anxiously at the girl— "unless you were really in love with him."

Terry shook her head. "No, I don't think so. I was awfully hurt, but I guess that was mostly pride. I danced with him at the Kermiss Ball last night, and I still think he's attractive." She leaned forward, her face flushed and earnest. "Oh, Annie, I had to talk to you. I seem to be all mixed up. Ned Deming is going to ask me to marry him, I'm sure. He tried to last night coming home in the cab, but I headed him off. He's a sweet person and ever so good and kind. I'm really awfully fond of him. Should I marry him, even though I'm not in love with him?"

Annie's face grew stern and her eyes darkened. She put her hand over Terry's and held it hard. "No. Don't do it, Terry. Don't marry anyone, no matter how kind and good he is, unless you love him. You won't be happy and I'm afraid you won't make him happy, either."

Terry suddenly wanted to tell her about Matt Regan, but actually, what was there to tell? She'd been drawn to him, they'd kissed, and for a month she'd thought about him and hoped for some word from him. Now, whatever there had been between them, was over if, indeed, there had been anything except what was in her own mind. Instead she suddenly said, "Where is my mother now, Annie? I haven't seen her since the night Father took me away."

Annie hesitated, then gave the girl a keen look. "She's got a room at Bess Fuller's place, Terry, down on the waterfront."

Annie offered to share her cab home with Terry, but the girl thanked her and decided to walk and to think about the things Annie had told her. She was deeply grateful to Annie for having helped her to understand her mother better, for having given her something to be proud of her for.

"I'll never be ashamed of her again. She's brave and unselfish, and if she did wrong, she's made up for it." And then a thought she'd never had before struck her. "Besides, didn't Father do wrong, too? Wasn't he as much to blame as Mother? Yet nobody points the finger of scorn at him. Why? Because he's a man, and rich and important? Why should he be happy and respected, while Mother is ostracized and has nothing, not even her own child she suffered so much for!"

She was suddenly filled with longing to see her mother, to tell her she loved her and was proud of her. Did she dare go to

156

Bess Fuller's place on the waterfront, in spite of her father's and Isobel's certain anger and disapproval, in spite of her mother's last words to her: "Good-by, baby, you're going to a fine, new life. Don't ever try to see me, Terry. Better to forget me."

But I didn't, I couldn't forget her. And what do I care if Isobel and Father are cross? If I could just see her, tell her I'm proud to be her daughter—— Tears misted her eyes as she walked slowly down the street, and her heart ached with an anguish which, for the first time, was mostly for another.

A hansom cab was drawn up to the curb, its bony bay horse drowsing, while the cabbie slumped over a newspaper on the box. In sudden, crisp decision, Terry tapped the cabbie's shoulder. He sat up with a start, scrambled out, and opened the door in back for her. He gave her a puzzled look when she told him the address.

"You sure that's where you want to go, miss?"

"Yes, I'm sure," she replied evenly.

He didn't take her to the door of the waterfront rooming house but drew up a block away. She said nothing, got out and paid him, and he seemed to be struggling to say something to her, but was put off by her dignity and aloofness. As she walked rapidly up the street, he stood on the pavement watching her and scratching his head. He got back into the cab, but he waited, keeping an eye on her.

A colored maid she didn't know answered Terry's ring and stared at her suspiciously. "Yes'm. What you want here?"

"I've come to see Miss Maizie La Tour," said Terry, fighting down a mounting panic, but looking at the maid with authority. "May I come in, please?"

"What you want wif Miss La Tour?" The coffee-colored girl had opened the door only a crack and did not respond to Terry's question. Her head was done up in a red handkerchief and gold hoops dangled from her ears.

"I hardly think that's your business," replied Terry coldly.

"Kindly tell her Miss Terry Compton is here to see her." She managed to keep her voice from shaking, but her heart was thundering.

"Cain't do that, miss." The maid shook her head so that the yellow hoops swung. Her voice was sullen, and she devoured Terry's face, figure, clothes with her opaque black eyes.

Terry's hand, clasping her purse, began to tremble, but she held her head high. "Then be so good as to call Mrs. Fuller to the door and I'll speak with her."

"Miz Fuller is out of town. An' Miss La Tour is at work." And with a high cackle the maid shut the door in Terry's face.

As Terry walked down the steps to the street, her head bent, the cab drew up at the curb, the driver sprang out and opened the door without a word, but his face was red with relief.

Thirteen

AFTER Compton had driven off with Terry in the rancher's buckboard bound for Anacortes and the boat to Seattle, Matt Regan had sat for a while on the riverbank, smoking his pipe, slapping at nosee-ums, the tiny, vicious black gnats that rise in dizzy little clouds above the river at dusk. The river ran swift and dark with a steady roar, its deep waters broken now and then by trout jumping at the gnats.

Off toward the ranch house where Compton had hired the wagon, a dog began to bark and presently the moon rose and shimmered mysteriously on the water. The woods were full of night noises; birds still calling and rustling in trees and bushes, mice skittering in the grass, moths coming out of the weeds to blunder softly about in the moonlight. An owl drifted over Matt's head on silent, ghostlike wings and a moment later there was the small squeak of the mouse caught by the shadowy hunter.

Matt was not physically tired from the long trip down the river, yet he felt oddly spent, as if the life had been drained out of him. There was a cruel ache in his heart that made him sigh heavily, as if he might dislodge the source of his pain, but to no avail. She was gone and when or whether he might ever see her again, he had no way of knowing.

He'd wasted their last few moments alone together in trying to tell her about himself, boasting what a great one he was, the wonders he was going to do. I should have kept my big boastful mouth shut and taken her in my arms and told her I love her, he berated himself. No matter that she was cool and faraway, like a Queen sitting on a cloud; her lips were warm and answering when I kissed her on the trail yesterday.

What has she done to me, the tall, quiet girl with the steady gray eyes? I've wanted a woman before. I've felt desire burning through me like fire. But there was never this pain in my heart, never this cruel ache, as if part of my very body had been torn at her going. Ah, Terry, Terry, you've wounded me sorely, you've brought Matt Regan low, the best high-climber, the fastest man in the ring, the hardest hitter in the Pacific Northwest—here he sits, weeping in his heart like a lovelorn schoolboy.

It was a mournful thing to sit alone by the river with his thoughts, with the moon drawing her silver net over the dark waters and the night birds calling. He'd meant to start back to camp that night and sleep on the riverbank, but now he decided to hike into Sedro-Woolley and find some diversion that might take away this affliction in his soul.

The Gem Café and Bar was still open when he hit town, and though he'd not eaten since noon when they stopped on the bank, his thirst was stronger than his hunger and he made for the bar. It was crowded with loggers and ranchers, but a scaler he knew hailed him and motioned him to take his place at the rail.

"I'm on my way home, Matt," he cried, clapping the topper's shoulder. "The little woman'll give me a bad time as it is, and her keepin' supper hot since six-thirty. Have a drink on me, chum, for luck. Patrick, my boy, what do I owe ye? Mr. Regan, here, is havin' a drink on me."

"I'll be having a drop of ale, then, thank ye, Bill," said Matt.

Matt took his glass of ale to a table in the dining room, and ordered dinner from the waitress, Rita, who came up with her slow, provocative smile and said softly, "Hello, stranger. When did you blow in?"

"Hello, yourself, Rita. I just now got in. I've had no dinner yet. Can I get a steak smothered in onions, fried spuds, a side dish of succotash or maybe stewed tomatoes, and a hunk of pie and coffee?"

Her eyes went over him, as caressing as ardent hands. She was handsome in her way, he thought, with her full-blown figure, ripe, sensual mouth, and black eyes. But there was a coarseness in her broad face with its high cheekbones, short, flattish nose, which now repelled him.

"If it was anyone but you, honey," she murmured, leaning one palm flat on the table before him, her other hand on her hip, "I'd say the kitchen is closed. But for Matt Regan I think I can get Wang to fry you a steak."

"Thanks, Rita. I'll remember ye in me will when I die." He grinned up at her and she gave him a long look, running the point of her tongue over her lips.

"You'd be no good to me dead, honey. But a lot of good alive. Know what I mean?" She winked and pressed her knee against his thigh.

He laughed. "All I know right now is that me stomach is hollow and the ale I've had is sharpening me appetite something terrible."

She tossed back her head, which seemed too small for the heavy, oily black braids wound about it. The gesture reminded him of a snake about to strike. "You men!" she snapped. "All you ever think of is your blankety-blank stomachs."

"Not quite all, sweetheart. The trouble with women is that they never learn that there's a time and place fer everything!"

She made a face at him, touched her thumb to her nose, and switched off to the kitchen, her hips swaying.

Clint Reber, a sawyer for Gus Steiner, came up and sat down with his beer at Matt's table while the big Irishman lit into his beefsteak. "Heard y' was talkin' about buyin' some timberland and settin' up yer own company, Matt. That right?"

"I may do that, Clint, if I can find what I want. It'll be small potatoes compared with Compton and Steiner, but I hanker to be on me own," said Matt, between bites. Lovesick he might be, but there was nothing the matter with his appetite. He wiped up the last of the good red beef juice with a hunk of bread and stuffed it into his mouth.

"You're smart, Regan. Wish I had yer guts. But I'll never be anything but a sawyer on somebody's payroll. Too scared to take the chance, or mebbe I don't like the notion of being tied down in one spot. I'm a rollin' stone, never stayed in one camp more'n three years." The sawyer, a good-looking young fellow with a broad back and a strong, full brown throat, shrugged and grinned, his roving dark eyes on Rita's figure as she set down a tray of beers at the next table.

"I've been a rolling stone since I was fourteen," said Matt, pushing away his dinner plate and reaching for his pie. "Now I'm tired of rolling. I'm tired of bosses, too. I want something of me own besides me climbing boots and bedroll."

"You wouldn't be thinkin' of settlin' down with a wife, would ye, Matt?" chuckled Clint, winking at Rita as she glanced over at them. She ignored him and gave Matt a strange look, two spots of color burning suddenly on her cheeks.

"Maybe that's not such a bad idea, Clint. I'll give it some thought once I've got me a good stand of timber and the logs are beginning to roll," smiled Matt, not noticing Rita's stare.

Reber tossed off his beer, pulled out tobacco sack and papers, and began to roll a cigarette with stubby, mutilated fingers. "Heard about something might interest ye, Matt. Heard about a stand of virgin timber, Sitka spruce and Douglas, some hemlock, too, I guess, over Port Blakely way. Old coot name of

Peter Metcalf owns it. The Weyerhausers have been nosin' round, but he's an independent cuss, don't like the smell of Eastern money. Metcalf's never done a thing with the land, seems he might sell to the right party."

"By glory, Reber, that sounds good." Matt leaned across the table, his face alight. "Where can I get ahold of this fella?"

"He's got an office in Anacortes, they tell me. Don't know that he's in much, but ye might write to him there."

"Write, nothing doing! I'll try to see him before I go back to camp. If he's not in Anacortes, I'll find out where he is. Dobie'll be sore at me fer taking the time, but this sounds too good to pass up. How about some of the Chinaman's tobacco juice?" Clint nodded and Matt called out, "Rita, will ye be a sweetheart and bring us a couple of coffees?"

She brought their coffee, managing to brush against Matt's shoulder as she put the cups on the table. Matt scarcely noticed her, but Clint reached out and patted her arm. She whirled and struck his hand away.

"Fresh guy, huh?" she muttered. "I don't like fresh guys."

"Aw, come on, baby, don't give me that. You didn't act that way last time I was down." Clint gave her a bold, insolent look. "We had a real nice time t'gether, remember? What time d'ye get off t'night?"

"I get off at ten-thirty, like I always do. But I *expect* to be busy," she said pointedly, fixing her black, opaque gaze on Matt.

Matt, who was thinking about Metcalf and his virgin timberland, was busy filling his pipe and unaware of her glance until the sawyer chuckled and said, "Excuse *me*, Regan. Didn't know I was hornin' in on yer party."

Matt looked up and met the flash of the girl's eyes as she flounced away. "*My* party, Clint? What the blazes're ye talking about?"

"I didn't know ye were datin' Rita t'night or I wouldn't have tried to bust it up."

Matt reddened and he drew his black brows together. "You're not busting up anything, Clint. I've got no date with Rita tonight or any night. I took her out once, before I knew she was Jack Dobie's girl, and I've had nought to do with her since. She's all yours, for all of me."

"She's taken a fancy to ye, ye handsome black Irishman," teased Clint. "Don't know if she'd look at me with you in town."

"Cut it out, Clint. She'll look at any man willing to spend money on her." He finished his coffee and changed the subject quickly. There had been a time when he'd have savored Clint's teasing about his prowess with women, but now, with Terry in his heart, he was impatient with such foolishness. "How're things over at Steiner's camp?"

"Uneasy. There's talk that Gus is plannin' to sell out to Weyerhauser." Reber leaned his arms on the table and gave Matt a sober glance. "I'm about ready to move on. If you start yer own outfit, Matt, and want a first-rate sawyer, let me know. I think I'd like workin' fer a guy like you, Regan."

"It's a deal, Clint. My big trouble will be trying to get a good crew t'gether. I won't be able to pay top wages at first, but ye know I'll give ye a fair shake." Matt pulled on his pipe thoughtfully, took it out of his mouth, and pointed it at Reber. "I've got a notion ye might like, Clint. How'd ye feel about being paid part in cash, part in stock in the company?"

"Would that mean I'd be part owner, in a small way?" Clint sipped his coffee, his slow mind working painfully. "It'd mean I'd be workin' fer myself, too, sort of, huh?"

"That's the idea, Clint. It'd be a bit of a risk, ye know. If I go broke, so do you. But if I make money, you do too, over and above your wages."

"By golly, that sounds okay. But I'd have to think it over, Matt."

"You do that. If ye don't want to take the risk, I'll pay ye what I can, spot cash, as long as it holds out."

164

"I'll keep in touch with y', Matt," said Clint, shaking hands and getting up to go.

Matt was tired in his very bones now, relaxed from the food, and it was a good feeling, for he knew he would sleep and not be tormented by the thought of gray eyes. Clint's information about the timberland had fired him with excitement and hope. Here was something he could put his mind to and know where he was. Tired as he was, a sense of exhilaration lifted his spirit. Well, Miss Terry, he thought, this may be the first step toward showing you what manner of man Matt Regan is. After that, who knows?

As he paid his bill and turned to leave the café, Rita sidled up to him. "Leaving so soon, honey?" she said softly.

He glanced down at her as he stuffed his change into his wallet. "Uh-huh," he replied. "Got to hit the hay, sweetheart. Big day t'morra. Got to be up bright and early."

"I got a new place, Matt, a nice little three-room flat over the butcher shop on Front Street. I fixed it up real nice."

"That's fine, Rita. Well, good night now. I'll be seeing ye." He turned to go, but her nails bit into his arm.

Her eyes smoldered and there was a stiff, dangerous smile on her red lips. "Mebbe you think y're too good fer me, now, eh, Matt? I hear y've been makin' time with the Boss's daughter. Went horseback ridin' all alone with her on the mountain."

He picked her hand off his arm as if it had been a scorpion. His face was dark with fury. "I never hit a woman in me life. But so help me, if ye ever come near me again, I'll give ye the back of me hand," and he pushed open the swinging doors and strode out into the street.

He slept like a log at the lumberman's hotel, but was awake at dawn to catch the first stage into Anacortes. It was a white, foggy morning with wetness dripping off the trees, but gossamer cobwebs in the fields along the road promised a hot, fine day by noon. In Anacortes, the air was fresh and pungent with the smell of the Sound and the docks. He strode up the street,

165

throwing out his great chest, breathing deeply and smiling at all the world. He had a feeling that he'd be lucky that day. He strengthened his luck by stopping at a clean little hole-in-the-wall restaurant for a fine breakfast of eggs, ham, fried potatoes, hot cakes and syrup, and three cups of coffee.

A few inquiries led him to a shabby office building near the docks and on the second floor at the end of a dark hall smelling of old wood, spittoons, human decay, and unaired, dusty offices he reached a door with *P. G. Metcalf, Attorney* in bold gold letters on the frosted glass window, and under, in smaller print, *Timber, Farm, and Mining Properties. Walk In* was written in a fine, Spencerian hand on a card stuck into the window frame. Matt Regan walked in.

At first he thought the tiny, dark office was empty, and then a shining bald head reared up from behind the old-fashioned roll-top desk and a pair of bright blue eyes, as blue as his own, twinkled at him.

"A good morning to ye, young fella," creaked an ancient voice, full of hemidemisemiquavers.

"And to yerself, sir," replied Matt, peering down at the shriveled bit of a man at the desk. "Would ye be Mr. Peter Metcalf, now, sir?"

"I would, indeed, and who else? And who might ye be, ye black young giant with the sweet sound of me own dear green Isle on yer lips?"

"Matt Regan is me name, sir. And the dear green Isle of which ye speak was me parents' homeland, God rest their souls."

"And may light perpetual shine upon them. Amen," said Peter Metcalf, bowing his head. "Draw up a chair and let's hear yer story, lad."

He looked like nothing so much as a very old, very dried-up leprechaun and once more Matt felt that luck was with him that day. Hadn't his poor mother often told him the great good luck attendant on meeting with a leprechaun if he took a fancy to you and you could win him over to be your friend? She'd warned that it was a tricky thing to do, needing goodness of heart, pure honesty, and a sweet tongue as well.

"I felt in me bones that I'd be in luck t'day," said Matt, with his engaging smile, pulling the chair up to the desk and fixing his blue gaze on the old gaffer. "But 'twas too much to hope that Peter Metcalf'd turn out to be from the ould sod!"

The old man chuckled, his bright eyes keen, for all their warmth. "Whist, boy! Save the blarney fer the Yankees. Ye can't fool another Irishman with yer sweet talk. Ye want something of me, so out with it and don't waste me valuable time. The story, lad, the story!"

"'Tis a simple story, sir. I heard ye've got a fine stand of timber up the Sound that ye might be persuaded to sell to the right party."

"That's as it may be. Go on, Matt Regan. I'm listening."

"I'm a logger, sir. I've been high-climbing fer the Compton Lumber Company at Skagit River."

"A good man, Compton. I know him. He's not greedy like some. He's got a proper respect fer the forests God has given us here in this great Northwest." Metcalf nodded, pulling out a battered oilskin tobacco pouch and reaching for a brier pipe on his desk.

"That he has, sir. I, too, have respect for the forests and I admire the way Compton logs. If I could be content to spend me life working for other men, I'd stick with him. But I've the itch to be me own man. The best boss in the world is still a boss, and a thorn in me spirit."

Metcalf chuckled. "No proper Irishman ever had much love in his heart fer a boss. Which the English have been finding out to their sorrow. So ye're wanting to set up fer yerself, Matt Regan? Is that it?"

"It is, indeed, sir. That's part of the story. Here's the rest of it, if ye'll permit me." The old man waved a hand, puffing on his pipe and regarding the young fellow sharply behind his smoke screen.

"Well, sir, me parents were poor Irish immigrants, forced out of Ireland by the evil days of the Famine. Dada lost his life in a Pennsylvania coal mine when I was going on fourteen. Mother died with her seventh child, a few months later, and the little one with her.

"I've been on me own ever since. I've worked as cookee, then faller, then high-climber in the Michigan camps. I hit the Klondike trail in '97 and was lucky enough to bring back a poke of gold which I put safe away in the Dexter Horton Bank in Seattle. I've saved a good part of me pay in the three years I've been with Compton. I've got twenty thousand dollars salted away and most of this year's wages coming to me."

"Not bad fer the son of poor Irish peasants, Matt Regan. Ye want to buy me timberland up the Sound, I gather."

" 'Tis been the desire of me heart, sir, since I heard it might be had," cried Matt passionately. "I heard, too, that a certain Eastern monopoly is after it, and that makes me soul shake, knowing fer sure that me own small grubstake can't match what they can offer ye."

"Devil and all his angels take the Eastern monopoly!" The old man bounced up from his chair and hopped about the room like an angry beetle. "Maybe ye also heard that next to Ireland, the Northwest is the place of me heart, and to me mind, 'twill be the ruination of our Western timber once we let them robber barons in!"

"I heard ye don't like the smell of Eastern money, sir," smiled Matt, leaning back and puffing contentedly on his pipe.

"I do not, Matt Regan. I like money as well as the next man, but I've got me principles. And, thank God, I'm so old and so near me blessed reward in heaven, I can't be tempted. How much can ye pay me fer the five hundred acres of beautiful, sound timberland, lad?"

Matt pulled on his pipe, looking steadily at the ancient leprechaun. "If I said more than ten thousand dollars, I'd be land-poor and unable to get the logs rolling."

"The Weyerhausers offered fifteen thousand dollars and I can jack them up to twice that." The old man's eyes were piercing as he paused in his gyrations around the room.

"Then I'll be taking me leave of ye, sir, and wishing ye good day and luck," cried Matt, pushing back his chair, his color rising.

"Keep yer shirt on, blast ye! Leave me a moment to consider this thing." Metcalf flapped his arms like wings at the young man. "Sit down, I tell ye! Possess yer soul in patience."

Matt sat down and Peter Metcalf sat again at his desk and busied himself with pencil and paper, stopping now and then to scratch his bald pate and screw up his monkey features. At last he threw down his pencil and slapped his palm on the desk.

"Seven thousand five hundred and twenty-five dollars is the very most ye can afford to pay me and not go broke the first year. And that's not figuring in layoffs because of bad weather, or accidents, fires, or acts of God."

"Ye'll never take that little fer virgin land ye can get three times that fer," said Matt sadly, glancing out of the corner of his eye at the old man.

"I'll take three thousand dollars cash on contract and the rest in a first mortgage against yer business. And I'll charge ye a stiff rate of interest, too. Five per cent till the first twenty-five hundred is paid off, three per cent thereafter. If ye go broke the first year from mismanagement, the whole outfit reverts to me. If ye get into a jam because of them rascally Easterners and their finaglings with the government, let me know and I'll lower the boom on them."

Matt couldn't believe his luck was that good, but he was not the man to question it. He was on his feet, towering over the wizened leprechaun, holding out his great hand. "Will ye shake hands on it, Peter Metcalf? Will ye believe me when I say ye'll not regret yer generosity?"

"I'll shake hands with ye, but go easy with that great fist. I've no mind to get me bones cracked," chuckled Metcalf. "And whether I'll regret me soft-headedness, we'll see."

Matt tried to press his thin, dry claw gently, but the old man winced and shook his fingers afterward. "Dear God in heaven, lad, ye've got the grip of a bear trap."

"Will ye take me check fer half the down payment as option money, sir, till I've had a chance to look over the timber?" asked Matt, reaching in his pocket for the checkbook he was so proud of that he always carried it with him.

Peter nodded approvingly. "I see ye're a man of sense, Matt Regan. I'll take yer check and I'll keep the land fer ye till ye make up yer mind, one way or t'other. Take yer time, lad, I'm in no rush to sell and with ye holding an option on it, nobody else has a right to buy."

There was no holding Matt's luck that day. He walked out of Peter Metcalf's office on wings, and it was a wonder he didn't soar clean over the housetops. The first person he met was Jack Dobie, who'd taken a log boom down-river to the Anacortes mill with Red. He seldom left camp except for an occasional week-end spree, but an aching tooth had been driving him crazy for a day and night, so he'd taken Jake's place on the boom to see his dentist in Anacortes.

Now the tooth was out, and the relief from pain so heady he was in a celebrating mood. He didn't seem surprised to run into Matt in town, but slapped his arm and invited him to have some coffee at the New York Saloon near the docks. It came into Matt's mind that perhaps the prospect of seeing Rita later might account for his jollity, poor devil.

The way his luck was running, Matt thought it would do no harm to tell Dobie he was taking a couple more days off to look over Metcalf's timber. Over their coffee in the airy, light, white-tiled saloon, the best in Skagit County and the safest for a logger or a seaman, since Anton Gereg, the big, bald Polack who ran it, kept his reputation as spotless as his shiny brass spittoons and clean, thick glasses and steins, Matt broached the matter.

"Sure, Matt, take the rest of the week off if you have to. We're way ahead of our mark this month. You've only taken one week end in the last six weeks." Dobie gave him an interested look. "I'd like to hear more about this plan of yours to set up your own company. I've got a few bucks cached away, Regan, and if this timber looks good and you'd like a silent partner, I might be willing to go in with you."

"Thanks, Jack, maybe I'll take ye up on that," said Matt heartily, but not committing himself further. It made good sense to have a partner to share the financial load and the responsibility, but even a silent partner would want to have his say, and Matt had dreamed too long of running the whole show, sink or swim. Then, too, he couldn't forget the feeling all the men in camp had that Dobie was unlucky, that everything he touched, business or love, when he went out for himself, went sour.

"Understand now," Dobie said earnestly, "you'd be boss, run everything your own way. I'd stay on with Compton, go into the deal purely as an investment, keep my nose out. I wouldn't even want my name on the books, it'd be between the two of us."

The poor devil knows he's unlucky, thought Matt, compassionately. Well, I've got enough luck for the two of us. What harm could his money do me? And maybe this would break his jinx.

"If ye're willing to take a chance on me, Jacko, I'd be proud to deal ye a hand on yer ante. But maybe after I've seen the stand, I'll be wishing I had me option money back." He laughed, and ordered more coffee for the both of them.

"No, Matt, I think it's going to be all right," said the foreman thoughtfully, turning his cup in his thin, freckled hands.

"I've got a hunch about you. I think you'll succeed in this deal and in anything else you try. As I get older it seems to me that some men are born lucky. Everything they touch turns out fine. And others"—he laughed bitterly, hunching his narrow shoulders—"well, for them, it works just the other way. No matter how they try, everything goes to pot for them." He drained his cup and set it down carefully on the table before him. "I'm beginning to think I'm one of the unlucky ones."

Matt was uneasy at all this talk of bad luck. He liked Dobie and he admired him for his fairness and industry as a foreman. But he was restless under his introspective, gloomy talk, and besides, he was eager to be off up the Sound to Port Blakely.

He got up and punched Dobie's shoulder affectionately. "That's no way to talk, Jacko. And if you're right that I'm a lucky one, maybe, if ye go in with me, some of me own luck'll rub off on you. Buck up, boyo, have yerself a toot before ye go back to camp. I'll get back as soon as I can."

He was gone a week. Metcalf's timber was a logger's dream, a virgin forest of Sitka spruce, Douglas fir and sound hemlock, running down to the Sound, about twenty miles above Port Blakely. There'd never been an ax laid to the woods. There was no camp, no road, no landing. The *Kitsap* put him off at a tiny fishing village in a cove about halfway between the Metcalf stand and the big mill town, and he had to make his way on foot along an old Indian trail.

He had an hour to wait for the stage to Sedro-Woolley after he landed back in Anacortes and he stopped in at Peter Metcalf's office, demanding to know what the catch was. "Is it that the woods are haunted, sir?"

The old man nodded. "Ah, you'd be the one to catch on, wouldn't ye, Matt Regan? Haunted they are, by the dear ghost of the sweet girl I went all the way back to County Cork to win for me bride." He sighed and the bright, mischievous eyes dimmed a little. "We took our wedding trip up the Sound, Matt, and she fell in love with that piece of God's green earth, so I bought it. We planned to build us our dream house there, far from the madding crowd, where we'd raise a great batch of lively, blue-eyed children to climb the trees and tumble on the beach. But she died trying to give me our first, and the wee girl with her, and since then, I've never laid eyes on them lovely woods."

"'Tis heart-scalded I am, sir, at yer sadness and yer loss," murmured Matt, honest tears in his eyes.

"Thank ye, my boy," replied the old man with dignity. "That was near fifty years ago and will ye believe it, the ache in me heart has been with me all the years, and there's never a day goes by that I don't long with all me soul to be taken to where she is?"

"I do believe it, sir," said Matt soberly, thinking of the ache in his own heart. "And it's humble I am ye'd think me good enough to take over those sacred woods from ye."

"Sacred they've been to me, boy, and it gladdens me heart to hear ye use the word. I know ye must cut the trees, ye must log and sell the timber, but I think ye'll be kind to the woods, lad, ye'll not be ruthless with me Mary's trees?"

"I give ye me sacred word on Our Lord's Body, on me hope of salvation, that I'll be kind to the trees, Peter Metcalf!" cried Matt.

The old man smiled and nodded. "I believe ye, boy. Ye've got the look of a true man on ye. May the Lord prosper the work of yer hands, lad, and send ye as great a happiness with a woman as I knew in the short time I had with my Mary."

Matt looked at him, got up, and stood hesitantly by his desk. "If ye'll forgive me for talking about me own affairs, sir, but I think the Lord has sent me the one woman out of all the world who can give me happiness. The only trouble is, I don't know if I'm the one she can be happy with. And there's this ache in me heart because of her and I think, whether she'll have me or no, my heart will never be whole again."

"If she's your true woman, Matt Regan, her heart is aching

173

for you, too," cried Peter Metcalf, "and if ye haven't told her what's in yer heart, ye better do it soon, for a woman is a fragile creature in many ways, and stronger than a man in others, but she cannot live without knowing her love loves her."

Matt got into camp the next morning. That night he tried to write a letter to Terry Compton. He labored over pages and pages, read them and balled them in his great hand, shot them into a corner. At last he gave up. He knew he could never tell her how he felt about her in a letter. He was ashamed of his big, round, childish scrawl, uncertain of his spelling, and besides, the written word was so cold and flat when the heart was warm and passionate. He could only hope that the Holy Mother, in her infinite compassion and wisdom, would help him, would let her know, somehow, of his undying, his desperate, his inarticulate love.

Fourteen

AFTER Merritt Compton had been assured by the family doctor that Terry's concussion wasn't serious and that with rest and quiet she'd be all right in a few weeks, he continued his inspection tour of his camps, returning from Grays Harbor in late July. Isobel had taken Terry to Green River Hot Springs, the fashionable watering place in Washington, for two weeks, shortly after the Kermiss Ball, and for a few days Merritt was alone in the house, except for Hannah and her daughter, Sadie, who looked after him competently, though in a more relaxed manner than when Isobel was there to keep them on their toes.

He was quite content to have the house to himself, to take his meals on a tray in his study, where he shut himself up with his notes, reports from his foremen, market quotations, and the daily papers. He was becoming increasingly concerned over the encroachments of Eastern interests in the Northwest lumber industry and the gradual capitulation of the smaller Western companies, who were either selling outright to the Eastern companies, or merging, which amounted to the same thing in the long run.

He was particularly disturbed over Beauchamp Deming's

disclosure that one of the sturdiest of the independents, the White River Lumber Company, after vainly fighting encirclement by the Weyerhausers, was in the process of merging with its powerful competitor.

"Weyerhauser and the Northern Pacific literally bottled them up, Merritt," Deming said. "The railroad gave Weyerhauser alternate strips of land along their right of way in return for a freight price agreement. First thing Olssen at White River knew, he was boxed in, with no way of getting his logs out. He had to agree to the merger or go out of business."

"If this goes on, Beau, there won't be a local outfit that can stand out against them!" Merritt paced the study, puffing angrily on his cigar. "Except, of course, Compton."

"And how long can Compton hold out, Merritt, with these big fellows pulling deals with the railroads and the railroads getting the government to condemn timberlands right and left, then buying them up for a song?"

Deming sat in the red leather Morris chair, cradling a sherry glass in both hands. He had a lawyer's cold, precise voice, which he seldom raised, and was as unlike his son, Ned, or Hugh, his brother, as possible, being a thin, tall, dry man with an almost ascetic face. Even in his office he wore a frock coat, gray waistcoat, and wing collar. Merritt, by contrast, looked burly and untidy in his rumpled tweeds.

"Teddy Roosevelt is getting after the Big Trusts. The Supreme Court has already declared the merger of the Northern Pacific and the Great Northern illegal. The Attorney General has just instituted proceedings against the Beef Trust. They'll get around to the lumber monopolies, too."

"In the meantime, we have a fight on our hands," said Deming gravely. "Fight or get swallowed up before T.R. gets around to us."

"We'll fight, all right, but the only way we can fight is to stick together. Work out some kind of merger, loose enough to let each of us keep his own entity, but strong enough to

176

battle them on their own ground." Compton sat down and poured himself a small glass of sherry. "I want to talk to Gus Steiner. He's too close to our Skagit River Camp for comfort and he's too much of a highball operator to suit me. We lost close to half a million feet of timber in his forest fire."

"You'll never get that pigheaded Dutchman to go in with a merger, Merritt. It wouldn't work if you did. You'd be at each other's throat from the word go. He doesn't give a hoot for the forests, all he cares about is a quick profit."

"I'd merge with the Devil himself if I thought it would save our timber from the Eastern monopolies. But what I want is to try to get Gus to sell me all the timberland adjoining our Skagit stand. Arrange a meeting with him tomorrow or as soon as possible, Beau, will you?"

As Deming was leaving, he turned to Compton, smiled, and held out his hand. "Well, Merritt, speaking of mergers. If my son, Ned, has his way, there'll be a happier kind of merger between our families."

Compton looked blank. "What d'ye mean, Beau?"

"Ned's in love with your daughter, didn't you know? He's asked my permission to propose. I, naturally, gave him my blessing and promised to set him up in business if and when he gets married. He wants to go into real estate. No doubt he'll be speaking to you soon if he can muster the courage." Deming laughed, beaming proudly. "Ned's a bit of all right, Merritt, even if he is my son."

Merritt gripped his hand, at a loss for words.

"Ned's a fine boy. We've always liked him, Beau. But it's entirely up to Terry, y'know. She's pretty young yet, doesn't know her own mind, and all that. I don't want her to rush into anything till she's sure."

Deming sensed his withdrawal and his face chilled. "Of course, Ned's no lady-killer and he hasn't a Harvard accent, but he'd never back out, once his word is given," and he turned and stalked out of the room.

Compton stood quietly and let the anger subside in him. That last remark wasn't worthy of Beauchamp, who prided himself on being a gentleman. But people were apt to forget their manners where their children were concerned and Merritt was sorry he had brushed off Ned so ungraciously. He *was* a good boy, salt of the earth, but as a husband for Terry? All that gray-eyed, long-limbed loveliness given forever to a stout, red-faced boy with a stutter? Hell, maybe he can make her happier than that tailor's dummy who thought he was too good for her. And Isobel keeps hammering away that our first duty to the girl is to find her a suitable husband.

But what about Terry? Merritt refilled his glass, sat down in the Morris chair Deming had vacated, and turned the glass in his hands. Suitable husband, blast! I want her to find a man she can love. I'd rather see her married to a real man like that cocky, virile logger, Regan, than to Ned Deming or Hal Forrester or any of these well-mannered, thin-blooded popinjays on the First Hill.

He remembered the way Terry had looked at Regan when he came down from the tree and swaggered up to them, the feeling he'd had of interrupting something intense between them when he came back with the wagon to take the girl to Anacortes. No, I don't want that, either. I've worked too hard to give her her proper place in society to let her throw herself away on an ignorant, reckless Irish lumberjack and live in a lumber camp in the woods.

The truth is, he thought, that there's nobody good enough for her, because I can't bear the thought of any man possessing her. But I want her to be happy and she can't be happy unless she finds the right man. I can't let her wither away, year after year, unloved by Isobel, loved too much by me. If she wants to marry Ned Deming, I won't stand in their way. At least, he'll be good to her.

Gus Steiner put him off until the end of the week and Merritt, unused to such treatment, was in a surly mood, nearly

178

snapping off Beauchamp's head when he told him Steiner would see him in his office in the Boston Block that Friday. "In *his* office, hey?" he cried. "Nothing doing. If he won't come here to my office, then we'll meet on neutral ground. Tell him to meet me for one o'clock lunch at the Butler as my guest. Tony can put us in a private dining room. I'll want you along and he'll probably bring that shyster, Clarey, with him. Hold on—any of your smart law clerks take shorthand?"

Deming, still smarting from the way Merritt had received the prospect of Ned as a son-in-law, smiled faintly and nodded. "Yes, as a matter of fact, young Forrester takes shorthand."

Merritt threw back his head and gave his lawyer one of his long, merciless, appraising stares. Then he grunted. "Sure it's not Greek or Sanskrit? Didn't know they taught anything as useful as shorthand at Harvard."

"Hal didn't learn it at college. He bought a book and taught himself."

"Clever fellow. Bring him along, then. Don't trust that big German or his shyster lawyer. I want a record of what goes on."

As it turned out, they didn't need Hal, after all. The fat German, with his iron-gray Prussian-cut hair and greedy little pig's eyes, stuffed himself with raw Olympia oysters, thick pea soup, roast goose, red cabbage, and beer, and sat picking his teeth and belching, while Merritt, who had taken nothing but half a cold cracked Dungeness crab and a glass of Chablis, stopped drawing circles on the tablecloth with his spoon and leaned across the table, his hooded, deep-set eyes piercing.

"Now let's get down to business."

"Ja. Suits me. Talk."

"I want to buy 150 acres of your timber stand on the Skagit, adjoining my camp. Name your price, within reason, and I'll meet it."

The waiter came in with coffee and Steiner helped himself to cream and sugar, sat stirring his coffee round and round until the waiter had left, then shook his head. "Too late, Compton. I don't own that stand any more. Sold out last week to Weyerhauser." He laughed and his belly shook like a malevolent Santa Claus's. "Paid me so good I can take Momma and the poys and go home to Chermany." He waggled his coffee spoon at Merritt. "Take my advice, Compton. Sell out, too, if you can. You're a fool if you try to fight."

Compton and Deming went back to Merritt's office on Pioneer Square together. Hal Forrester left them in front of the hotel to go to the courthouse.

"Thanks for lunch, Mr. Compton," he said politely. "Sorry I wasn't able to be of use."

Merritt gave him a brief glance and nodded curtly. He didn't offer to shake hands. "Appreciate your coming, Forrester."

"Well, that's that," said Beauchamp, as they walked down First Avenue in the shimmering July sunshine.

"Now we've really got to fight, Beau. We've got to get to the other independent lumbermen before Weyerhauser does. I'm going down to see the Schafer brothers at Hoquiam tomorrow. I want you to get in touch with Johanssen at Humptulips and McGraw in Snohomish. We'll have a meeting as soon as I get back."

"May I remind you, Merritt, that though I may be your lawyer, I also have a private practice? I've got court cases coming up next week," said Deming touchily, annoyed at being treated like a secretary.

"What the devil, Beau! You're also a stockholder in the Compton Lumber Company. Let those clever young men in your office handle your court cases till we get this thing rolling. Unless, of course, you'd prefer that I engage another counsel." Merritt's voice was edged and he gave Deming a measuring look.

The lawyer flushed under Merritt's gaze. "All right, keep your shirt on. I'll contact Johanssen and McGraw, but I warn you, this merger thing may take time. The other lumbermen may be afraid you're trying to swallow them up. It's going to take a while, first of all, to get ahold of them—they're hardly ever in their Seattle offices. Then it'll take time to convince them you're right. They're an independent lot, and they'll want to chew it over for months."

"I don't expect to set up a merger overnight," snapped Merritt. "But the longer we wait, the closer the danger gets. If I could get an agreement with these fellows to hold off on any propositions Weyerhauser or the other Eastern outfits may make for at least six months, we'd have a chance to talk sense to them."

When Merritt got home that night, Isobel and Terry had returned from Hot Springs. Dinner was laid in the dining room with the proper linen, silver, glasses; and Sadie, who took his hat and stick at the door, was prim and subdued in her black uniform, stiff white cap, and starched organdy apron with the butterfly ties.

"Mrs. Compton and Miss Terry are back, sir," she said in a discreet whisper.

He laughed. "No need to tell me, Sadie. One look at you is enough. The holiday's over, eh?"

She blushed and hid a smile. "Oh, Mr. Compton, sir. You won't be after telling on us, would you?"

"Not if you don't tell on *me*," he grinned, and strode into the sitting room where Isobel was arranging pink La France roses, white snapdragons, and lavender stock for the mantel. He smiled. There'd not been a flower in the house while she was gone.

"Welcome home, my dear," he cried, and put his arms around her.

"Oh, it's you, Merritt," she said, over her shoulder. "Do be careful, you'll make me spoil this arrangement."

"I don't give a hoot about your arrangement. I've missed you, Belle, and I want a kiss." He squeezed her waist. "By golly, Hot Springs did you good. You've lost a couple of inches around the middle."

She turned, her face flushed. "Oh, *do* you think so?" and she let him kiss her cheek. "Did you really miss me?" she pouted.

"Honest Injun. Nobody to tell me not to smoke my nasty cigars in the parlor. Nobody to make me put my coat on for dinner." He chuckled and she pushed him away.

"You did not, Merritt Compton. You had a fine time all by yourself and probably spoiled the servants rotten. We could have stayed another week and you'd never have known the difference. Anyhow, there was no point in staying longer. Terry was getting bored."

She sighed and shook her head. "*I* don't understand your daughter, Merritt. There was a fine, jolly crowd of young people at the hotel, but after the first few days, Terry would go off on a horse by herself right after breakfast and be gone for hours. At first I thought she was lonesome for Ned, who's been so attentive since she came home from her trip with you. But Ned came down over the week end and she didn't seem a bit impressed. Oh, she was nice enough to him, let him ride with her, went to the hotel dance on Saturday night. But she didn't even get up the next morning to say good-by to him, though he sent a huge basket of American Beauty roses up to her room and wanted to have breakfast with her on the terrace. Instead of annexing a new beau at Hot Springs, she's come home with a dog!"

"Good Lord! What kind of a dog?" He smiled at Isobel's seriousness, thinking, of course, that's what the poor kiddie should have had long ago, a dog. Something to follow her around, something all her own.

"Oh, I don't know. Some kind of hunting dog, I guess. He's not a puppy, he's half grown, a great shaggy brown creature with hound's ears and a white blaze on his chest. He *smells*, too!" Isobel made a disgusted face.

There was a scuffle on the stairs, a dog's nails scrabbling the polished floor, a young woman's warm, happy laughter, an excited bark, and Terry, in a short pleated blue linen skirt that exposed her slender ankles, and a white tailored shirtwaist of tucked lawn, came into the sitting room, followed by a large brown dog, laughing and wagging his long tail, but decorously observing her command to heel.

Terry embraced Merritt warmly, not giving her cheek as his wife had done, but kissing him on his hard, dry mouth. Then she turned, held out her hand to the dog, who had paused uncertainly on the threshold, and said, "Come, Mac, I want you to meet my father."

The dog responded instantly and galloped across the room, skidded on the highly polished floor, and covered up his embarrassment by putting his forepaws on Terry's chest and licking her chin ecstatically.

"How do you like him, Father? He's got a lot to learn, but he's an utter lamb."

"Where did you get him?" asked Merritt, putting down his hand for the dog to smell and nuzzle.

"I found him when I was out riding near the hotel. He was tied up in a mean little back yard and he looked so miserable that I pulled up to the fence and spoke to him. He nearly tore down the fence, he was so glad for a friendly word, and when I started to leave he gave me a look that broke my heart."

"So you came back and bought him," he said, with an indulgent smile.

"I didn't know if he was for sale, but I got off my horse and went into the house and asked the woman if I could have him. She said he'd belonged to her husband who had died a few weeks before and that he was a one-man dog and she couldn't handle him. She didn't even want to take my money, she was so glad to get rid of him. I made her take five dollars."

Compton bent over the dog, fondled his ears, held his muzzle, and ran a knowing hand over his deep chest and straight back. "You've bought yourself a good dog, kiddie," he said, as he stood up. "This is no mutt, Terry. He's a Chesapeake Bay retriever and he looks pure-bred to me. There's no better duck dog in the country than a Chesapeake. I had one when I was a kid that never missed a bird."

Terry knelt and put her arms around the dog's neck and he nuzzled her cheek. "I'd love him even if he *were* a mutt. I'll let you hunt with him, Father, but, remember, he's my dog. He knows he belongs to me now and I don't want to confuse him." She looked up and gave Merritt a strange, direct look, her eyes wide and dark. "It's important to know just where you belong, Father."

"You're quite right, Terry," he replied gently. "You handle your dog in your own way."

"All very well," broke in Isobel firmly. "But I've told Terry he's not to have the run of the house. If she insists, he may sleep in her room, but during the day, he belongs outside." She wrinkled up her nose distastefully. "Why on earth you want a great, clumsy, smelly creature like that, Terry, instead of a pretty little Pom or a pug, I can't see."

Terry smiled and stroked Mac's head. "Maybe it's because I'm big and like the outdoors, and he's a big, outdoors dog. I can't stand little dogs. Anyway, the minute I saw him, I knew we belonged together, and I think Mac knew it, too." The dog sat motionless, his odd, golden eyes gazing into her face as if there were no one else in the room. "Come on, old boy, I'll put you in the back yard. It's fenced in, so you won't have to be tied."

"From the way he looks at you, kiddie, I don't think he'd budge from the place without you," smiled Merritt, watching as she walked with her long, graceful step out of the room, the dog close at her heels.

As he listened to Isobel prattling on about the people she'd met at Hot Springs and the agonies she'd endured to lose five pounds, he kept thinking of what Terry had said about knowing where you belong, and pondering the meaning back of her words and the strange look she'd given him.

Didn't she feel that she knew where she belonged, even after almost nine years as his daughter? Was she still lost between her mother's world and his? In a flash of insight he understood why she had had to have the dog. Terry herself was probably not aware of it, but she had wanted to free the fine dog from his chains and give him a place of his own with her because she longed to be free, too; free of the restrictions and narrowness of a life that had been imposed on her by Isobel and himself; she, too, was waiting to find her own place and to be claimed by love. And there is nothing I can do to help, he thought sadly.

Fifteen

THE summer ended, though the fine weather continued on into early October with very little rain. Merritt Compton worried about the dry forests and went off again in September to his camps to check and recheck his fire-prevention rules; ordered a swamper at Grays Harbor discharged for leaving slashings burning with no one to watch.

At the Skagit Camp, he found Dobie laid up with an infected throat and Regan as acting foreman and apparently doing a good job. The Irishman asked about Terry, and Compton told him bruskly that she was quite recovered and dancing every night. Matt's face went tight and he said he was that glad she'd suffered no ill effects from the tumble and would Mr. Compton be good enough to give Miss Compton his regards and best wishes. Merritt said he would, and promptly and deliberately forgot about it.

His plans for combating the Eastern companies moved slowly, much too slowly to suit him. The Schafer brothers turned down the plan for a Western merger but assured him they could hold their own against Weyerhauser or any other lumber monopoly. Talks went on from time to time with other local lumbermen, and McGraw of Snohomish, at least, showed some interest, while the stubborn Norwegian, Johanssen at Humptulips, said he didn't need any help yet, but Compton needn't worry about him, no Minnesota German would take him over.

Ned Deming summoned the nerve to ask his permission to court Terry, and Merritt told him that if he thought he could make her happy it was all right with him. But Ned, though he was as faithful as the big Chesapeake, got no further than holding Terry's hand under an Indian blanket at a football game between the University of Washington and Leland Stanford.

Terry was a bridesmaid at Milly Fox's fashionable wedding at St. Mark's and envied the radiant bride, not her blonde loveliness, though Marguerite Brookes wrote in the *Argus* that she was the most beautiful bride to be married in Seattle in a decade, nor her exquisite cream lace gown and heirloom veil, but the look of happiness and assurance on her smiling face as she turned from the altar and put her hand on the arm of her good-looking, adoring husband and walked up the aisle.

Hal Forrester, who was an usher, drank too much champagne at the reception and, finding Terry alone for a moment in the conservatory, tried to kiss her, and when she rebuffed him, told her that all during the ceremony he'd been thinking of her. To which she replied easily that the champagne had gone to his head and she hoped he'd feel ashamed of himself in the morning.

During the fine, blue October days, Terry took long walks with her dog. The Chesapeake went everywhere with her, except to parties and church. His responsive love gave her a wonderful new confidence. There was a great dignity to the animal which she loved and admired. There was nothing abject about him, he never pleaded for her affection. He waited, with his nose on his paws, and when she spoke to him, lifted his noble head and regarded her with a look of understanding and alertness that recognized her claim on him, but asserted his own integrity.

Yet, many times as she sat by her bedroom window lost in thought and swept by longing and sadness, the dog, who had been asleep in the corner, would silently get up, pad over to her, and lay his heavy, warm muzzle on her knee. It was as if the understanding between them was so complete that, animal though he was, the weight of her unhappiness lay on his spirit, too.

October ended in one of the most violent equinoctial storms the West Coast had known. Two of Hugh Deming's North Star steamers foundered in the Strait of Juan de Fuca, and the asters in Isobel's garden which she'd been saving for her "at home" were beaten down by wind and rain. There were floods in the lowlands around Puyallup and Kent and telephone wires were down all over the city. Compton rejoiced that the fire hazard to his forests was ended for another year.

The Comptons entertained the Beauchamp Demings at Thanksgiving dinner and Isobel introduced a brand-new dessert, peach Melba, which had been created in the East to honor the great Australian diva, Nellie Melba. After stuffing themselves with crab bisque, roast turkey, creamed oysters, corn pudding, boiled onions, hothouse asparagus, all manner of relishes, preserves, jellies, condiments, pickles, Hannah's famous pecan rolls, pumpkin pie, and Isobel's new dessert, they engaged in a new parlor game, Diabolo, which soon had the older folks gasping and puffing.

Isobel prevailed upon Terry to sit down at the piano, and she gave them MacDowell's "To a Wild Rose," a Chopin mazurka, and her father's favorite, "Narcissus." Then, fearing the gentlemen were falling asleep, she swung into the popular favorite, "Henrietta," which brought Ned up to turn the pages for her and to sing the words in his surprisingly clear, true tenor. They romped through a couple of other popular numbers, "After the Ball" and "The Strawberry Blond," and then Terry swung round on the piano stool, slammed down the lid of the upright, and said to Ned with a yawn, "For heaven's sake, let's take a walk. I'll go to sleep if I don't get some fresh air. And I promised my dog a turn in the park."

There was a fine, cold mist in the air that Terry lifted her face to gratefully. Far down the Sound a lonely steamer hooted through the fog. The mist had a pungent smell of the tide flats and kelp that was a wonderful antidote to the afternoon's stodginess. Family dinner parties were deadly, but Thanksgiving Day, with its orgiastic bounty of food, was stupefying.

It was unfortunate but typical of Ned, Terry thought, that he should choose that day, after they'd circled the park and were sitting on a bench, watching Mac stalk a squirrel, to propose.

Oh, heavens, thought Terry, if I marry Ned I'll be committed to these horrible, overfed, flannel-wool affairs, year after year, for the rest of my life. I can just see us arriving with our children, all fat, rosy, pop-eyed little editions of Ned, sitting down at dinner and gorging ourselves on Hannah's good food.

She hated hurting good, dear, kind Ned, so she took his hand and pressed it softly before she spoke. But, of course, that didn't soften the blow for him, though she refused him in the gentlest, most loving voice. "Oh, Ned, I *do* thank you most awfully for asking me. But I can't marry you, even though you're the very nicest, dearest man I know." She looked at him directly, her eyes very clear and honest and unhappy for his pain. "You see, Ned, I'm not in love with you. I like you more than anyone. But I don't think people should marry unless they're terribly in love."

He didn't, as she'd feared, go to pieces. He got even pinker than usual and swallowed and looked off across the lawn, but when he spoke there was no trace of a stutter. "I know you

189

don't love me, Terry," he said quietly. "But I think you like me. Sometimes love comes after—people are married. If you ever change your mind, I'll be waiting."

"No, Ned," she cried, in a sudden passion. "That's not fair. I don't want you hanging around waiting for me and missing out on life. I want you to find a nice girl and be happy. You're so good, Ned, you *should* be happy."

"There'll never be anyone for me but you, Terry," he said simply.

He had a genuine dignity, born of an honest emotion, and as he got up and gave her his arm, she wished with all her heart that she could have accepted him. For a moment she thought of telling him she'd changed her mind, that his love would be enough, that maybe, if they were married, she could come to love him. So she did an outrageous thing, a cruel thing, but she had to be sure. She suddenly turned to him and said, "Ned. Will you kiss me?"

He blinked and his arm under her hand trembled, but he bent and gently pressed his lips to hers. Then he straightened up, looked steadfastly ahead, and they walked along in silence, while the dog foraged a few paces beyond.

Presently Terry, with her head down, said in a faint voice, "That's why I can't marry you, Ned. Kissing you is like kissing my brother, if I had one."

"Then let me act as your brother, Terry, and take you wherever you want to go and look out for you—unless, of course, you have a more interesting escort," he said humbly.

So nothing was very much changed. Ned was still Terry's faithful escort to the Christmas and New Year's parties and they seemed to be even better friends than before. She did not tell Isobel or her father that he had proposed and that she had refused him, and since he was as attentive as ever, Isobel seemed quite certain that all would be well.

Mable Fisher took her to meetings of the Mission Circle and she helped the Baptist ladies sew chaste, long-sleeved gray flannel nightgowns for the Mission School at Umiak, Alaska, where Mable's saintly young missionary was stationed.

She went with her stepmother to Morning Prayer at 11 o'clock every Sunday at St. Mark's Episcopal Church, and once a month took Communion at the early service alone, and wished she could keep the exalted and purified feeling she came away with, but which was gradually dissipated by dinnertime. It was an uneventful winter and all the time Terry had the curious feeling that she was waiting for something to happen. But whether it was to be good or bad, she had no clue.

Then, one evening early in May just before dinner, the telephone, which had been so newly installed that Hannah was afraid to touch it, rang, and Terry, answering, heard Annie Jordan saying, "Terry? I have some bad news for you, my dear. Try to be brave. Your mother is very sick and isn't expected to live. She sent word to me that if you could come to see her before she—goes, it would make her very happy."

Was this, then, what she had been waiting for? Was it tragedy instead of happiness that had been preparing for her? "Oh, Annie," she whispered. "Of course I'll come."

"If you can be ready in ten minutes I'll come for you in the motor, Terry," Annie was saying.

Hannah, who always expected the voice of doom from this new, devilish device, saw her face, white and pinched with pain, as she fled past her upstairs for her coat, and went back to her kitchen to say a Hail Mary and ask the Holy Mother's help for the poor child in whatever trouble that black machine with the gaping mouth hanging on the wall had brought to her.

When Terry flew downstairs in her coat, Isobel met her in the hall, frowning. "For pity sakes, Terry, you're not going off someplace at this hour? Dinner will be on the table the minute your father gets home."

Terry gave her a dazzled, unseeing look. "Mrs. Bauer is coming for me. My mother is dying. I must go to her."

Isobel pressed her hand to her throat and went a little pale.

"You're not going to—to that awful part of town, Terry? You can't! What if you should be seen by some of our friends?"

"Do you think I care about that when my mother is dying?" cried the girl passionately, her lips trembling.

"When she gave you up to us, she promised never to see you again. I forbid you to go. She can mean nothing to you now."

"She means everything to me!" If Isobel touches me, I think I must hit her.

Isobel moved toward her, as if to bar the way. "Your father would never permit you to set foot on that street. Do you hear me, Terry? You may *not* go!"

Through the hall window Terry saw Annie's big red automobile, one of the first in town, coming up the driveway. She brushed by her stepmother without another word, opened the front door, and ran down the steps. John, Annie's chauffeur, sprang out and helped her into the tonneau, where Annie reached for her hand in silence.

"What is the matter with my mother?" the girl asked in a low, tense voice.

"It's her lungs, Terry. She had pneumonia a year ago and she didn't take care of herself. Now it's gone into consumption."

"Thank you for coming for me, Annie," said Terry, and then she sat in silence the rest of the way and Annie did not try to talk to her. Terry stared at the back of John's head as they drove along Boren Avenue to James Street, crept in second gear down the steep hills with the yellow cable cars clanging up and down on their almost perpendicular tracks, to Yesler Avenue. Her eyes felt hard and dry and from time to time she drew a deep breath, as if there were a weight on her chest that made it hard to breathe.

Just before they reached the boardinghouse, Terry said in a queer, tight voice, "I tried to see Mother last summer. The day we had tea across from the park. But the maid wouldn't let me in."

192

"If you can, it would be nice to tell her, Terry," said Annie. She spoke to her driver. "John, this is the place. Please wait for us."

The maid must have been on the watch for them. She opened the door before Annie could press the bell, and with a scared, subdued look on her dark, subtle face, whispered, "You the ladies come to see Miss La Tour? Right this way, then. Through the hall, all the way to the back."

The enormously fat woman in a flamboyant green-and-purple Japanese kimono held together by a wide yellow sash, her hair, still a startling pink, done in tight, short curls all over her head, opened the door at Annie's knock. The moment she caught sight of Terry, she held out both pudgy, beringed hands.

"Oh, Terry girl, thank heaven you've come!" she cried in a deep, emotional voice. "I was sure you would, bless your heart, even if you're a lady now and far above the likes of your poor ma and fat old Bess Fuller."

Terry, in a sudden rush of feeling, found herself unable to utter a word. She disregarded the outstretched hands and embraced her mother's old friend, her heart burning within her. The sight of the kind, still pretty face buried in the mass of flesh brought back memories lost for years. Dear Bess, who took us in when we had no place to go, who bought me a doll with real hair on my birthday—oh, Bess!

There were tears in Bess Fuller's eyes as she held Terry away from her to look at her. "Oh, it's good to see you, girlie dear. And what a lovely young woman you've grown to be. Your dear ma will be proud."

"It's good to see you, Bess," said Terry, her throat tight with tears she would not shed. "And I'll never be above you or Mother, nor ever want to be."

"Bless you, honey. I think you mean that!" Bess dabbed at her eyes with a soiled lace handkerchief she fetched from her capacious bosom, then she sniffed, smiled at Annie. "I hope you'll excuse me receiving you in my dressing gown. I was just changing when Maizie got took bad and the doc said I best send for her kinfolks."

"It's true, then, Bess," said Annie softly, putting her hand on Terry's arm. "Maizie isn't going to get well?"

Bess sighed and shook her head. "The doc says she hasn't got a chance. Poor lamb, she don't have much longer to go. In a way, it's a blessing for her."

"Is she—in there?" whispered Terry, indicating the room beyond Bess's massive figure.

"Land sakes, child, yes. And here I stand, keeping you from her! Come on in, both of you," cried Mrs. Fuller, drawing Terry into the room with her. "She's over yonder, behind that screen. This is my private apartment, y'know, and when Maizie got so sick, I had her moved down here so's I could look after her. The Sisters from Providence Hospital come in every day, too."

The apartment was oppressively warm, with a Franklin stove humming in the corner and all the windows tightly shut. "Let me take your wraps," Bess said. "It's awful hot in here, but poor Maizie complains so of the cold."

It was a large, high-ceilinged room, shaped like an inverted L, with the sitting room near the door, the sleeping quarters at the other end, hidden by a huge, magnificent Chinese screen of teak overlaid with lotus flowers in gold leaf and mother-of-pearl.

Bess tossed their wraps on a large sofa which was covered with a handsome throw made of black sealskins. "I been sleeping on this couch since I put Maizie in my bed," explained Bess. "See that cover? Got it when I took my vaudeville company up to Nome in '98. One of my admirers presented me with a king's ransom in furs he got off some Eskimo hunter. I had a jacket made of some of the skins, the rest I had sewed up to make a couch cover. The crazy things you do when you're young and beautiful!"

She suddenly lowered her voice, as if aware for the first time of the dying woman behind the screen. "Now you both sit down and make yourselves to home. I'll go see if Maizie is awake and tell her you've come to see her."

Terry couldn't make herself "to home." She stood, her eyes fixed on the Chinese screen, her whole body tense with dread, with anguish.

Annie Jordan sat on the couch, her hands loosely clasped in her lap, her bright head bent, a look of almost unbearable sadness on her strong, beautiful face.

It all seemed unreal to Terry. The sudden summons in the midst of a quiet spring evening, the silent ride in Annie's car, even the fact that her mother was dying behind the exotic Chinese screen, Annie sitting there, withdrawn into her own mysterious thoughts—all too unrelated, too bizarre for her to understand or accept. She suddenly wished she were anywhere but here.

She wished to be home, at dinner with Isobel and her father, with Sadie handing round the soup. She realized that though she had longed to see her mother again, she didn't know what to say to her. She was trembling when Bess came back and nodded gravely and said, "You may go in now, Terry. She's awake and very happy that you've come."

Maizie La Tour was lying on a great black walnut bed with a headboard carved in the shape of an enormous swan. She was propped up by three eggshell satin pillows and covered with a luxurious pale blue satin comforter. The bed was a shock, as were the opulent apricot velvet curtains looped across the bedroom windows. But the greatest shock to Terry was the woman who turned her great, smoke-gray eyes, stained underneath by deep blue shadows, and put out a white, emaciated hand in greeting.

The abundant chestnut hair that Terry remembered as falling in a silky, shining cascade on her mother's pillow was now shot with gray and plaited in two neat braids like a schoolgirl's.

The lovely, laughing face, once so full of warmth and life, was bloodless and gaunt, the full, sensuous lips pale and dry, the cheekbones sharp under the tightly drawn skin. Only the splendid eyes had not changed, and as they met Terry's, they shone with a light so intense and wonderful that they transfigured her poor disease-riddled face. "Oh, Terry!" she said in a rough whisper. "I'm so glad you've come."

Terry was bound by an agonizing shyness. Her heart was beating so hard that it was a pain in her breast. This dying woman was not her mother, not the mother she had remembered all the years, yet she was; the eyes, the voice were hers. *I must not cry, and I must say something warm and comforting. I must not let her see how shocked I am.*

As if understanding her shyness, Maizie said, "I'm sorry you have to see me looking like this. Doesn't my hair look silly? But the nurse says it's easier to keep neat this way."

"I don't know what to say to you, Mother," Terry suddenly cried, unable to pretend or to say meaningless things when she might never see her mother again.

"I know, baby. It's been so long. I'm like a stranger to you now, I suppose." The hand that Terry had clasped pressed hers faintly, then, as if exhausted, fell away and lay inert on the satin quilt. "Don't worry about it, dearest. You don't have to say anything. Just let me look at you." The bright, full eyes devoured the girl's face. "You're lovely, Terry girl. You've grown up into a beautiful woman. I'm so proud."

"Mother, I want to—to tell you——" Terry struggled desperately to say all that she had meant to say last summer. "I came to see you last summer, but the maid turned me away."

"You came to see me?" A wave of warmth went over the bloodless face. "You—*wanted* to see me?"

"Yes, Mother. More than anything. I wanted to tell you how proud I was of you for having been so brave. Annie Jordan told me how brave you were. And about what it must have meant for you to let Father take me."

"You were proud of me, Terry?" The smile that trembled over the pale lips was heartbreaking. Terry could not look at it. She had to look down at her own tightly clasped hands.

"Very proud, Mother."

"God bless you, my darling. You've made me so happy. But are you happy, Terry? Is Compton good to you, is his wife kind?" The frail hand reached out again in a vague, helpless gesture and Terry covered it with her own young, warm, alive one.

"Yes, Mother, I'm very happy. I have everything. Father and Isobel are very good to me." I can give her this, if nothing else, thought the girl with a sudden mature insight. It is too late to ask her help or wisdom. It is for me, now, to reassure her, to let her know that her suffering was not in vain.

"Annie tells me that you will marry soon, the pick of the First Hill families."

"I—I hope so, Mother." With those bright, anguished eyes on her, she could say nothing to disturb the dying woman.

"Of course you will, honey. You're so beautiful. I used to be beautiful, too, but you've got more than I had—you've got class." Maizie's hand dropped away from Terry's; she lay back on the nest of pillows and her breathing was slow and labored.

It seemed to Terry that she was dying then, before her eyes, and all at once all her shyness and strangeness melted away and she was a child again, wanting her mother, wanting to be held close against that warm, loving bosom, wanting to be reassured of love.

"Oh, Mother!" she cried, and burst into hard tears. "Mother, Mother, don't go away from me, don't leave me. Oh, Mother, I love you. I love you!" And the tears that she had not shed all evening poured down her cheeks in a sudden burst of grief. All at once she was on her knees beside her mother's bed, her arms were around the thin shoulders and her head was buried on her mother's breast, and two frail, infinitely tender hands were pressed gently on her head.

"My baby, my precious girl, my little Terry," crooned Maizie ecstatically, her face blazing with love. "If I die this next minute I'll be happy to go, knowing you love me."

She held the sobbing girl until Terry was able to stem the tide of her emotion and to move out of her mother's arms and stand alone, not ashamed of her grief but thankful that the shyness that had held her captive had given way to the very real emotion she truly felt.

"I must go now, Mother," she said gently. "I'm afraid I've tired you."

"Yes, Terry, best you should go. I'm not tired, but I never know when I'll have a bad time, and I don't want you to see me like that." Maizie, with great effort, reached around her neck and unclasped a thin gold chain which was attached to a gold, heart-shaped locket. "I want you to have this," she said, putting it into Terry's hand. "Your father gave it to me years ago. It was the first present he gave me, when he was very much in love. He gave me others, more valuable, but this I kept. I want you to have it to remember me by."

Bess Fuller tapped on the Chinese screen. "The doctor is here, Maizie."

Terry, clasping the locket in her hand, turned a wild, dark, frantic gaze on her mother. "Good-by," she said, her throat aching with grief.

"Good-by, my dearest," said Maizie tenderly, her thin, pale face soft with happiness and love. "Be happy, Terry. That's all I ask. Be happy."

Terry did not kiss her mother good-by, she did not look back at her, but walked quickly out of the room with her head high and her face set in the heroic lines of accepted grief that was her final tribute to her mother's courage.

Annie took her arm and directed her out of the apartment and down the long, dark hall to the street. As they went out the door, a hansom cab drew up at the curb and Merritt Compton pounded up the steps.

"Terry, my dear!" he cried in a strangely soft, shaken voice, and put his hand on her arm.

Terry, blind with tears, looked at him without recognition, and shook off his hand, turned, and went down the steps with Annie to the red motorcar waiting at the curb to take her home.

Sixteen

MAlZIE died that night, a few hours after Merritt Compton had left her. Her death was not as painful to him as had been the sight of her lying on that bed, her beauty wasted, squandered, ravaged. He had seen her only once since the night he took Terry away, and that had been nearly four years later, at the theater, when she had passed him in the foyer during intermission, beautifully gowned and handsome, on the arm of a well-dressed older man. They had smiled at each other, but passed without speaking. He was not prepared for the pitiful, wasted creature dying in Bess Fuller's preposterous bed.

Better dead than like that, oh, much better dead, poor Maizie, poor, lost girl. Once my delight and my torment and now, saddest of all, nothing to me except a reproach to haunt me for a little while, and then, because a man cannot live with a reproach all his days, to be mercifully forgotten.

Worst of all, he thought, as he rode downtown the next morning to the undertakers' parlor to select a coffin and arrange for the funeral, a gesture whose irony he was as well aware of as was Bess Fuller, who had allowed him the privilege with a bitter smile, her death is a great relief to me. Shameful to feel that, he knew, but the truth, so it must be faced. So long as she lived, her unhappy life would cast its shadow over the bright future of his darling, his Terry.

Maizie's death had shocked the girl grievously, he realized. She had not even known him last night on the steps of Bess's house. This morning when he had gone into her room, while she was still in bed, to tell her that Maizie was gone, she had stared at him with wide, accusing eyes, as if by bringing her the news he was in some way responsible.

She had not cried. She had not even spoken, and when he sat on the edge of her bed and took her hand in his, there had been no answering pressure. So he had kissed the cold hand gently, touched her unbound hair, and left her. He'd looked back before going out the door and had seen her dog get up from where he had been asleep beside her bed and lay his muzzle on her arm, and the girl had suddenly leaned over and put her arms around the Chesapeake's neck. A twinge of bitterness had twisted his heart. I cannot comfort her, but the dog can.

But she will get over it, he thought, she's very young and in a few weeks life and youth will ease this sorrowful memory. Then, perhaps, I can talk to her, as I should have done before, help her to understand her mother's life and death and my part in it all. If I can't altogether justify myself to her, since I can't justify myself to my own conscience, I can at least make her understand.

Terry did not go to the funeral, which was held in the small Roman Catholic mission on the waterfront. It was only the year before, when she had nearly died of pneumonia, that Maizie had been baptized and had taken instruction, though she had often gone with the Variety girls to Mass. She was buried in the Roman cemetery in South Seattle, overlooking the bay, and Compton put up a handsome headstone and arranged with the cemetery officials for "perpetual care." Another irony, he thought, in self-castigation.

When her father asked Terry if she wished to attend the

funeral, she had shaken her head and looked at him as if he were not there. "No. I said good-by to Mother while she was still alive. I don't want to see her put in the ground."

Isobel, to his surprise, insisted upon accompanying him. It wasn't until she said, with lowered eyes and flushed cheeks, "I think it would look better if I went with you, Merritt," that he realized it was not out of respect for the woman he had once loved, nor as a gesture toward Terry, but because she was afraid "people would talk" if he were seen at Maizie's funeral without her.

It was a pitifully small cortege that followed Maizie to her last resting place. Compton and Isobel went in their own carriage, and Annie Jordan, in her motorcar, alone, so the undertakers had only three carriages to provide, besides the hearse, in which the priest in cassock and biretta rode with the body. Bess Fuller and four of Maizie's friends from the old Variety, subdued and tearful in respectable black, wearing huge cartwheel hats with heavy black veils, occupied one; two sea captains in blue uniforms with brass buttons, the Greek who ran Jake's Place, uncomfortable in a shiny black broadcloth suit, obviously worn only at weddings and funerals and obviously too tight for his opulent figure, in another; the two middle-aged nuns from Providence Hospital, who had nursed Maizie in her final illness, shared the third with Jim Petley, editor of the *Argus*, whose sharp, ironic gaze flickered briefly over the faces of Isobel and Merritt as they left the mission church.

Isobel, disturbed at seeing the newspaperman, whispered to Merritt to ask him to ride back from the cemetery with them. Petley, though he had found the nuns excellent company and a source of information about the deceased, accepted Merritt's invitation with a faint smile. On the way back, when Isobel leaned forward and asked him delicately if he was planning to print an item about the funeral in his paper, he nodded.

"Certainly, Mrs. Compton. Maizie was a very popular actress in her day, and a great friend of mine. There will be a lot of people in Seattle who will be sorry to hear that she has left us. I intend to give her a good send-off." He glanced at her mischievously over the cigarette he was lighting. "But don't worry, ma'am, I shan't mention the names of the mourners."

The next issue of the *Argus* carried a front-page story about the death and theatrical career of Maizie La Tour (born Maizie Thomsen), the "former beautiful and popular star of Considine's Variety Theater, whose untimely passing of the 'galloping consumption' will be mourned by her many friends and admirers, both on the waterfront and on the First Hill."

There was no mention of her decline, but the story paid tribute to her warmhearted generosity to waterfront unfortunates in her palmy days, to the legend that she had been so tenderhearted that once, on being approached by a beggar at the stage door, and having no change in her purse, she had impetuously stripped off a valuable bracelet from her arm and thrust it into his hand. Her marriage to Merritt Compton was also omitted. The obituary ended with the cryptic words, "There are no survivors."

Terry read and reread the item, cut it out of the paper, and locked it in her desk drawer with the only picture she had of her mother, a rather stagy photograph taken when she was Considine's star, in a sequin dress and a headdress of ostrich feathers. Until she read Jim Petley's story, Terry had never known what her mother's real name was.

As she sat by her bedroom window, stroking Mac's head and staring at the red hawthorn just coming into bloom, she realized sadly that she had never really known her mother. She knew nothing about her life before she came to Seattle—where she was born, who her parents were, why she had gone on the stage. Nothing, nothing, she grieved. Mother never talked about the past, only about today or the day after. And I never asked. She felt that she had failed her mother not to have known, not to have asked.

She fingered the gold locket, which she had worn ever since the night her mother gave it to her. The locket, the photograph, and the newspaper clipping were all she had left of her beautiful, loving, warmhearted mother. It had hurt to read in Mr. Petley's story that Maizie had "left no survivors." At first she thought he might not have known about her. Then she reasoned that if he could have ferreted out her mother's real name he must have known she had a child, that she had been married to Terry's father. That he chose not to mention it could mean either that he knew Terry was accepted as Merritt Compton's daughter and wished to spare her the embarrassment of being publicly proclaimed as the child of a former Variety girl, or else her father had influenced him to ignore the fact.

Terry chose to believe the latter. The question of her father's responsibility in her mother's tragedy which had come into her mind so suddenly last summer had, with Maizie's death, become an obsession with her. It was not only the shock of her grief that had made her refuse to recognize him as she was leaving Bess Fuller's boardinghouse and fail to respond to his efforts to comfort her when he came to her room to tell her that her mother was dead. It was the shock of the final and inescapable realization of the great injustice that had been done her mother and that now, in her anguish, she blamed on her father.

She believed now that she hated Merritt, and she could not bear to have him touch her. She could not talk to him without restraint and dreaded the moment when he came home and it was necessary for her to greet him. With all the single-mindedness of the young, the inexperienced, the cruelly honest, she rejected her father because he was alive and rich and successful and happy, while her mother, who had been spurned, neglected, and allowed to suffer, was dead.

Annie tried to talk to her, to explain that while her father was certainly responsible for her conception, he was not completely to blame for the disaster of Maizie's life.

"I know you loved your mother. I loved her, too. When I was a little girl, she was my ideal. But without any disrespect for the dead, Terry, we can be honest, can't we, and face the facts about Maizie? Long before she met your father, circumstance and her own nature had shaped her life. If she had not met, loved, and married your father and then lost him, her life might have been different. But then you would not be here, or if you were, you would be a different person."

The girl sat in Annie's pleasant upstairs sitting room, stroking the gray cat, staring at the floor. Annie felt that she had deliberately closed her mind against all argument or explanation, that her bitterness toward her father was actually the impotent anger of one as yet unreconciled to grief who must have a specific object to assail to save herself from utter desolation.

"Perhaps that would have been better," said Terry bitterly. "I'm not pleased with the person I am, nor the circumstances of my being alive and in this world. I don't think I like this world very much, Annie."

"Yet it *is* our world and we are alive in it, you and I, and since we can't change it, isn't it better to learn to live in it and not to fill ourselves with bitterness because it isn't heaven?"

"I don't ask that it be heaven, Annie," cried Terry, raising her stricken young face. "I only ask that justice be done, and that kind, loving people like my mother be allowed to live and be safe and happy."

"Ah, but my dear, you *are* asking for heaven!" sighed Annie.

"Perhaps so. But why should Father escape?"

Annie gave her a long, thoughtful look. "*Has* he escaped, Terry? Do you know that he has? I saw him at your mother's funeral and he did not look to me like a man who had escaped."

Merritt Compton made an attempt to penetrate the wall which Terry had put up between them. Isobel was at a whist party and he came home early from the office and found Terry in the little summerhouse in the back garden. Her dog was at her feet and she was sitting in a high-backed wicker lawn chair, reading. The summerhouse was covered by Virginia creeper, newly green, and the sunlight through the bright leaves cast a tremulous radiance over her serious young face. The two great lilac bushes were heavy with purple bloom and their fragrance scented the warm spring air.

The dog, seeing him first, lifted his head and thumped his tail on the floor. Terry looked up. Merritt felt that if she had seen him coming she would have escaped, and a flicker of pain went through him. He smiled and paused, before bending his head and entering the little pavilion.

"May I intrude on your peaceful privacy, Terry?"

"Certainly, Father," she answered soberly, and closed her book.

He eased his length down into the companion chair to hers and glanced at the title of her book. "Browning, eh? You like poetry?"

"Very much. Much better than novels." Her voice was distant and polite.

"I would have thought Browning a little obscure for a young girl."

A ghost of a smile reached her eyes. "I'm not *that* young, Father. Anyway, it's only in the way he puts things that Browning is obscure. His philosophy is almost too simple."

"Oh? And what is, if I may ask, your idea of his philosophy?"

She made an impatient gesture. "Hopelessly optimistic. 'God's in his heaven: all's right with the world.'"

"You don't agree with him?"

She flashed him a somberly intense look. "Do you?"

He drew a long breath and gazed off across the sun-splashed

lawn. "At moments like this, with the smell of those lilacs in the air, the sun just warm enough to be pleasant, that little breeze refreshing my cheek, and my well-beloved daughter beside me, looking so beautiful, yes, I'm inclined to agree with Robert Browning."

"How utterly selfish!" she cried, and faced him with the same accusing eyes that had greeted him days ago when he told her Maizie had died in the night. "How can all be right with a world that is so full of injustice and pain and sorrow and sin!" Her face flamed with passionate color.

"Dear child, the world has always been filled with misery, but men have been able to live in it without going mad with despair exactly because they could accept moments like this and enjoy them." He turned his hooded eyes on her with an almost pleading look. "Is that so selfish?"

But she gave him no mercy. "Yes. Selfish, blind, unfeeling. What you mean is, all's right with *your* world. But what about my mother's world?"

He put his long, narrow hand over his eyes as if her piercing gaze had blinded him. Presently he said gently, "All's right with your mother's world, now, Terry. Her sufferings are over and she is at peace."

For several minutes she did not speak. She had turned her face away from him and was staring unseeing at the shimmer of sun on the dark madroña leaves. "Yes," she whispered at last, in a desperate, choked voice, "because she is dead and no one can hurt her any more. But why did she have to suffer so much when she was alive?"

"Terry, Terry," he murmured in pity, "no matter what our lives are, all of us must suffer. It is true, some people, because of circumstances or bad luck or their own mistakes, suffer more, or seem to. There *is* injustice in all this, though perhaps not as much as we may think, not understanding very much of the laws that govern our lives."

He took his hand from his eyes and compelled her, by the

force of his gaze, to look at him. "Don't think your mother's life was all suffering. I never knew anyone who loved life more or who found it more exciting. Why, she lived every moment to the hilt. If you could ask her now if she had enjoyed her life, I think she would say yes, with all its ups and downs, its strange turns, even its suffering and tragedy, *yes, yes!*" His dark, brooding eyes glowed strangely. "It was her joy in life, not only her beauty, that made me fall in love with Maizie."

"If you loved my mother, why did you divorce her and marry Isobel?" The words created a little eddy of silence between them. As soon as she had uttered them Terry wished them unsaid. This question, which she now knew had tormented her for years, should never have been asked.

"I could say, Terry," he replied slowly, as if feeling his way, "that what kept your mother and me apart were two totally different ways of life. Or I could say that my family would have disowned me if I had stayed married to an actress from the Variety Theater. Or that Isobel was from my world, Maizie was not." He gave her a long, thoughtful look, frowning slightly, not at her so much as at his groping to make her understand.

"Or I could say that I was very young and selfish. All true. But do you believe that Maizie would have been happy as my wife, committed to the teas, the 'at homes,' the luncheons, the church bazaars, the dinners that make up Isobel's life?"

"I'm sorry, Father," Terry murmured, looking down at her tightly clasped hands. "I should never have asked that question."

"You should never have had to ask it, Terry. Long ago I should have talked to you frankly about your mother and myself. God forgive me, I was too cowardly. I was afraid to lose your love." He looked at her with eyes that seemed sadder than her mother's eyes as she lay dying. "Have I lost it, Terry?"

She met his gaze and remembered Annie's words, *But has he escaped?* She could not bear the weight of his pain, his sorrow, and his pleading. All at once she felt very young and immature and unsure. She wanted, quite suddenly, to be free of grief, even the grief of her mother's death. She wished he would go and leave her alone. "I don't know, Father."

As if sensing her distress, he got up and left her, strode across the lawn, and disappeared into the house. She lay back in the wicker chair with her eyes closed, wishing for Ned, or Mable, or someone her own age to come and talk to her about silly, young things. A thrush lighted on the Virginia creeper, set it to swaying, and began to sing. As she listened to the pure, trilling, joyful notes, tears came to her eyes and gently her overburdened heart let go its load of sorrow. It seemed that there was nothing in the world but this happy, exquisite song. Is this what Father means, what Browning meant?

Merritt wanted to ask Terry to come with him when he set off for his spring inspection tour of the camps, but the wall between them, while not so high nor so impregnable as before their talk in the summerhouse, still stood. Any further attempt to break it down would have to come from her. It would come eventually, he felt, but he dared not try to force it.

He announced that he was leaving one night at dinner, and Isobel sighed, as she always did, and protested, "I don't know why you think you have to make these trips, Merritt. Why can't you hire competent foremen to look after the camps, the way other lumbermen do, instead of wearing yourself out checking up on them?"

"My foremen are the most competent in the industry, Isobel. It just happens that I like to spend some time in my camps with the men. As a matter of fact, my trips don't wear me out at all, they keep me fit."

Terry said nothing, did not glance his way, though she felt her father's gaze on her. If he had asked her, she would have said yes. Since he did not, she couldn't suggest it herself. Merritt took her silence for a sign she didn't want him to ask her because it would be embarrassing for her to refuse. At the end of the week he left for Skagit River before Terry and Isobel were up, eating a hasty breakfast in the kitchen with Hannah and Sadie, which would have shocked Isobel had she known.

That same evening after dinner, Beauchamp Deming dropped by at the house to see Merritt. Terry, who was alone, Isobel having gone to the theater with Mrs. Struther, whose husband was also out of town, met him at the door. Hannah and Sadie had left immediately after washing up, to attend the wake of a cousin in South Seattle.

Mr. Deming seemed distressed when she told him her father had already left for the Skagit Camp. Something very important had come up while he was on a case in Olympia, he said, and he hadn't found out about it until he reached his office late that afternoon. He'd tried to reach Compton's office by telephone but there'd been no answer. Evidently Merritt's secretary had left early.

Terry prevailed upon him to accept a glass of sherry in the parlor. "The devil of it is, Terry," he said, looking worried and rather old, "I can't reach him by telephone at camp, and it's imperative that he return immediately and deal with this situation. I'd go after him myself, but I've got to appear in court on Monday. I suppose I'll have to send one of my clerks."

"No, don't do that, Mr. Deming. I doubt if there's one of your clerks who could find his way up the Skagit without a guide. But I could."

"You, Terry?"

She smiled. "I've been going up to the Skagit Camp with Father for years. I wouldn't have the least trouble."

"But you couldn't go alone, child. Mrs. Compton would never approve." She's quite a girl, Deming was thinking, rather too much for Ned, I'm afraid, though I'd be delighted if he could win her.

"If you'll give me the message you wish delivered to Father,

I'll start first thing tomorrow morning. There's a boat for Anacortes at six-thirty."

"If there weren't so much at stake, I'd never consent to it, Terry. But neither of my two bright young men is much of a woodsman, and we can't waste time having them get lost and wandering all over the country looking for your father. Very well, if you think you can do it, more power to you."

He put down his glass, leaned forward, and gazed at her earnestly. "Tell Merritt that Weyerhauser and the Northern Pacific are trying to squeeze him out at Grays Harbor, as they did the White River Company. I've already moved to get an injunction. Also, Johanssen at Humptulips has been approached to sell out by an Eastern company. Only Merritt's influence can stop it. Tell him to get back here as soon as possible or his chance of a merger is lost."

As soon as Mr. Deming left, Terry flew upstairs, packed a bag, hurried down again before Isobel would return, and phoned for a cab to pick her up in the morning in time to make the Anacortes boat. She composed a note to Isobel telling her where she was going and why, which she would leave for her to find in the morning. There was no point, she felt, in asking her stepmother's permission, for she knew Isobel would be appalled, and though Terry meant to go anyway, there was no sense in having a row.

She was in bed, but not asleep, when Isobel returned from the theater, and after she was sure her stepmother had retired, she crept downstairs to Hannah's room. Hannah and Sadie hadn't got in from their cousin's wake until some time after Isobel had turned off her light. Hannah had just got off her knees from saying her prayers when Terry tapped at her door, and she was embarrassed at having the girl see her in her long white outing-flannel nightgown, her gray hair in a wispy braid down her back.

"God save us, Miss Terry! Is something wrong?" she whispered, wide-eyed, her hand at her throat.

"No, Hannah. I'm sorry to disturb you. But I must take the boat to Anacortes tomorrow morning at six-thirty and I was afraid I might not wake up in time. A cab is coming for me, and I want you to wake me at five-thirty, without fail. I'm going to Skagit River to deliver a very important message to my father."

"Saints preserve us, child! You're not going all the way into that wilderness by yerself?"

Terry smiled. "Yes, Hannah dear, I must. But it's all right. I know the way. Isobel doesn't know I'm going and I can't risk her trying to stop me. So promise you'll say nothing till I'm gone. I'll leave her a note explaining everything."

"She'll half kill me if she finds out I knew and didn't tell her!"

"She'll not find out, Hannah. Don't worry. I'll take my dog for protection. Now, remember, five-thirty, Hannah, not a minute later. Promise?"

"I do. And I'll pray for ye, dear lamb, till you're back safe."

Hannah kept faith, waked Terry at five-fifteen, bringing her a tray with tea, toast, and a boiled egg. "I thought 'twould save ye time, miss. Now eat yer breakfast like a good girl." She gave her a conspiratorial smile. "The missus is sleeping like a baby. She'll not wake for hours yet. You'll take care, darlin'?"

"I will, Hannah, and thanks." She gave the housekeeper a quick hug. "Bless you." She thrust the note to Isobel into her hand. "Will you put this at my stepmother's place on the dining table so she'll see it first thing? And if she questions you, just say you don't know a thing."

"I'll do it, Miss Terry. And if me conscience bothers me, I'll say an extra Hail Mary!"

Hannah was on the lookout for the cab, and in the half darkness of the May dawn Terry, carrying her bag, with Mac on a leash, crept downstairs and out of the house to the cab, and at six-thirty was safely aboard the *Potlach* bound for Anacortes.

She spent the night at the lumberman's hotel, where she and her father had often stayed, and by pressing a dollar bill into the room clerk's hand was able to keep the dog in her room. In Sedro-Woolley, she looked up old Joe Samish in his tumble-down shanty. The half-breed was friendly, but disconsolate because he couldn't accompany her up the trail. Rheumatism had crippled him so much during the past winter that he was practically an invalid, and he had sent his nephew, young Joe, with her father two days ago.

But he let her take the buckskin pony, King, and she set off in midmorning, with her luggage tied to the saddle, the big Chesapeake trotting beside the horse, a packet of ham sandwiches, put up by Joe's broad-faced, smiling wife, in her pocket, proud and excited at being on her own, at knowing she could accomplish this important mission, and grateful to her father's generosity in the matter of her allowance, so that she didn't have to ask Isobel for money to make the trip.

Spring was in full tide, the trail was lush with green growth, with sweet-scented blossom, with bird song. When she reached the place where the river sprang into view, glinting silver in the sun, full-throated, filling the air with its mountain coolness, she drew rein and dismounted and she and Mac, who came up with tongue lolling and tail wagging, shared Mrs. Joe Samish's excellent, thick sandwiches and drank from the snow-cold river, while the pony lipped at red clover beside the trail.

They made good time on trail, unencumbered by the pack mule that usually slowed them down, though Terry stopped from time to time to give the dog a rest. By nightfall, the wilderness had closed in, and though she was not afraid, she would have been clutched by sudden loneliness after the sun went down if it hadn't been for Mac. The dog was at her heels constantly, while she tethered the pony, made camp, built her careful, squaw fire for supper. She talked to him all the time, as much for her own comfort as for his. He did not leave her for a moment, though his ears rose and his nose quivered at the rank, wild, tantalizing scents of unseen forest creatures attracted by the smell of the horse, or perhaps by Terry's small fire. When she rolled herself into her blankets on the bare ground, not bothering to cut fir boughs, being too weary for such luxuries, Mac curled himself at her feet.

Twice during the night her deep oblivion was vaguely disturbed by the pony's whinny and low, menacing growls from the dog, but she was quite unable to rouse herself to action and sank back again into sleep, thinking she might have been dreaming. But in the morning, while she was foraging for dry wood for her breakfast fire, she saw the prints of the cougar in the soft earth just beyond her campfire, and she went cold all over.

Shortly before noon the next day, she rode into the Skagit Camp and was met by Matt Regan, who, coming across the clearing toward the cookhouse, stopped to shield his eyes against the sun, staring at her as if she were an apparition. When she raised an arm in greeting, being so grateful to have arrived and to have seen a familiar face, he ran toward her and caught her pony's bridle, and his arms received her as she slid down out of the saddle.

Seventeen

IT wasn't until Matt Regan put up his hands and lifted her bodily off the pony's back that Terry realized how tired and keyed up she was, and how deeply grateful to be in camp at last.

To her discomfiture, she began to tremble the moment he touched her, and she leaned against him for a moment, all her bravery and independence at making the long, hazardous trip alone dissolving into very feminine weakness. It would have been easy to cry when he said incredulously, "Is it yerself, or am I dreaming? Sure, and did ye make the trip alone, girl, or did the angels bring ye?"

"I came alone, but there must have been angels around. There was a cougar last night," she whispered, shivering against him in a sort of delayed reaction to her peril. "I saw his tracks this morning. If it hadn't been for my dog, Mac——"

"Oh, my God!" he cried softly, and his hands tightened on her arms. " 'Twas a desperate thing for ye to do, Terry. Why did ye come alone and not with yer father?"

At that, she remembered why she had come, having for a second or two almost let herself believe it had been to see this man again. She moved quickly away from him and brushed the hair off her forehead with a shaking hand. Was it the fatigue of the trip and the relief of safe arrival that made her tremble, or was it being close to him?

"My father," she said quickly. "Where is he? I must see him at once."

"He's not here. He left this morning to ride over the ridge to Steiner's old camp to talk to the new boss there."

"But he's got to go back to Seattle at once. I have an important message for him. That's why I came." She was close to tears. To have come all this way and not find her father here to meet her! She had been counting on this meeting with him, for he would know, she was sure, that her reason for coming herself, instead of letting Mr. Deming send someone else, was because the wall between them was down, she had forgiven him and wanted to be friends again.

"We must send someone after him! Take me to Mr. Dobie, please, and I'll explain it all to him."

Matt's face was somber. "Ah, I can't do that, Miss Terry, though I wish with all me heart I could. But poor Jack Dobie is dead."

"Dead? Oh, no!"

Matt nodded and stared at the ground. "He was killed two weeks ago by a sidewinder. I was topping the spar and it twisted as it came down. He was standing too close, I could see it falling wrong, and I shouted, but he didn't hear me. He had begun to get a wee bit hard of hearing of late. It was an awful thing." His voice was dark and broken with remembered horror. His great hands kept clenching and unclenching and when he lifted his eyes to hers, they were haunted. "An awful thing."

In quick pity, she put her hand on his arm. "Oh, Matt, I'm so sorry. What a terrible thing! For poor Mr. Dobie, of course, but for you, too. But you mustn't blame yourself. I'm sure it wasn't your fault."

"Thanks, Miss Terry. There are those who don't feel that

216

way." He turned suddenly and reached for the pony's bridle. "I'll just turn this animal into the corral. Noon dinner will be any minute now, but I'd think ye'd like a rest and a tray in the cabin, now."

"Yes, I think I would. But I must see the new foreman, or whoever is taking Mr. Dobie's place, and arrange for someone to go for my father."

He looked at her over his shoulder, one hand gently stroking the pony. "Set yer mind at rest, ma'am. I'm foreman now, and I'll send Red or Tommy to fetch Mr. Compton."

"Oh," she said. "I suppose I should congratulate you, Matt." He winced and met her eyes. "No. I wish you wouldn't. It's given me no cause for rejoicing. It gives me no pleasure to be stepping into Jack Dobie's boots."

Ole Olssen, the cook, brought her tray to her cabin himself and after he'd set it down on the deal table that served as a desk, he shook hands with Terry and paused in the doorway to chat.

"You hear yet about poor Yack Dobie, Miss Terry? Yack bane one goot man, but he never had no luck. Yust one t'ing after anodder. But Matt Regan bane goot man, too. He one fine foreman. Ever'body like Matt, except dot no goot Swede Peterson, an' onc-two odder soreheads."

"Matt told me, Ole, and I think it's terrible. Mr. Dobie was such a fine man. My father was devoted to him. But nobody blames Matt Regan, I hope. It couldn't have been his fault."

"You're right, Miss Terry. Dem sidewinders can happen any time, to anybody. But dot fool Peterson, he tell Mr. Compton Matt done it on purpose, placed undercut wrong so it hit Dobie. Starts yellin' 'Murder!' "

"But why should Matt want to kill Dobie, Ole? They were good friends. I've heard Mr. Dobie tell my father so."

"Matt never want Dobie dead. Dot's all fool talk of Swede." The cook hesitated, then whispered behind his big hand. "Dere bane woman in case, Miss Terry. Cheap liddle Sedro-

Woolley waitress, Rita. No goot. She bane Dobie's girl after his wife and kid die. But she take shine to Matt Regan. Peterson, he take shine to Rita. Peterson can't make time wit Rita, so he tell Compton Matt wanted Rita, so kill Dobie. Phooey!" Ole spat out the door in disgust.

Terry felt her face reddening, remembering what she had heard from her hiding place in the tree. "Did Matt take a—a shine to this Rita?"

Ole burst into laughter. "Golly, no! Beggin' yer pardon, Miss Terry. Oh, mebbe he flirt a liddle, take her dancing. What harm? When he find out she's Dobie's girl he quit—yust like that!" Ole snapped his fingers to indicate how it was. "But Rita, she don't quit. She come to camp, pester Matt. Matt tell her get out. She and Peterson get togedder—Rita sore at Matt because he quit, Swede sore at Matt because Rita likes him better than Swede. Swede bring Rita here last night to lie to Mr. Compton dot Matt want take her from Dobie."

"But my father didn't believe her, did he, Ole?"

Ole chuckled. "You bet not. Yer fadder no fool. He don't believe Rita. He don't believe Axel Peterson. He believe Matt Regan, Ole Olssen, Red, Tommy, Yake, Slim. Compton make Matt foreman. He tell Rita get out, don't come back." The cook darted a sharp glance at her. "I don' t'ink Rita go. I t'ink she hang around camp, in woods, mebbe. I tell Regan, watch out now, dot woman sore at you. Mebbe she got knife. She got hot blood."

Before he left, Ole admired Mac, petted him, and told Terry to bring him to the cookhouse for a good meal of scraps. "I yust hope he don't chase cats, Miss Terry! My Loki bane hard on dogs."

Terry shared her dinner with the dog, then lay down for a nap. It was nearly three o'clock when she wakened with the strange feeling of not knowing where she was. She got up, poured water from the old-fashioned china pitcher into the wide, flowered washbowl on the commode, and gave herself a

218

sponge bath. Then she changed from her riding skirt and flannel shirt to the white duck yachting costume she'd worn on the *Kelpie*. She took down her hair, gave it a long, thorough brushing, and coiled it again in a low knot on her neck. She touched lavender toilet water to her brow and wrists, glad she'd remembered to toss it into her bag. Feeling refreshed and renewed in body and spirit, she went out into the quiet, balmy afternoon, where the mountains, so near, had already begun to cast long, blue shadows over the sunny clearing.

The camp was deserted. The rough-hewn buildings, soon to be abandoned when Compton moved the camp in the fall, drowsed in sun and shade, as if already empty of life. Ole's tiger cat, Loki, lay stretched out on the cookhouse steps, only the tip of his tail alive. The smell of cut timber, sawdust, resin, and drying grasses was sweet and sleepy in the still, warm air. On a line strung between two spruces behind the bunkhouse, several pairs of faded blue jeans, work shirts, and long cotton drawers hung motionless in the still air.

Terry, with Mac at her heels, crossed the clearing and struck off past the corral, where the pony, King, lifted his head with clover dribbling from his velvety lips, twitched his long, silver tail and nickered softly in greeting. She paused to speak to him and he came up to the rail fence to have his nose stroked, then galloped off again in sudden caprice.

Mac, tormented by a thousand fascinating scents, fidgeted at her side until she laughed and gave him leave to run. He broke away and tore into the brush, only to come back with his head on one side and his tail waving, to make sure she was coming.

There was a narrow, overgrown trail that wound beyond the pasture to a little rise crowned by a stand of young hemlocks. Along the way, Terry nibbled at wild strawberries she found in the long, pale grasses, sweet and hot and winy, staining her lips and fingers. When she reached the hemlocks she sat down, clasped her knees, and gazed bemused down at the corral and the camp buildings, feeling more at peace than she had since a year ago when she had come to camp with her father.

Since the urgency of her mission had been halted by her father's absence, a delicious sense of lassitude and ease had overtaken her. Until Merritt returned, there was nothing she could do but enjoy the freedom and peace of the woods. Even the tragic news of Dobie's death and the disturbing things Ole had told her about Matt, the Swede, and Rita didn't impinge too sharply on her serenity. Nor did any thoughts of her mother's death disturb her complete relaxation. This was the great power of the woods; they laid a calm, firm hand on her uneasy spirit and made all the small frustrations and busynesses of the world seem unimportant.

Mac, who had been lying beside her, his nose on his paws, suddenly lifted his head and growled. Terry turned, looked behind her into the brush, and met the implacable gaze of two black eyes, hard as stones with hatred, was aware of a woman's face and figure melting away into the darkness of the woods, and was only just quick enough to reach out and grasp Mac's collar.

"Be quiet, Mac," she said, holding him fast, though he strained against her hand, his hackles on end, ears alert and lips curled in a menacing snarl. He turned a pleading look on her, whined, gave a few short, exasperated barks, and gradually, under her urging, subsided and lay down, but he kept his gaze fixed on the spot where she had seen, or thought she had seen, the apparition of the black-eyed woman.

Terry was quite sure that she had seen the waitress, Rita, and she remembered now what Ole had said. Why was this woman, cast off by Matt, ordered to leave by Compton, still lurking in the woods? Ole had said she might have a knife. She had testified against Matt in the matter of Dobie's death. Suddenly Terry was frightened. Not for herself but for Matt Regan. I must warn him, she thought, and started back down the trail.

Halfway down, she met him coming up, looking for her. "So, there ye are. I was worried about ye. No one had seen ye since Ole brought yer dinner to ye. I feel responsible, with yer father away and all."

"I'm quite all right, thanks," she replied crisply, surprised at the swift rush of relief and happiness she felt at seeing him.

"But I'm afraid you're not."

"Now what might ye be meaning, ma'am?"

They stood facing each other on the narrow trail, and Terry looked so pale and undone that he took her arm and gently led her to a fallen log, saying, "Shall we sit down fer a bit?" He looked at her in concern. "Something has frightened you. You must tell me what it is."

"I'm not afraid for myself, Matt, but for you," she said, turning her troubled gaze upon him. "Ole told me about Swede and Rita. He said she might be dangerous."

"Oh, Rita——" He laughed. "Your father gave her the bum's rush last night. Don't be upset by her, ma'am."

"She's here, Matt, hiding in the woods. I saw her just now."

"Did ye now? Did ye?" He turned instinctively and scanned the brush behind them. Then he said lightly, "Well, let her stay, poor soul. She can do me no harm. But I'll not have her bothering you, Miss Terry."

"Oh, you fool!" she cried, turning to him with blazing eyes. "Don't you see? She's in love with you, Ole told me, and the only reason she testified against you in Dobie's death is because you tired of her and cast her off. Why should she bother me? But she may try to kill you!"

He reached out and took her wrist and held it tight. "You haven't got it straight, my girl. I never cast Rita off, because she was never anything to me but, God forgive me, a moment's relaxation after months of hard work. I didn't know she was Dobie's woman when I took her out, and after I found out, I never went near her again."

"It's nothing to me what your relations were with her. I'm

only trying to warn you," she flared. "Be so good as to let my wrist go, you're hurting me."

He let go her wrist but took her hand in both of his and held her eyes with his bright, intense gaze. "From the moment I laid eyes on you, Terry Compton, there's been no woman I could look at or bear to touch. I tried to tell you that when we were alone there by the river, before your father came back with the wagon."

"You did not!" she cried hotly, all the months of resentment against him storming through her. "You did nothing but talk about yourself and how you were going to be somebody. But not a word did you say about me, Matt Regan."

"Ah, I was getting round to that, after I'd built up me own case to you, but Compton came back too soon."

"So you did nothing, and if I hadn't come up to fetch my father, you'd never have tried to see me again, nor written. You could at least have written to find out if I was all right. But oh no, not you——"

A slow smile spread over his mouth and he said almost gaily, "Ah, so you wanted to hear from me then, Terry Compton? Then I must mean something to you, for you're angry at me, and you'd not be angry with a man who meant nothing to you."

She would not answer him. She turned away her head and he released her hand. She was quite unprepared to deal with the torrent of emotions rushing over her. She was angry at him and afraid for his safety. There was something debonair and independent about him that made her want to laugh. Even when he was telling a woman she was the only one for him, he was still himself, Matt Regan, and he'd be no one's slave, not even for love. And that was what made her want to laugh and say, Good for you, Matt. I don't want a slave, nor yet a master, but a man who knows his own worth and lets it go at that. Yet it would have been easy to cry, too, knowing that much as he might love a woman there would be always a part of him she could never reach.

He sat looking at his clasped hands, saying in a bemused voice, as if to himself, "So I made you angry by not sending some word. And all the while I was thinking of you all my waking moments, yes, and dreaming about you, too. I wanted to write, but I don't spell very well and I write a clumsy hand. I didn't want to shame meself in yer eyes. I sent word by yer father last fall when he was up that I hoped you were well and all. He said you were fine and dancing every night."

"Indeed I was, though he never gave me your message."

"Perhaps he doesn't think me good enough to look at you."

She raised her head and drew herself up proudly, meeting his eyes. "I love and respect my father, but no one can rule my heart and mind."

He flashed her an odd little crooked smile. "I imagine ye've got the pick of all the fine young fellas in Seattle. I imagine there's one of them ye've set your mind on for a husband?"

She stood up so suddenly that the dog at her feet was startled. "No," she cried angrily. "There's no one in Seattle or anywhere else that I've set my mind on."

He got up, too, and from his great height was smiling down at her, his eyes so blue they hurt. "And ye'd look at an Irish logger who is too ignorant to write you a proper love letter, but who loves you just the same, with all his heart and soul and body?"

"Yes," she whispered, her heart beating wildly as she met his gaze, "I would look at him."

Before he could reach out for her, she started down the trail ahead of him. Had she stayed, she knew she would have been in his arms the next moment, and what would happen then, she did not know, but with her limbs turning to water, she was afraid to find out.

She sat beside Matt that evening at supper and from his

manner no one would have guessed what had passed between them earlier. He was relaxed and pleasant, with just the proper deference toward her as the Boss's daughter, careful not to let his eyes linger too long on her face.

The state fire inspector, newly appointed by the governor, who had arrived in camp without warning that afternoon while Matt and Terry were on the trail, sat on her left, and she directed most of her conversation to him, not trusting herself to glance too often in Matt's direction.

The fire inspector was an agreeable young man who evidently considered it great good luck to find an attractive young lady in camp. He had taken forestry at the University of Washington and knew several of Terry's acquaintances, so it was easy to talk to him. He had been shown around camp by Matt before supper and was favorably impressed by Compton's fire-prevention measures.

"I wish all our logging camps in the state were run so efficiently in regard to fire prevention, Miss Compton," he said.

"My father is almost a fanatic on the subject, Mr. Furth," replied Terry proudly. "He was one of the first to ask the governor for fire marshals and inspectors for the camps. He once told me that if he had his way, any logger found guilty of setting a fire, whether by carelessness or design, should be treated like a horse thief and strung up."

"I agree with your father heartily," he said, thinking how much more interesting she was to talk to than most of the scatterbrained young things he knew in the city. "I am sorry not to have a chance to talk to him this trip, but I understand he won't be back in camp till tomorrow and I must be on my way right after supper. I'm due at the Weyerhauser Camp over the divide in the morning."

"But that's where Father is now," said Terry, "and he should be starting back early tomorrow. Surely you don't intend to travel over the divide at night."

"I'll have at least three hours of daylight if I leave in half an hour. I'll make camp on trail and start out again at dawn. It's a great temptation to stay and enjoy your charming company, Miss Compton, but my schedule is heavy and I have a lot of territory to cover before dry weather sets in."

Matt Regan, it occurred to Terry, while he treated the inspector with courtesy, didn't try to persuade him to linger and seemed relieved when he excused himself from the table before Terry had finished her supper, and departed. Matt left the table, too, and saw him out the door, where his Indian guide was waiting with the horses.

When he came back, Matt slid into his seat beside Terry and asked the bull cook for more coffee and pie. "Too bad Mr. Furth couldn't stay longer," he said cheerfully. "He seemed a good sort, didn't ye think?"

"He was charming," smiled Terry. "But you didn't put yourself out to encourage him to spend the night here."

"Did I not?" He pretended surprise and concern, his eyes sparkling. "Ah, but he was so set on doing his duty. What could I do, when even you couldn't persuade him?"

She turned away to hide a smile and caught the pale, white-lashed eyes of the albino, Swede Peterson, staring at her with a queer, twisted grin on his face. Though she felt her color rising, she stared him down coldly until he pushed back his chair and shuffled out of the room. *He knows about Matt and me,* she thought in panic, and he hates us both. Was he lurking in the woods when we met on the trail, or did Rita spy on us and tell him?

"Is something the matter?" asked Matt in a low voice, having sensed her uneasiness.

She thought of telling him about the look she'd seen on the Swede's face but was afraid to condemn a man when it might have been her own intensified imagination that seemed to be aware of every eye trying to ferret out the feelings she was trying hard to hide.

She shook her head. "It's nothing. I guess I'm tired. How long will it take Red to reach my father?"

"He left right after noon dinner and I warned him to hump himself. But the trail over the divide and down the canyon is dangerous and slow. The camp horse he's riding is about as heavy-footed as the one I rode that morning with you. He can't possibly get to Steiner's camp before nightfall."

"Then they can't get back here till tomorrow afternoon?"

"Say, not till suppertime, at best. It's slower coming up the trail, you know." He looked at her soberly. "You're not afraid to stay the night in the cabin alone? You'll be quite safe, I promise you."

Her cheeks flamed and she gave him a cool glance. "Thank you, but I'm not in the least afraid. I have my dog, you know. And I have your protection."

"You have that, indeed." He bowed slightly; his voice held only politeness but his eyes accused her of cruelty.

Terry and Mac walked till dark by the brook, and Matt Regan didn't come near them. In spite of the necessity to maintain the proper dignity before the men, she had felt sure that when he saw her take the dog and strike out along the stream Matt would follow her, meet her, perhaps past the big spruce where she'd been trapped last year, where they would have been hidden from the camp.

If he loves me with all his heart and soul and body, as he said, why does he stay away from me? He knows I can't go to him, and tomorrow Father will be back, and the next day we will have to leave for Seattle. Oh, God, she thought as she crossed the clearing to the cabin, if he leaves me like this and says no more, what am I to do? I can't go to him and tell him that I love him, that I'll marry him if he asks me. I've said all I dare to say. If I had not turned away from him on the trail today, if I had let him take me in his arms, would it now all be settled and the both of us at peace? Or would something dreadful have happened? I do not know him, I do not know what he is truly like, or what he wants of me.

He was waiting for her in front of the cabin. He came toward her out of the dark and spoke her name. The dog, surprisingly, ran up to him, wagging his tail, and made no protest when the man took his young mistress in his arms. Terry, forgetting everything but that Matt was here, waiting for her, went to him and lifted her face for his kiss.

"My darling, my beautiful darling," he whispered, and held her gently, but close enough so that she could feel the terrible pounding of his heart against her.

It was as it had been on the trail that morning when he lifted her in his arms and she came back to life and felt his lips on hers, a thing of gentleness and such sweet anguish that her eyes were wet. "Oh, Matt," she breathed, "do you love me? Do you truly love me?"

"I've never loved so truly in my life, dear heart. You are my own true love, forever and ever, amen." He laid his cheek against hers and murmured softly, "I'll be good to ye, Terry mine, and I'll make ye proud of me."

"If you ever leave me, Matt," she said suddenly, "I think I shall die."

"When I leave ye, my queen, my rose of the world, 'twill be to go to my grave."

They kissed again, and suddenly the dog growled and whined, and they broke apart. "I'll speak to yer father tomorrow," he said, letting her go, but keeping her hand to kiss and hold to his heart. "And God bless ye this night!"

She turned and took a few steps away from him, then flew back to his arms, and pressed her face against his great chest. "Oh, Matt Regan, I do love you!"

Presently she went into the cabin, the dog going ahead of her, and she leaned against the door after she'd closed it and let the soft tears of happiness and love fall down her cheeks.

The only time she'd known such happiness was when she lay in the canoe, watching Matt from under her half-closed eyelids, remembering the first time he'd kissed her.

And then Mac stiffened, growling ominously. There was a rustle and a sharp intake of breath. Terry whirled, her heart thumping. Someone was in the cabin. "Who's there?" she cried.

No one answered, but she was aware of light rapid breathing in the corner. There were matches and a candle on the window sill by the door and she quickly made a light, held the candle high.

The room slowly swam into focus as the candle flame steadied and Terry saw a woman standing behind the table, shrinking away from the big, threatening dog.

Eighteen

THOUGH she had not even been sure she had actually seen the woman on the trail, Terry instantly recognized the black, stony gaze that met hers in the candlelight. She set the candlestick on the table between them and grabbed Mac's collar, pulling him against her. The other woman was obviously far more frightened of the dog than Terry had been at finding an intruder in the cabin, though a little prickle of apprehension went over her, remembering what Ole had said about the knife.

"Be quiet, Mac," she commanded softly, and the dog's rumblings diminished to an uneasy mutter.

"Blast ye, that's a mean critter. He'd of gone for me if you wasn't here," gasped the woman indignantly. "Don't take your hand off'n his collar or he'll jump me."

"Not if I tell him not to," replied Terry meaningfully. "He isn't mean except when he thinks I'm in danger."

"Well, I ain't gonna hurt you. I just come to tell you somethin' fer your own good." The woman gave a shrug of bravado.

"I suppose you're Rita."

In the flickering light, Terry could see that she was a small, full-bosomed woman probably a few years older than herself, with a broad, sensual face, which was not without a kind of

229

primitive allure. Her heavy black hair braided about her head gave her a look of pride. The most striking thing about her was the aura of intensity that almost transfigured her coarse features. Only her eyes were cold and filled with hatred.

"Oh, so you know about me, huh?" Rita bridled and put both hands on her hips.

"Yes," replied Terry evenly. "Ole Olssen told me about you."

"All? Did he tell you about Matt Regan and me?"

"He told me something and Matt himself told me the rest. There wasn't much to tell, you know." Terry's voice was cool and unemotional and she felt embarrassed for both of them, oddly more embarrassed for the waitress than for herself.

"Not much to tell, eh?" Rita laughed. "Listen, Miss Terry, there's plenty to tell, and you're gonna hear it right here and now." She leaned both palms on the table and stared at the girl.

"I'm not interested in anything you have to tell me about Matt." Terry didn't flinch under the other woman's steady gaze.

"Sure, sure. He's been givin' you that ole Irish blarney of his. I heard him outside before you came in. I know how 'tis. Didn't I fall for it, too? He made me think he was crazy about me and he tossed me aside when he seen he could do better."

Terry began to tremble inside, but she held herself proudly erect. "I don't want to hear any more. Matt loves me and wants to marry me. And I believe him."

"He wants to marry you because you're the Boss's daughter, you poor little fool. He wants to be a big man and he knows you can help him." Rita's smile was cruel. "Oh, he's got big plans, Matt has, and Rita's not good enough now that he's seen you."

For a moment Terry thought she was going to reach out and slap the woman's face, or that she would burst into tears from the sudden helplessness and shame she felt in the midst of so

230

much ill will. But she did neither. She suddenly began to laugh and her laugh was so hearty and free that the small, dark woman's triumph crumbled at the ringing sound of it.

"Oh, Rita," she cried, "if only you knew how wrong you are! Matt Regan wouldn't take any help from my father or me if it was handed to him on a silver platter. He's as independent as a hog on ice."

At that moment the door was flung open and the big black Irishman himself towered in the doorway. He stared at the two women, unable to grasp the situation. "I don't know what you're doing here, Rita," he cried, frowning, "but y'd better get out, if y' value yer skin."

"Don't go threatenin' me, Matt Regan!" yelled Rita. "I ain't skeered of you. I just got through settin' yer girl friend here straight about you and I. She puts up a good bluff, bein' a lady and all, but I hope I've put a spoke in yer wheel."

"I've got no time to waste on talk. The woods are afire and ye'd better clear out while ye can, the best way ye can. There's not a man in camp'd lift a finger to help ye, except maybe yer fine pal, Axel. But if ye've been tellin' my girl a pack of lies, I'll take a whip to ye if I ever see ye again."

"What d'ye mean, Matt?" Rita's face had paled and there was fear in her opaque eyes.

"I mean Peterson has set a forest fire in the Sitka spruce just this side of the divide. Jake caught him with a kerosene can, sneaking into the brush. The whole stand is afire and unless we can stop it, the camp will go, too."

"That fool Swede! I told him to wait till I left. Let me out of here!" She turned to Terry, her voice terrified. "Hold off your dog and let me go, for pity's sake!"

Terry held Mac's collar, and the woman slid past them and disappeared into the night. Matt shut the door after her and took Terry in his arms. "What did that tramp say to you, Terry?"

"A lot of foolishness. I didn't believe a word," she replied stoutly. Then, suddenly, she was weeping against his breast. "Oh, Matt, you do love me just for myself, don't you? And not because I'm Merritt Compton's daughter?"

"Oh God, she did hurt you, the creature! My darling, I'd love you if you'd never had a father or a mother." He kissed her and she whispered, "I was sure, but I—I had to hear you say it."

Suddenly he put her away from him. "You must leave too, dear heart. Ole Olssen is taking my canoe and going by the river. He'll take you down to safety."

Terry shook her head. "No, Matt. I'm not leaving you."

"I order you to go, Terry," he cried, frowning. "I'm foreman here, now."

She smiled and shook her head again. "But I'm the Boss's daughter, remember. You can't order me to go. I'm staying."

There was no mistaking her stubbornness and no time to argue. "Then you'll do me the favor of keeping to this cabin," he said angrily. "If things get out of control, I'll take ye downriver myself, willy-nilly. There's a log boom all ready to float and ye can escape on that."

"Why is Ole leaving, Matt? Who will feed the men if he's gone?"

"The bull cook is his nephew and the boy's scared. Ole promised his sister to look after the lad. I told him to take him to safety. We'll manage someway without Ole."

Tommy shouted outside and Matt had only time to give Terry an angry, exasperated look, and then rushed out. Terry stood at the open door and smelled the smoke, as yet only a faint, not unpleasant strangeness tainting the clear, cool air. But off toward the divide, the night sky was curiously bright, though there was no moon.

Presently, she went back into the cabin, lit a lamp, blew out the candle and, very deliberately, changed her white yachting costume for the sensible covert cloth divided skirt, the flannel shirt, and the thin sneakers for the calfskin high laced boots.

As she twisted up her hair under a blue scarf, she listened to the quick tramp of heavy boots going past, the shouts, sharp commands, as Matt marshaled his forces to fight the fire. There was the sputter of the pump, which was Compton's latest fire-fighting innovation, and from the window she could see the lanterns swaying back and forth up the trail as the men poured out of camp to the divide where the ominous brightness was.

The sputtering of the pump settled down to a steady throb as it sucked up water from the river into the two large storage tanks beside the bunkhouse. It was operated by one of the stationary donkey engines, which had to be stoked with short fire wood. There was a hose attachment, which was useless for saving the timber beyond camp, but which could be played on the buildings and the logs at the landing station to keep them from catching fire from wind-blown sparks. The real job of saving the timber was done with axes, hacking away the burning branches and underbrush, with shovels, digging fire ditches, with water-soaked burlap bags to beat the low growth, and in extremity, the setting of backfires.

Terry knew that two men were being kept from the actual fire fighting to protect her and the camp, one to stoke the donkey, another to tend the pump and, if necessary, the hose. Her first impulse was to run out and tell them to let the pump go and help save the timber. Then she thought of Matt's angry words, "I'm foreman here, now," and she knew he would never forgive her. He might not even forgive her for disobeying his order to leave with Ole in the canoe, or for reminding him that she was the Boss's daughter and would do as she pleased. His voice had been cold with anger and he had flung her a furious look as he dashed out the door. She had no right to interfere with his orders to the men, and she doubted, anyway, if they'd listen to her, once Matt had set them their task.

But she had no intention of staying in the cabin, waiting, doing nothing. She waited until the clatter of boots outside had ceased and the lanterns bobbing up the trail were lost in the trees, and then she turned the lamp low, lit the lantern, called Mac to heel, and went quickly across the clearing to the cookhouse.

The air had a murky quality like a heavy fog, and the smell of smoke was more pungent and biting. It made her nostrils feel pinched and dry and Mac sneezed several times and shook his head. The cookhouse was unlocked, but dark, and she swung the lantern ahead of her to see her way. In the kitchen, she hung the lantern on a hook by the back door, found a lamp and matches and set the lighted lamp on the worktable. The fire in the huge iron range, which took up one whole wall of the kitchen, was not quite out.

She shook down the grates, plied the embers carefully with stove wood from the gigantic pile in the lean-to, and when the range was humming, shut the dampers and put on the great black coffee kettle, guessing at the measurements of coffee and water, but feeling that to err on the coffee side would not be amiss for men stumbling in, exhausted from fire fighting.

In the food safe she found a boiled ham, a boiled tongue, and a great yellow cheese wrapped in a damp cloth, butter in a huge tin. Ole had baked that morning, so there were a dozen loaves of fresh bread on the cupboard under cloths. Mac lay in a corner as far as possible from the heat of the range, and watched her slice bread, meat, and cheese and build up a mountain of sandwiches.

She worked swiftly, spreading the thick sandwiches generously with butter. Once she cut her finger slicing the ham with Ole's razor-sharp carving knife, but she wound her handkerchief about the cut and forgot it. When the sandwiches were made, enough for a "shanty crew," she lit lamps in the mess hall and carried the sandwiches in on platters, covered with dampened kitchen towels. She got out cups, spoons, sugar bowls, and cans of evaporated milk.

When the first of the men stumbled back into camp for a

234

break, she was ready for them. Seeing lights in the mess hall, they paused at the door, and Terry threw it open. "Come on in, boys," she cried. "I've got sandwiches and coffee waiting for you." For a moment they stared at her in surprise, smoke-grimed, haggard, their eyes bloodshot. Then they filed in, grinning and murmuring thanks, and began grabbing for the food, not waiting to sit down.

"God bless you, ma'am," said a grizzled faller with a face as black as the pit. "You sure saved our lives. We knew Ole had left and we thought there'd be no one to cook for us."

"I'll cook for you, John, but get somebody to give me a hand pouring coffee, will you?"

Two of the younger men came out to the kitchen, grimy, smelling of smoke, and even in this emergency shy of the Boss's daughter. She filled pitchers with the hot strong coffee for them to carry into the mess hall. As she handed one to the boy she recognized as Tommy, she asked him, "Tell me. How is it going?"

"It's touch and go, miss. Matt set backfires and had us digging ditches and we've got it under control on the left side near the divide. It's still nasty on the right toward the mountain."

"Where is Matt? Didn't he come down with you?" Her hand was steady as she went on pouring out coffee, and her voice was almost casual.

"Oh, he's in the thick of it, roaring like a bull and working like the devil himself, you may be sure." Tommy grinned. "He wouldn't leave to take a break. He and half the crew are trying to keep the fire out of the Douglas stand. A couple of the swampers got knocked out by smoke, so we had to bring them in."

"Tommy, will you help me take sandwiches and coffee up to Matt and the others, after you've eaten and had a chance to rest?"

"You, Miss Compton? You'd go up there?" The blond boy stared at her. "Ain't you scared of the fire?"

"Of course I am," she laughed. "But so are you, and you're going back, aren't you?"

He nodded. "Well, sure. But that's my job."

"I think it's my job to help, too, by bringing them food. You'll help me?"

"Yes, *ma'am*. You kin count on me. I'll get Slim to help, too."

The sound of the fire, as they neared the divide, was like the roar of surf, interspersed with sudden, explosive cracklings as the flames leaped from tree to tree, snaking up the branches. The smoke was so dense that the lurid flicker of the flames seemed like the veiled fires of a distant Inferno. The dark figures of men leaped about in the smoke in wild devilish capers.

Burning twigs and sparks fell all about Terry and the returning men. They had covered their mouths and noses with handkerchiefs soaked in water to protect them from the stinging smoke, but there was no protection for their smarting, streaming eyes. Choking, weeping from the smoke, stumbling in the murky darkness, Terry clung to her hamper of food, while Tommy and Slim toiled behind her, carrying the buckets of hot coffee. Old John brought tin cups in a burlap bag over his shoulder.

"This is far enough, ma'am," said Tommy. "It'd be dangerous for you to get any closer and you'd only be in the way, too. You wait here with the grub and I'll go tell the boys to come and get it."

She was glad to stop, not sure she could take another step. They had reached a sort of plateau, halfway up the trail, where the timber had been partly cleared off. Terry put down the hamper and sank for a moment on a fallen log, gasping for breath, wiping the tears from her eyes with her sleeve. Then she got up, took the cups out of the bag the faller had dumped at her feet, and by the light of two lanterns set up her canteen on the uneven ground.

236

The men staggered down the trail, choking, coughing, wiping their eyes, silently taking the cups of strong, sweetened coffee, the thick sandwiches she held out to them. If they were amazed to see her, they gave no sign, only muttered thanks, sprawled out on the ground, almost too exhausted to eat.

The ones who had come into camp and had been fed and momentarily refreshed took their places. Terry kept looking for Matt, but he didn't appear. She called to a logger who was just starting back up the slope. "Tell Matt Regan to come down and get something to eat. Make him come." The logger nodded.

She sat down again to rest after the men had eaten and drunk cup after cup of the strong coffee and gone back. Suddenly there was a crashing on the trail behind her and an angry voice bellowing, "Terry! What are you doing here? I told you to stay in the cabin!"

She closed her eyes for a moment in swift, grateful relief and when she opened them Matt was standing over her, naked to the waist, his face and body streaked with smoke and sweat.

"Sit down, Matt," she said calmly, "and have some coffee, though I'm afraid it's not very hot, now. Here's a ham sandwich and there's tongue and cheese, too."

"Sit down, she says, as if she was serving tea in her own parlor. 'Sit down, Matt, and have a ham sandwich!'" he roared. "I ought to turn ye over me knee, willful, headstrong, stubborn creature that ye are."

"Time enough for that, darling, after we're married," she replied, smiling at him. "Do stop roaring, please, and have something to eat. The sandwiches are very good."

"I'm marrying no woman who sets herself against me express orders, Miss Compton, me girl. Get that into yer pretty, stubborn head."

She dipped a cup into the coffee bucket, thrust it and a ham sandwich into his grimy hands. "Who wants to marry an ugly brute of a man without the manners to say thank you to a woman for nearly slicing off her finger to fix him a bite of supper?"

He looked helplessly around for a place to put his cup and sandwich, having seen the bloody handkerchief tied around her hand. "No," she commanded, "eat your sandwich. You're not to touch me. You can kiss my poor cut finger tomorrow when the fire's out."

He gulped down the coffee, ate the sandwich in two ravenous bites, held out his cup and hand for more. "By golly, girl, ye can cook. Best coffee I ever tasted. Good sandwiches, too." He ate a tongue and cheese sandwich, drank two more cups of coffee, then, with a cavernous sigh, stretched out on the ground, face down, and went limp, as if all life had gone out of him.

Terry longed to touch him, but she knew he needed those few moments of utter oblivion. Five minutes later he was on his feet. He stood over her, frowning. "Ye disobeyed me and I don't like that. But I'm proud of what ye've done this night. I'll never forget it, nor will the crew. We needed what ye brought us. It's put new life in all of us. Ye have me thanks. Now I'll take ye back to the cabin, where I'll be hoping ye'll stay."

"No, Matt," she said, looking up at him. "You want to get back to the fire. I can take myself down to camp. And I'll promise to stay there. Only you must promise me to be careful."

"I've never been careful in me life, darlin'. Ask me anything else but that." He smiled at her and touched her hair lightly. "I'd like to hold ye tight in me arms, Terry mine, but I'm filthy with smoke and sweat. Now take yer lantern and be-gone."

She took her lantern, leaving the remains of the food and coffee for the men, and groped her way slowly down the trail. It seemed to her when she reached camp that the air had turned fresher, the smoke was no longer so thick. Perhaps the wind has changed, she thought, and prayed that it was so.

Mac, whom she'd shut in the cabin before setting out up the trail, leaped on her when she opened the door. She gave him a hug and let him outside to run, but he was soon back, asking to be let in, whimpering and uneasy at the strange smell in the air. Terry was lightheaded with weariness, but she knew if she lay down even for a moment she'd be lost to the world, and she wanted to be on hand to cook breakfast for the men, who would be ravenous in a few hours, in spite of the sandwiches and coffee.

To keep herself awake, she washed herself, took down her hair and brushed it free of bits of leaves, twigs, and charcoal, wound it into a snug knot at her neck. She changed back into her low sneakers, after soaking her tired feet in cold water. When she started back to the cookhouse to stir up the range fire, her watch, pinned on her blouse, said four o'clock, but the smoke held the darkness low over camp.

Jake, one of the men assigned to the pump, called out to her as she went out to the lean-to for more wood to stoke the range. "Wind's changed, ma'am. Feels like it might rain, too. Reckon I could leave Bill, here, with the pump, and give ye a hand it ye need help."

"Thanks, I could use a hand. I'm going to get breakfast started. I imagine some of the crew will be taking a break soon."

Ashes were still drifting through the air when the sky brightened enough for them to blow out all but one of the lamps. With Jake's help, Terry had made another Gargantuan kettle of coffee, got bacon sliced and sizzling on the huge skillet, potatoes peeled, sliced, and frying in the bacon fat, eggs ready to be slid onto the tremendous griddle the moment the men clattered into the mess hall, mountains of bread cut, butter and plum jam ready on the tables. She was beginning to have

239

an enormous respect for Ole Olssen, who had the job to do three times a day.

The men came trooping in, by twos and threes, groggy with fatigue, and for a solid hour Terry and Jake ran back and forth between kitchen and mess hall with piled-up platters and pitchers of coffee. Matt was the last to arrive. He had stopped outside at the pump and washed his face and hands, put on his shirt, but his face was white and drawn with exhaustion.

Terry served him in silence and in silence he ate. She brought her own plate and cup to his table and ate with him. Only after he pushed back his plate, sighed, and dropped his head in his hands, did she speak. "Matt, is it all right? Is the fire out?"

He lifted his head and stared at her with bloodshot eyes. "It's not out. It's under control. The wind has shifted and if it doesn't shift again, I think we're safe. Anyway, we can do no more. The men are dead on their feet. They've got to get some sleep. If the Holy Mother would send us rain, I could lie down and take some rest. If not, it's back again we go as soon as we can move."

She filled his coffee cup again and when he'd drunk, he looked at her with sudden realization of her tiredness. Her face was drained of color, there were dark stains under her eyes, and her hand shook as she lifted her own cup to her lips.

"Put down that cup," he ordered. "You look all in. I'm taking you to the cabin and putting you to bed."

As they started across the clearing, a sudden spatter of great cold drops struck them in the face. They paused, hand in hand, and looked up at the sky, which had grown black and still. The wind had died completely. As they looked, the drops came faster and faster until they became a downpour.

"It's raining, Terry! God be praised. This'll be the end of Swede Peterson's fire!" cried Matt exultantly, squeezing her hand.

"Yes, God be praised," whispered Terry, and, as if this were the signal she had been waiting for, went limp against him.

He carried her across the clearing and into the cabin, kicking shut the door behind him. He laid her on the bed and chafed her wrists, but she was in a dead faint. Her clothes were soaked to the skin, and the dawn was cold. He stripped off her wet shoes and blouse with hands that seemed all thumbs, turned back the covers, and gently eased her between the blankets. The dog scratched at the door and whined, so he let him in. He saw that there was no one in sight and the camp, with the lamps out in both mess hall and bunkhouse, looked deserted.

Mac put his paws on the bed, sniffed at his mistress, and whined, looking up at the man. "It's all right, boy," he said softly. "She's just worn out."

Terry sighed then, moved her head on the pillow, and opened her eyes. Matt knelt swiftly beside her and took her hand in both of his. "Terry, dear heart! Are ye all right?"

"I guess so," she said, smiling. "But I'm so tired, Matt. Did I faint?"

"And why not, me darlin', with all ye've been through this night and far into the morning. Ye're a strong, fine, brave girl, and no shame to ye that ye should let go now that it's all over and all's safe," he whispered tenderly, pressing her hand to his lips.

She lay still for a moment, closing her eyes, then she put up a hand and felt her bare shoulder, looked at him with slow color coming into her white cheeks. "How did I get here, Matt? In bed, I mean."

He looked confused and kept his eyes averted. "I—I carried ye here, darlin', and since ye were in a cold faint and soaking wet, I—I took the liberty of taking off yer shoes and blouse and putting you under the covers. Ye're not offended at me? I—I meant no harm, Terry."

Her cheeks were still rosy, but she laughed. "I'm sure you

didn't, Matt, and I'm not in the least offended. If you'd left me lying here in my soaking wet clothes till I was able to undress myself, I might have caught pneumonia."

"That's what I thought." He rose to his feet. "And now, I'll go and let ye sleep, dear one."

Her eyes went suddenly dark with fear and she caught at his hand. "Oh, don't go yet, Matt. Stay with me till I go to sleep. I wasn't afraid before, but now I am. It's so silly, and I'm ashamed, because now there's nothing to be afraid of. I guess I'm just now realizing the danger we all were in." She began to weep silently, the tears trickling down her face, and she turned her head to try to hide them.

"I'll stay as long as ye want, my darlin'," he cried, and drew a chair up beside the bed, found her hand again and held it tight.

She turned, looked full into his face, and put her free hand on his cheek. "You're so cold, darling. And you smell of smoke. Oh, Matt, I love you so much. Kiss me, so I'll sleep?"

He held her against his breast, kissed her gently, murmured, "I love you, Terry darlin', with me whole heart. Do ye sleep now, dear one." And with a sigh she lay back on the pillow and was instantly asleep.

It tore out his heart to leave her, and when he had gently, gently eased her head onto the pillow and slipped his arm free, he felt that he was leaving a part of himself and that his heart and flesh would ache until they were together again.

He blew out the lamp and went out into the pale, cold morning light, acrid with the smell of smoke and wet ashes. The rain had dwindled to a light, persistent drizzle, and as he looked instinctively toward the divide, he saw only gray wisps of smoke trailing skyward, last remnants of the holocaust. The battle was over and now he could, with gratitude, take the rest that he had earned.

As he pushed himself toward the cookhouse, Matt saw that the camp was as dead and silent as if it had already been abandoned. He slipped into the bunkhouse where men lay sprawled, some half dressed on their bunks, snoring, twitching in their sleep, the pale light revealing faces sunken with exhaustion, every one dead to the world. Matt crept under his blankets, naked, and for the first time in years offered up a prayer of thanksgiving and knew no more until Tommy woke him to tell him that Compton had been sighted coming down the trail.

Nineteen

MATT was there to meet Terry's father, when he and Red rode into camp. Compton's face was grim as he got off his horse and swung to face the big Irishman. "Is my daughter safe?" were his first words.

"She is, sir. Still asleep, I imagine. She was up all night, fixing coffee and sandwiches for the men."

"Thank God she's all right." Compton let out his breath in a great sigh and laid his hand heavily on Matt's shoulder. "I didn't know what I'd find when I got here. We saw the blaze from Steiner's camp. I wanted to start then, but Red was afraid the horses would bolt when they smelled the smoke and saw the flames. Cartwright, the new foreman the Weyerhauser outfit put in when they took over Steiner's stand, kept his fire crew ready in case the wind shifted toward them."

" 'Twouldn't have hurt him to have sent over some of his boys to help us out," observed Matt sourly. "With some extra hands we might've been able to save the spruce."

"I asked him to send some help, but he said he had no authority to ask his men to risk their lives for another company's timber. Nice neighbors we've got, eh? Red and I were so mad, we wouldn't sleep under his roof, spent the night dozing on the bunkhouse steps, watching the divide. We left at dawn and didn't even stop for lunch."

"Then ye'll no doubt be wanting some grub, sir." Matt had warmed to the man because of his worry over Terry. He loves her, too, he thought. "We've no cook, now. Ole left to take his nephew, the bull cook, to safety last night. But I'll get Jake to rustle up something for you and Red."

"Good." Suddenly Compton whirled, his face angry. "Why didn't you send Terry to safety, too, along with Ole and his nephew, Regan?"

Matt grinned. "I tried to, sir. But she wouldn't go. Your daughter has a mind of her own."

The anger left Merritt's eyes and he shook his head. "I guess she has. She ought to be spanked."

"The thought did occur to me, sir," replied Matt, "but I wasn't sure ye'd take kindly to the notion."

Compton laughed, put out his hand and gripped Matt's. "I want to congratulate you for handling the fire as you did, Regan. The way it looked from the other side, we were afraid not only would the whole Compton stand go, but that it would sweep down the gulch into the Weyerhauser Camp, too."

"The men worked like demons, sir. And then the wind shifted to the north and the rain came. The Sitka spruce is in a bad way, but we kept it out of the Douglas."

"How the devil did it get started? We've not had our usual heavy spring rains, but the woods aren't that dry."

Matt gave him a stern, steady look. "It was set, Mr. Compton, by one of our own men. I'll rustle you some grub and take it to your office. Then I'll give you the full report."

With Ole gone, Matt pressed Jake into service as cook, with Tommy as his helper. Jake had once worked as cook on a tugboat and promised to do his best till Ole got back. He made a plate of sandwiches, a pot of coffee, and found a wedge of Ole's apple pie for Compton's lunch, promising a real dinner for the whole camp at five.

While Merritt ate at the desk in the office, Matt sat smoking his pipe, and reported on the fire. Compton's only word of criticism was that the Swede hadn't been locked up. Jake had knocked him out when he found him with the kerosene can, and had left him where he'd fallen to spread the alarm. He might have escaped down the trail, or perished in the blaze. No one had seen him since the fire started.

"I could hope that he burned to a crisp, the skunk," cried Merritt, "except that I'd like to bring him to justice. As soon as I get down to Sedro-Woolley, I'll have a warrant issued for his arrest, and I'll post his name with every lumber company, every hiring agency in the Northwest. Even if we don't catch him, he'll never work in a logging camp again."

Matt had promised Terry to speak to her father as soon as he arrived, but he felt the moment hadn't come. The man was dog-tired and upset, his mind was full of wrath at the Swede and thoughts of the fire. Matt decided to wait till after dinner. There was another matter on his mind, now, too. He'd heard Rita's accusation that he wanted to marry Terry only to further himself as Compton's son-in-law. He saw that others might put the same construction on it. The hackles of his pride rose at the thought.

For some time he'd had his plans made to start out for himself. He'd already put down option money on a fine stand of Douglas, hemlock, and Sitka spruce above Port Blakely, where the logs could be easily tugged down the Sound to the huge Port Blakely mills. It had been his intention to quit Compton last year and begin his own operations, but he had held off, and now he knew it was because of Terry. If he'd left Compton then, he might never have seen her again.

But now, things were different. He'd won his woman, he could start his own company with no help from Compton, and no one could say he was beholden to him or to any man. He would give Compton notice before he spoke for Terry, so there'd be no doubt in Merritt's mind, but he'd stay on as foreman till Compton could replace him. As a common logger, working for him, Compton might not take kindly to his courting his daughter, but as an independent lumberman with his own holdings, even though he hadn't got his company started, Matt Regan was no beggar.

Compton finished his meal, lit a cigar, thanked Matt for a clear report, and went to the cabin to see Terry. Matt's heart went with him in longing for a glimpse of her sweet, drowsy face on waking. Ah, he thought tenderly, I'd like to be the one to wake you, my darling, to kiss the sleep out of your eyes and to feel your arms about my neck again. He had little time to spend in dreaming, since there were hours of work to do, clearing away the ravages of the fire, and he must wait to see her at dinner. He got his crew together and set off up the trail.

Terry was up and dressed when her father rapped on the cabin door. She turned from the mirror above the bureau, where she'd been coiling her hair, with a sweet weakness in her limbs, thinking it might be Matt. She started to call out his name, but checked herself in time. "Come in," she said, and her father opened the door, stepped inside, and without a word, put his arms around her, saying, "Oh, Terry girl. You're a sight for sore eyes!"

This meeting, which might have meant so much to her, had lost its importance and meaning to her, now. She was glad to see her father, glad that she no longer was separated from him by the barrier of bitterness and grief, but even as she returned his embrace, she knew that she was separated from him forever, not by a wall of anger or restraint or accusation, but by her love for Matt Regan. For she had found what neither her father nor her mother could give her; she had found her true home, her own place, the direction of her life which she had been seeking, in knowing that she loved and was loved by a man who suddenly filled all the blank places in her imagination.

Even as she realized this, swift pity for her father, who loved her and who did not know that he had lost her, made her tender with him. She kissed his cheek and cried, "Oh, Father, I'm so glad to see you! I've been awfully lazy. I only just now got up."

"I know, kiddie. Matt Regan told me how you worked all night, feeding the men. That was grand of you, Terry. Just grand!" He held her away and smiled at her. "And look at you, fresh as a daisy. And so pretty. I don't think I've ever seen you looking so pretty, or your eyes so bright."

She wanted to say, That's because I'm happy, Father, and in love, and safe, and I know where I'm going at last. Instead she said, shyly, "Oh, so you've seen Matt?" She turned away, on pretext of adding another hairpin to her chignon, her heart pounding, wondering if Matt had "spoken" to him.

"We had a long session just now in the office. He gave me a full report on the fire. He did a fine job of controlling it, I'll say that for him. I doubt if Dobie, God rest his soul, could have handled it as well."

So he hasn't told him yet, she thought. "Oh, he was wonderful, Father. He worked like a madman. He wouldn't even stop to have coffee, until I brought it up the trail. He gave the other men time to rest and eat, but he took not more than five minutes himself."

Something in her voice made him look at her in quick appraisal. He nodded. "He saved the best timber, the Douglas stand. I think he deserves some kind of bonus."

"I don't think he'd take it, Father!" she cried swiftly, thinking, All he wants is your consent to our marriage.

"We'll see. At least I can offer him something. But I want to talk to you about what brought you up here. Red said that I was needed back in Seattle."

"Yes, Father. Mr. Deming said it was imperative that you return as soon as possible." She sat on the bed and he on the chair where Matt had sat, and Terry gave her father Deming's message.

When she had finished, Merritt's face was grave and frowning. He got up, thrust his hands in his jacket pockets, and took a turn around the room. "This is a fine time for me to leave. But the situation down there sounds bad. We'll have to start at dawn tomorrow. Better get packed tonight."

Terry saw Matt at supper, but his glance, meeting hers, was only momentarily warm and did not linger. She knew he was thinking of her father and the men. She found it hard to eat, knowing he was so close, on the other side of Compton, though Jake's stew was as good as Ole's.

Immediately after the meal, Matt and her father disappeared into the office, and she, restless and unable to sit still after packing her grip, took Mac and went for a walk by the brook, which had bits of burned twigs floating in it. She saw neither her father nor Matt again that night. When she was in camp, Compton slept in the foreman's shack, and Matt, though he had taken Dobie's place, had never moved into it, but bunked with the men, which they seemed to like.

For a while Terry lay awake after she'd gone to bed, listening to the owls hooting in the woods and to the scream of a cougar far off up the mountain. She wondered if it was the same one who had left his footprints beside her campfire. She wondered what Matt was saying to her father, since she knew from the way he'd looked at her as he said good night and followed Compton to the office that he was going to tell him that they were in love. What her father's reaction would be, she didn't know. He was a complex person, on the one hand, hearty and impatient with insincerity and show; on the other, proud and given to unreasonable prejudices. It doesn't really matter, though, she thought, whether he likes it or not, Matt is the man I'm going to marry.

The moment Merritt offered Matt a hundred-dollar bonus for saving the camp and the stand of Douglas fir, the Irishman's back stiffened. His blue eyes glinted dangerously, but his voice was soft and courteous. "It's generous of ye, sir, and I

249

thank ye. But I can accept no bonus fer doin' me duty. Should I have let the timber burn, then?" His Irish accent came out strongly, as Dobie had often noticed it did whenever he was trying to keep his temper.

"Don't be a stiff-necked Irishman, Regan," snapped Compton, annoyed that his gesture had been rebuffed. "I'm trying to show my gratitude in the only way I can."

"And I thank ye, sir. But I can't accept it."

"Terry said you wouldn't." Compton shifted in his chair, his hooded eyes intent on the foreman's face, which had softened curiously at mention of Terry's name.

"She knows me better then than ye do, Mr. Compton."

There was something in the Irishman's voice and eyes that bothered Merritt. He wondered if his offer of a bonus hadn't been good enough. "All right, forget the bonus. But I don't want to be in your debt. I feel that I owe not only my camp and timber to you, but my daughter's safety. What would you say to a better job, to being supervisor of all my camps, making the inspection tours that I'm getting a bit old for and that annoy my wife? I'd pay you twice what you're getting now, plus expenses."

"Ye're a generous man, sir, and I'm grateful. It'd be a most temptin' offer, if I didn't have other plans," said Matt quietly, pulling on his pipe.

Compton stared at him, playing nervously with his watch charm, a gold nugget from the Klondike. He was not a nervous man, but there was something about Regan that disturbed him. He and Dobie had been friends, yet Jack had always made him aware that he, Merritt, was the Boss. This fellow, while he was respectful and courteous enough, looked him squarely in the eye, measuring him, and Compton was sure that he didn't give a tinker's dam for him as the Boss, that Regan considered himself as good a man, if not better, and that the wrong word or tone would be enough to make him throw up his job. "What plans, Matt? If I may ask?"

250

"You may, sir, as I was about to tell you anyway." Matt knocked out his pipe on his shoe and laid it on the desk. "For some time now I've been thinking of striking out on my own. I've laid down option money on some fine timber land up the Sound, near Port Blakely. If Dobie hadn't died, I'd have left this month. But I wouldn't leave you in the lurch without a foreman. I'll not now. I'll stay through the summer till you can get a man to replace me."

Compton was silent while he lit a fresh cigar. Then he said, "Well, Regan, this is quite a surprise, but I'd not stand in a man's way to bettering himself. From what I've seen of your work, I'm sure you'll run a first-rate logging camp. We'll be competitors, but I wish you success," and he reached out his hand to clasp Matt's.

"Thank you, sir. And I may say that I've learned some fine things through working for you these four years. There's no lumberman in the Northwest that I have more respect for."

"That's very nice, Matt. Thanks. Let me give you a word of warning. The Eastern monopolies are trying hard to run us local men out of the timber. Be smart. Don't let them get a toe hold with your outfit."

"You may be sure, sir. I worked for a Michigan company before I hit the Klondike trail, so I know something about how they operate."

"I'll tell you frankly, Regan, that the only way I see for us to beat them out is to get together to fight. As a matter of fact, I've got to leave in the morning for Seattle because the situation is getting bad. I've been working on a merger of several Western companies, on a very loose basis, but tight enough to give us a combined strength. You may want to come in with us when you get your company going."

"I may, indeed, sir. I'm an independent man, I may say, and I don't like being dictated to, but I can see the merit in what you've got in mind." Matt smiled. "However, there's time to think about that, later. I've yet to get myself organized."

251

"Right you are, Regan. And more power to you." Compton pulled open a desk drawer and brought out a bottle. "I think this calls for a drink, don't you?"

Matt picked up his pipe and very slowly began to fill it from his tobacco bag. "I'd be proud to drink with you, sir, but there's one thing more." He tamped the tobacco down into his pipe with a long forefinger, lit it with several puffs, then he got up and paced the floor, while Compton watched him curiously. He came to rest with one great hand flat on the desk before Compton, his eyes fixed on Merritt's face. "I have the honor to ask your permission to marry your daughter, sir."

Compton's hand, which had been about to uncork the bottle, fell to the desk. His deep-set eyes suddenly went hard and cold. "What did you say, Regan?"

"I love your daughter, Terry, and she loves me. We want to be married, sir."

The anger gathering behind Compton's eyes suddenly burst forth. He hit the desk violently with his open palm. "Why, you blasted, ignorant upstart lumberjack! How dare you? You're not good enough to clean her boots. Just because you've saved a few dollars and can buy a few acres of timber, don't think that puts you in her class."

Matt drew back as if he'd been hit, and under his tan his strong face went white. He clenched his fists at his sides, and his eyes, meeting Compton's, were like bits of blue ice. "Everything you say is true, Compton. I'm an ignorant lumberjack. My parents died in poverty. Neither of them could read or write. But I've managed to teach myself a number of things, and I can tell you this—I'm going to be somebody, no matter. I know I'm not in Terry's class, but that doesn't seem to matter to her. She is willing to take me as I am. And ye'd be surprised what I'll be able to do with me few acres of timber." He turned and walked toward the door.

"Just a minute, Regan."

Matt kept on going until he had his hand on the doorknob,

then he glanced back over his shoulder at Compton. "Well, sir? Do I have yer permission to marry yer daughter, or must we go against yer wishes, sir?" His brogue was so thick it was almost unintelligible.

"You do not have my permission, either to marry my daughter or to speak to her again. I'm warning you—stay away from Terry. I don't know what tricks you've been up to while she was here alone with you. She's an innocent, trusting girl, and if you've hurt her, I'll kill you, Regan. But get this straight, I'll never give my consent to your so much as seeing her again. And in case you might be thinking of disobeying my order, Terry is going to marry the son of my lawyer. I expect to announce their engagement this summer."

Matt swung all the way around and his face was tight, a muscle in his taut cheek twitched. His hand, leaving the doorknob, tightened into a fist, then opened and fell limply against his thigh. "I've been up to no tricks, as you say, with Terry, Compton." His voice, which had been so confident and strong before, was now no more than a whisper. "Ask her, and she'll tell you. As I just said, I love her, and I thought she loved me. But if I'd known she was already spoken for and that she had given her promise, I'd not have troubled you."

He took a deep breath, and a little color came back into his face. "But under the circumstances, Compton, I'll not wait for you till you find another foreman. I'm quitting, as of now. I'll be gone before you leave in the morning."

After he'd gone, slamming the door behind him, Merritt Compton sat a long time with his hands clenched on the desk. He was deeply disturbed. Regan had done him a great service, at the risk of his own safety, in saving the timber and the camp. Yes, and Terry, too. His strong sense of justice had impelled him to try to compensate the Irishman for doing his duty. He had been surprised at Regan's refusal of a bonus, at his disclosure of his plan for starting his own company, but knowing the Irishman's independence, had rather welcomed

253

it, as another bulwark against the Eastern infiltration. He had been shocked out of any sense of justice, reason, or proportion by Matt's request to marry Terry.

His reaction had been purely instinctive and defensive, based on an unconscious antagonism toward Regan because of his independence, cockiness, and, he had to admit, his evident superiority, which, in some vague way, he felt threatened his position.

He had no idea why he had lied to Regan about Terry's being engaged, other than, knowing the Irishman's touchy pride, it seemed the only thing that would keep him away from the girl. He refused to let himself believe that she might be in love with Matt. No doubt she had been attracted to him, he was a virile, handsome devil, with a recklessness that appealed to women, but Compton felt sure that if Regan left her alone, she'd soon forget him. "Ned would make her a good husband, even if he is a bit heavy. What kind of life could Matt Regan give her, a girl who's been used to the best?" Yet he remembered how bright her eyes had been, how glowing she had looked earlier that day, and he was uneasy and not quite satisfied with the way he'd handled Regan. "I wish I hadn't lied to him. That was cheap."

He woke Terry at dawn and she was ready by the time Red brought up the horses. "We'll eat breakfast on the trail," he said, and helped her mount. In the half darkness before sunup, they rode out of camp. Terry kept looking back as they went.

"What's the matter, Terry?" he asked at length, bothered by her uneasiness.

"I wanted to say good-by to Matt Regan, Father," she answered frankly. "I thought he'd be up to see us off."

"Regan quit last night. He said he'd be gone before we started today."

She turned and stared at him, wordless, stunned, her eyes bewildered.

"He told me he was leaving to start his own logging outfit.

Turned down a hundred-dollar bonus and a better job as camp inspector. Left me in the lurch without a foreman."

"But I—I don't understand, Father! Why did he quit so suddenly?"

He did not like the look on her face at all. She had the strange, confused expression of a blind person left alone in an unfamiliar room, afraid to take a step for fear of running into an obstacle. "Why? How should I know? He's been planning to leave and go it on his own for over a year. Suddenly he makes up his mind to go now. Just like an Irishman, they're all a restless, unpredictable lot." His uneasiness made him speak sharply.

"Did you and Matt quarrel, Father? Is that why he quit without warning?"

Blast the girl's persistence. If he wasn't careful, she'd worm the whole story out of him! "We had words. He turned down my effort to reward him for saving the camp and the timber in a rather cavalier fashion, I thought. He's an arrogant fellow and I don't like impertinence. I was abrupt with him and he flared up."

"It—it wasn't about me that you quarreled, was it, Father?"

"What d'ye mean, girl? Certainly not!" He covered up his confusion at her coming so close to the mark by gazing at her sternly.

Terry didn't answer. Her eyes dropped away from his, and she bent to pat the pony's neck, to speak to the dog trotting beside her. All the way down to Sedro-Woolley, she rode in silence, except when Compton spoke to her and she had to answer. She ate very little when they stopped for breakfast and lunch and seemed to take none of her usual delight in the sights and sounds and smells of the trail.

On the boat down to Seattle, she sat on deck, wrapped in her blue wool cloak, with the Chesapeake lying at her feet, and stared out at the water. She came into the dining salon with her father, but scarcely touched the deviled Dungeness crab

255

he'd asked the cook to prepare specially for her. When he urged her to eat, she got up and said she had a headache and wanted to lie down in her stateroom.

Compton paced the deck with his cigar and his thoughts. The wall between them had been down when he embraced her in the cabin the day after the fire. She had been warm and loving and happy to see him. Now, there was no wall, but he could not reach her. She was simply not there. Had she fallen in love with that cocky Irishman, after all?

Twenty

THE letter Terry sent Matt in care of the Skagit River Camp marked "Please Forward," came back in ten days stamped, "Not Here. Address Unknown." She had waited nearly a month before writing it, thinking he would surely send her some word. She knew he didn't like to write letters, as he hated doing anything he couldn't do well. He was a proud man, but he must know that she was desperate to hear from him and would be happy with only a penciled scrawl, no matter how clumsily written.

She had tried to understand why, even if he had quarreled with her father, he hadn't tried to see her before she left camp. For a while she'd had the feeling that it *was* about her that they had fallen out, but her father had never lied to her and why should he not tell her if Matt had asked for her and in his anger Compton had wounded his pride? It must be that they had, as her father said, quarreled over the matter of the bonus, and Matt, in a fit of rage, had left without speaking to him about her.

She tried to account for his silence with the thought that if he was organizing his own company Matt would be too busy to write or try to see her. Or that he wanted to wait till he was established and could come to Compton proudly, as an equal. But she felt she could not wait any longer to hear from him. She conquered her own pride and wrote to him, certain that it would bring instant response.

It was a rather emotional letter that brought tears to her eyes as she wrote it. She begged him not to let his pride or his quarrel with her father keep him from her. She told him she loved him, that she had been unable to think of anything but him, that she could not endure not hearing from him. She had never written such a letter in her life. It was her first love letter, and she put all her heart into it.

The returned letter was lying in the silver tray on the hall table where Hannah always put the mail, when Terry came home from making afternoon calls with Isobel. She snatched it up before Isobel could see it and took it to her room. There, without taking off her hat or gloves, she tore it into tiny bits, which she dropped into her wastebasket. Her heart burned with shame for having written it.

The impersonal rebuff of the post office's heartless, terse, stamped message stung more, she thought, than might have a scrawled line from Matt, giving her her *congé*. It was intolerable not knowing where he was or how to reach him. An overwhelming impulse urged her to speak to her father, to demand to know what had happened between them the last night in camp, to tell him she loved Matt and that if he cared anything about her happiness he must help her find him.

She decided to speak to him the moment he came home from the office, to meet him in the hall and ask him to go into the study with her where they could talk without being overheard by Isobel. But he telephoned from the office at six, saying he had to leave at once for Olympia and wouldn't be back for a week.

Merritt Compton returned home while Terry was out shopping with Mable Fisher, helping her select material for her wedding gown. Dear, good, homely Mable was marrying her dedicated young missionary and going off to Alaska.

When Terry got home, Isobel told her that her father had left on the afternoon train for Chicago to attend an important lumberman's meeting. He would be gone over a month, since he intended going down to Washington, D.C., for a conference with the President on conservation of the Western forests.

By now, Terry had given up hoping for word from Matt. She was convinced that something a great deal more than angry pride over her father's offer of a bonus was keeping Matt from her. It was inconceivable that her father should lie to her, but the feeling she'd had on the trail, that he was keeping back something, grew as she waited for his return from the East.

Yet there were Rita's bitter words about Matt's blarney that she couldn't forget. She remembered Gen Lansing's warning of two years ago, "Don't wear your heart on your sleeve. Never let a man be sure of you until you're sure of him." Did I lose Matt because I forgot the rules and let him know I loved him? Was I diminished in his eyes for asking him to hold me the morning after the fire? But I thought I could be sure of Matt.

The month Merritt was away Terry began to go out in society again. While she still hoped to hear from Matt, she had declined nearly every invitation, now she deliberately accepted them. There was nothing so time-consuming and thought-deadening as the social whirl.

It was at a *thé dansant* at the Firlock Club that she met Hal Forrester for the first time since Milly Fox's wedding. Tea dances had become the rage that summer and were particularly popular with unattached girls since it was permissible for them to attend unescorted.

Terry had gone alone and so had Hal. His romance with Gen had fallen through when Mrs. Lansing had taken her to England that June in pursuit of Lord Claverly, a mild young nobleman who had visited the Struthers last fall, to whom he was related on his mother's side.

When Hal saw Terry standing uncertainly on the clubhouse lawn, he had put down his drink, which was not tea, and left the terrace where he was sitting by himself and hurried to greet her. "Terry! Are you alone?"

She turned and looked at him with that clear, frank gaze that had always intrigued him, and said, "Why, hello, Hal. Yes, I'm alone."

He thought he had never seen her looking so attractive. Her beauty, which had been a little too uncomplicated and *jeune fille* when he first saw her at her debut, had definite distinction now. There was still that remarkable quality of candor in her face and in the unstudied grace of her movements, but with his instinctive understanding of women, he saw at once that she had matured.

What a fool I was, he thought, not to have known she'd turn out like this. Having lived, by now, long enough in the West to have learned that there were few even of the "best families" without at least a minor skeleton in their closets, he had come to regret his stuffiness about Terry's mother and his haste to break things off. Also, his action had not been well received in many of the circles in which he wished to be accepted and he had the uneasy feeling that it had definitely hurt his career in Seattle.

As he studied her, moving toward him, half in sun, half in leafy shade, graceful, naturally poised, lovely in a simple frock of orchid lawn and a wide-brimmed, drooping leghorn hat trimmed with streamers of orchid ribbon, he decided she was the most distinguished-looking, probably the most beautiful girl he'd seen in the West. The waltz music floating out from the lounge where dancing was in progress seemed created as a background for her charming appearance. Certainly all the other women on the club terrace seemed commonplace beside her.

It would be very easy to fall in love with her now, he

thought, noticing how the simple, girlish frock outlined subtly the rich, full curves of her womanly figure. He had not been in love with her while they were engaged, only attracted to her youth and freshness, to the wealth and prestige of her father, the glamour of the great house where he'd first seen her. He had not really considered her apart from them until now.

"I'm alone, too, so let's join forces," he cried, taking her hand and tucking it under his arm. "They're dancing inside, but the air is so pleasant out on the terrace. Shall I order tea for you? There's an innocuous concoction which goes by the name of claret cup being served, if you'd like that, instead."

"Thank you," said Terry, smiling, "but I don't care for tea. I think I'll have the punch."

"Yes," he exclaimed eagerly, "that's exactly what you should want, in that charming frock and hat, looking like someone out of a Viennese waltz."

She let him lead her out onto the terrace and seat her at his table, and was both amused and rather touched that he managed to indicate by his eagerness and solicitude that he had been waiting for her to appear, that she was his invited guest. He does have beautiful manners, she thought, and noticed that the curious eyes that had appraised her while she stood alone on the lawn were no longer speculative, though heads had turned as she and Hal sat down together.

When the punch arrived, Hal raised his glass and smiled at Terry. "To you, Terry. You are more beautiful than ever."

She met his eyes with a faintly ironic smile. "To you, Hal. You are just as charming as ever." She took a sip from her glass and said, "Don't drink too much punch now. I remember the last time you did, you got quite carried away."

"It may have been the punch that time," he replied, "but this time, I assure you, I could be carried away even if I hadn't drunk a drop."

His dark eyes were ardent and his voice subtly caressing.

What a charmer you are, she thought, meeting his eyes with a smile. No wonder I fancied myself in love with you two years ago.

They danced presently, and Terry realized that she had forgotten how easy it was to let the music and the rhythm float one away, so that pain and grief and bitterness sank to the bottom of one's heart like heavy stones, and one was conscious only of the foam on the waves, the dancing sunlight, the white blossom dropped on the surface of the dark waters, spinning round and round in the shimmering eddy. Yet the heavy stones were not dissolved by the music, nor by Hal's arm about her waist, his smile bending to hers, and when she was home again in her room, she felt them weighing her down.

Hal had taken her home in a cab and had exacted her promise to go to the August cotillions with him. He had made it clear, without committing himself too much, that he was free of entanglements and, since she seemed to be, too, that they should take up again where they had left off. She, finding him an amusing and attractive escort, and now that she had no illusions about him or her feelings toward him, was quite agreeable to let him beau her around.

"Why not, Hal?" she responded casually. "As you say, we're both at loose ends, so we might as well have fun together." There had been something so cold, so close to cynicism under her light laugh, that he had felt uneasy. In a sudden moment of insight he wondered if this time round he might not be the one who would be hurt.

Isobel wasn't at all sure that she approved of Terry's taking up with Hal Forrester again. "After the way he treated you, I don't see how you could bear to be decent to him."

"Heavens, Isobel, that's all water over the dam," laughed Terry. "I was a starry-eyed schoolgirl when I first knew him. I didn't have sense enough to come in out of the rain. But I do, now."

"Well, I just hope you won't get too serious about him,

Terry. Of course, everyone will remember you were once engaged to him and will be wondering if you're going to take him back again."

Terry sat curled on the window seat in her room, buffing her nails, while Isobel, in a low rocker, ran blue baby ribbon through one of her own chemises. "I rather think Hal is wondering, too," said the girl with an ironic smile.

Hal came around the next evening to call and asked Terry to go walking in the park. He was looking harassed and tense.

"I'd love to, Hal," she replied cheerfully. "I was going to take Mac out for a run, anyway."

It was truly poetic justice that he should have chosen the very same bench near the sunken garden where he'd asked to be released from their engagement two years before (only two years? she thought, it seems a lifetime ago) to propose to her again.

Terry had unsnapped Mac's leash and was sitting watching the big dog quarter over the leaf-strewn grass. The park was pleasant in the early fall sunlight. A light breeze came up and sent a few more leaves spiraling down through the blue air. There was a scent of dry grass and pine needles. The good smell of fall, she thought. Summer was over, but zinnias and marigolds still made a bright splash along the walks.

"How nice it is here," she said dreamily. "I love the park and autumn is my favorite season."

"I love you, Terry," he said abruptly, staring at the ground, his hands tightly clasped over his knee. "I love you desperately and I want to marry you." He turned and looked at her, his face sharp with feeling.

"Oh, but you told me that once before, Hal, do you recall? And then you changed your mind." She smiled at him a little sadly, half sorry for him.

He took her hand and clasped it in both of his. "I was a stupid young fool, Terry. Can you ever forgive me?"

"No," she answered thoughtfully, "I don't suppose I can. I

was quite a nice young girl when you first pretended that you loved me. I don't think I can forgive you for breaking that nice young girl's heart."

His eyes entreated her and he pressed her hand beseechingly. "Oh, Terry, I'm so ashamed of the way I treated you. I was a stuffy ass, but I've learned a lot since then. Can you possibly understand?"

"Oh, yes, I think I understand," she said, giving him a direct, uncompromising glance. "I understand a great deal that I didn't two years ago."

"To understand is to forgive, Terry," he murmured, letting her hand go.

And suddenly, she did forgive him. If he hadn't broken her heart she'd never have known and loved Matt Regan. No matter what happened, she would always be grateful that she hadn't married Hal, and that Matt had held her in his arms and told her he loved her.

"You're right, Hal, and I do forgive you. But I can't marry you."

"Because I hurt you too deeply," he said miserably.

But she wouldn't leave him even that melancholy consolation. "No, Hal, because I'm in love with someone else."

Two days later, Compton got home from his trip. Terry waited until after dinner, when Isobel had gone to her Evening Guild meeting at St. Mark's and her father had shut himself in the study with brandy and all the correspondence that had piled up since he'd left.

She tapped on the door and he called out irritably, "Yes? Who is it?"

"It's Terry, Father. May I come in for a talk?"

He opened the door for her himself, delighted that she should want to see him alone. He took her arm and led her to the big leather armchair beside his desk.

"I hope I'm not disturbing you," she said.

"My dear girl, you could never disturb me. I'm flattered and

264

pleased that you want to visit with me. Sit down, and tell me what you've been doing while I've been away." He gave her shoulders a little squeeze. "Everything all right, I hope? You've been well and happy?"

"No, Father," she replied quietly. "I've been quite unhappy and confused. That's why I felt I must talk to you."

"Tell me what's troubling you, kiddie," he said softly, meeting her steady gray eyes and noticing with a shock how deeply shadowed they were and how thin her face had grown. "Perhaps your old father can help. You know there's nothing in the world I wouldn't do to make you happy, Terry."

"I wonder," she murmured.

He put out his hand and touched hers, which lay in her lap. "Try me and see, my dear."

Twenty-one

I WANT to know the real reason why Matt Regan left camp so suddenly last spring, and why I've never heard from him since," said Terry evenly, her eyes on her father's face.

"Matt Regan!" Merritt cried, completely taken aback. He had all but forgotten the incident and had taken for granted that she had. "You can't mean that he's the cause of your unhappiness, Terry?"

"Yes, Father. And I'm quite sure you didn't tell me the truth the first time." There was a frightening quietness about her manner. He knew he could not lie to her again. "It wasn't just over the bonus that you quarreled, was it?"

Compton felt his face get hot and, for a moment, could not bear the intensity of his daughter's clear gaze. He took a cigar out of the inlaid Chinese box on his desk, carefully cut and lit it before looking at her again. "No," he said at last, "it wasn't about the bonus. Regan had the impertinence to ask my consent to his marrying you."

"Then he *did* ask for me!" she cried softly, warmth coming into her cheeks. "Why didn't you tell me, Father?"

"I wanted you to forget him as quickly as possible!" he replied angrily. "I was sure he couldn't mean anything to you

266

other than a momentary crush. Why, Terry, he's nothing but a common logger."

Her eyes went dark and there was scorn in her voice. "You were quite wrong, Father. Matt Regan is not a common logger and I will never forget him." She got up from the armchair and began to pace the room, her hands clasped tightly. It was a mannerism which Merritt instantly recognized as his own and was torn by pity and love.

Presently she turned and faced him, her eyes accusing. "I suppose you refused your consent and told him to clear out?"

"I refused my consent, naturally," he answered. "But it was his own idea to leave without seeing you again."

"Why? I know Matt, Father. I know he loved me. He's not a man to be put off by you or anyone else. He'd not give me up that easily, unless there's something more that you haven't told me."

Her voice was cold and clear and insistent. It was very like his own when he was determined to get to the root of a question. He thought he might have been able to handle her if she'd broken down and wept or acted feminine and emotional. But he was faced now with his own flesh and blood, his own ruthless impatience with hedging and evasion. If he was to retrieve any shred of her love and respect for him, he must admit his lie and hope for her forgiveness.

"Yes, there is something more." He met her scrutiny squarely. "I lied to him. I told him you were already engaged to Ned Deming and I was announcing your engagement when we got back to Seattle."

She stood perfectly still, staring at him, and the tears flashed in her eyes for the first time. She turned as if she could not bear to look at him and went to the window and leaned her forehead against the pane.

"I meant it for the best, Terry," he said bleakly, longing to go to her and take her in his arms, but not daring.

She came back and sat down again in the armchair. Her face

was composed and her voice steady. "Perhaps you meant it for the best, according to your plans for me, Father, so I will try not to hate you for it. But you have done both of us a great wrong."

"If so, I am sorry," he said, looking at the long ash on the end of his cigar, as stiff and unrelenting as she, though he wished he might have begged her forgiveness for having caused her pain. I'd cut off my right hand before making her unhappy!

"You said that perhaps you could help me in my trouble," she went on, as if he hadn't spoken. "The only way you can help me, Father, is to find Matt Regan and bring him to me. I wrote him, but the letter was returned, address unknown. If I knew where to go, I'd find him myself."

He banged his fist hard on the desk. "I'd lock you up rather than let you go after this man and throw yourself at him!"

She raised her head and looked at him with pity and sorrow. "It's no good, Father. You can't lock me up and I'll never forget Matt Regan. Will you find him for me?" She got up and went to the door, turning with her hand on the knob. "Or must I go down the skid road, asking the loggers and the drifters where to find him?"

"I believe you'd do that, Terry." His voice was gray with defeat.

She looked very slim and young and alone, but there was a strength in her that he had not been prepared for. "Why, yes, Father. Now that I know the truth, now that I know why he went away, of course I would."

"I'll never willingly let this man marry you, Terry, but I'll find him for you." Compton rose from his chair and stood looking down at her gravely. "And I shall be hoping with all my heart that when I find him and bring him to you either he won't want you any more or you will realize you have made a mistake."

268

A shadow went over her face for an instant, then she smiled. "You are hoping for the impossible, Father."

Three weeks later Merritt Compton came home late. He tapped on the door of Terry's room and she opened it in her dressing gown. For a moment he couldn't speak, stood looking at her oddly. With her chestnut hair unbound, floating in shining waves nearly to her waist, her gray eyes bright and expectant, she looked so much like her mother it gave him a turn.

"I—I hope I'm not disturbing you," he said.

"Oh no, I've been reading." She stood back for him to enter. The lamp above her writing table was lit and a small limp leather volume lay open on the desk. "Take the rocker, Father, and I'll sit on the desk chair."

He smiled faintly. "Browning, again?"

She shook her head. "Not the same Browning. Elizabeth Barrett. The *Sonnets from the Portuguese*. Do you know them?"

"Once I did. When I was young and romantic." He stretched out his hand and, flushing, she handed him the volume. He glanced at a page which had been faintly marked in pencil. In a low voice he began to read, " 'How do I love thee? Let me count the ways. I love thee to the depth and height my soul can reach——' "

"Don't!" she cried sharply, and snatched the book away from him. "I'm sorry, Father, but that's a very special poem to me."

"I'm sorry, too. I didn't mean to intrude." He got up. "I only wanted to tell you I've located Matt Regan." His face was closed and dark and his voice remote and cold.

She put her hand on his arm in sudden contrition. "I didn't mean to be rude. Please, tell me about Matt. Have you seen him? Is he well? Did he send me a message?"

"I didn't see or talk to him. I found out he's running his own camp up the Sound near Port Blakely."

The eagerness died out in her face and she let her hand drop to her side. "I—I see."

"He's doing pretty well, from what I hear, though he's operating on a shoestring. But you were right on one score. Regan's not just another logger. He's managed to buy Metcalf's stand of five hundred acres that I've tried for years to get the old fellow to sell, and he's got a good crew of men working for him."

Warmth came back into her face and her eyes flashed with pride. "I told you, Father," she said quietly. "So, now that you've found him, what?"

"I'm calling a meeting in a few weeks of some of the independent Western lumbermen to talk over the merger I've been working on to protect our interests against the Weyerhausers. I've sent word to Regan that I'd like to have him attend. The meeting will be here. I'll get Isobel to give the men a good dinner and then we'll talk business. If Regan isn't too pigheaded to accept my invitation, you'll see him then."

"Thank you, Father," said Terry softly, her eyes bright.

"Don't thank me yet," he cried impatiently. "He may not come at all. You can't tell what an Irishman will do."

Isobel took special pains with the dinner, fussing over the hollandaise sauce for the hothouse asparagus, making the baking-powder biscuits herself, with Hannah muttering to Sadie at the sink and sighing, till at last her mistress, catching sight of the clock, rushed upstairs to change.

"Your father says we won't be dressing tonight," she'd told Terry earlier, "since it's a business meeting. But I shall wear my black velvet and diamonds. Men are always so impressed by black velvet and diamonds, especially those who aren't quite gentlemen, like Mr. Johanssen from Humptulips. It always helps a man for his womenfolks to look nice. You may borrow my amethysts, if you like."

"Thanks, Isobel, but I thought I'd wear the pearls Father gave me, and my little orchid lawn," said Terry. "It's a simple frock, but quite becoming, and I think one of us looking impressive is enough." She wanted to look her best for Matt, but she didn't want to overwhelm him with elegance. After all, he'd never seen her in anything but the simple clothes she wore in camp.

If he comes, she thought. There had been no answer to Merritt's invitation to the dinner meeting. All the other men had agreed to come. Oh, the Irish, Terry thought, stubborn, touchy, unpredictable. Perhaps Father is right. Perhaps he won't come. Or maybe he never did get the word Father sent him, if indeed the word was sent. Yet she was sure, now, that her father was being honest with her. He had given his word.

The night of the meeting Compton was late getting home from the office and was changing his linen, while Isobel was still struggling into her corset, when the doorbell rang and Terry heard Sadie hurry out of the kitchen to the front hall. Terry had been ready for half an hour and had been trying to suppress her nervousness and excitement by playing solitaire in her room. At the sound of the doorbell, she sprang up so suddenly she brushed the cards off the writing table onto the floor.

For a moment she stared at herself in the mirror. Wide-eyed, pale one moment, blushing the next, her reflection stared back at her. Then she went quickly out of the room and down the long stairs to the hall.

Sadie was just closing the door of the drawing room. "Oh, Miss Terry!" she breathed, looking round. "There's the grandest gentleman just arrived. He's got the bluest eyes and the blackest curls. And oh, what shoulders!" She sighed ecstatically. "Oh, he's that elegant in his tails and boiled shirt. I told him the master and mistress was still dressin' and would he wait in the drawin' room."

And who but Matt Regan would fit such a description,

271

thought Terry. Except for the tails. It seemed hard to imagine Matt in an evening suit. Father must have forgotten to tell him not to dress, or did he forget on purpose? What a shabby trick to embarrass him and make him ill at ease from the start!

As she opened the drawing-room door, the big man standing before the fireplace, looking at a portrait above the mantel, turned, his dark head bent slightly, as if he found the high-ceilinged room too low for him. The portrait was of Terry painted in her coming-out gown and he had been smiling tenderly as he gazed at it. The smile was still in his eyes as he looked across the room at the girl standing against the closed door.

In silence they stared at each other, as if the wonder of seeing each other's face was too great to be broken by words. Then, impelled by the same implacable impulse, they moved toward each other.

It was Matt who checked himself first. The low table with the decanter of sherry, the silver tray of imported English biscuits, and the box of Merritt's Havana cigars got in his way. As though trapped by the table and all it represented, he stopped short.

"It's yourself, is it, Terry? I didn't expect to find you here," he cried in a low, rough voice.

"Yes, Matt," she smiled. "I live here, you know."

"I thought you'd be married and in yer own place by now. Your father told me last spring you were engaged." The hunger and tenderness that had been in his face when he turned from her portrait and saw her at the door had vanished and his eyes were cold.

"He lied to you, Matt!" she cried, putting her hand out to him. "I wasn't engaged then. Would I have promised myself to you if my word had been given to another man?"

He started toward her, bumped into the coffee table, and at that moment Merritt Compton opened the door and came in, shaking down his cuffs. He had only time to glance at the two of them, to shake hands with Matt, who gave him a strange, dark look, and to ask Terry, over his shoulder, to do them the honors with the sherry, when Sadie ushered in Beauchamp Deming and Oscar Johanssen of Humptulips.

Twenty-two

IF it had been Compton's intention to put Matt Regan at a disadvantage by not telling him that the dinner was informal and the other men would be in business suits, his strategy failed. From the moment Terry walked into the room, Matt had forgotten he was wearing the grand "soup-and-fish" he'd spent a good deal of money to have made for him by Irving and Cannon in the Boston Block, the finest tailors in Seattle. He scarcely noticed that he was the only man in evening clothes, and cared not a whit. If anything, the fine broadcloth coat, which fitted him like his own skin, gave him a feeling of ease and confidence, so that he wasn't overawed by the great house with its crystal chandeliers and thick Oriental rugs.

After he'd met the others, Matt retreated to the mantel where he observed what was going on and brooded over what Terry had told him. So Compton lied to me last spring. She wasn't playing fast and loose with me, like I thought. Oh, Matt Regan, what a blind fool ye were, to be sure, doubting that girl's honesty and taking the word of Merritt Compton, the Big Boss, when never in yer life have ye trusted a boss.

If I hadn't let me blasted pride rule in place of me heart, I'd have gone to her and asked for the truth and 'twould have been there in her great gray eyes, clear as a bell. I let her go away with no word and what must she have thought and felt? Heart-scalded and bewildered, after that time we had together, waiting months on end and not hearing. And now, after the way I treated her in me blind pride, she must have nought in her heart for me but contempt.

He dared not dwell at all on how her father had betrayed them both by his lie, lest the quick anger unleash the devil that constantly prowled within him and he go after Merritt Compton with his two bare hands. But he took note of Compton's smooth urbanity to himself and Johanssen, and he thought, Oho, me fine bucko, now the shoe's on the other foot and it's Mr. Compton that's wanting something of Matt Regan, who mayn't be an easy fellow to bring round, considering.

He couldn't take his eyes off Terry's tall, slender figure in the soft, orchid-colored frock, looking like a flower, as she handed round biscuits and sherry, and he found it hard to keep his mind on Mrs. Compton's small talk when she came up graciously to put him at his ease. He agreed with her that it had been a beautiful fall, that it was wonderful how Teddy Roosevelt had got the Japs and the Russians to sign a peace treaty, said no, he wasn't related to the Timothy Regans of San Francisco, and tossed off the glass of sherry she proffered him in one gulp, without looking at it. He was relieved when at last she gave him up as a bad job.

Terry must have felt the burning impact of his gaze, for she turned once and met Matt's eyes in a strange, wild look. It was the same look he'd seen once in the eyes of a young gray fox caught in a trap. He'd set the fox free, though he'd planned to sell its pelt to buy new boots which he sorely needed. After that he'd broken up the trap and set no more.

Only once more did she look his way. It was during dinner, after the entree had been removed and the maid had set down a lace-paper doily and a small cut-glass bowl of water on the handsome gold-edged service plate before him. He had done all right with the bewildering array of silver at his place, though he'd found it awkward reaching around to serve himself from the vegetable dishes the maid offered him, and in an effort not to take too much had taken too little and was still hungry. But what in the name of all the Irish saints was he supposed to do with the silly little bowl of water? Drink it? But how could he when there was a rose petal floating in it?

He frowned down at it and then looked across the table where Terry was sitting beside Compton's lawyer, and she glanced up and met his eyes. In the candlelight her face was warm and tender, and still keeping her gaze on his, she deliberately lifted the bowl and the doily and set them aside. He carefully did as she had done and looked at her for approval. She smiled softly, nodded faintly, and then the maid was at her elbow with a fancy dessert of ice cream and ladyfingers.

Coffee was served at table in cups that held little more than a swallow, and then Mrs. Compton excused herself and left the room, taking Terry with her. All the men rose, clutching their napkins, and after the ladies had gone, their host led them into the drawing room for chartreuse and cigars.

Matt kept looking toward the door through which Terry had disappeared. All during dinner he had been hoping to see her alone, to ask her forgiveness for doubting her, to ask the painful, fearful question—had he lost her? Did she hate him for making her suffer? But Mrs. Compton had bidden them a gracious good night, and though Terry's eyes had sought his in bright, sudden intensity, he could not decipher their message.

His first impulse had been to rush after her, take her in his arms, beg her to come away with him that very night, knocking down anyone, including her father, who might get in their way. That was what a proper man in a simpler age might have done. But we've bartered our manhood for monkey suits and thingamagig finger bowls and dainty manners and I must sit and watch the girl of my heart walk away from me with my soul bursting within me.

276

He sat with the others in the handsome drawing room, sipping his chartreuse, only half listening to the discussion of the merger, remembering Compton's words the night he asked for Terry. They had meant nothing to him then, fresh from her arms, but now they assumed a heavy authority. Compton was right, what have I got to offer her?

He saw her now, for the first time, in her own background, surrounded by fine furniture, cut-glass decanters of Spanish sherry, maids in uniform handing round silver dishes, jewels on her throat and arms, and his heart failed him. She couldn't have known what she was saying when she told me she loved me. How could she, reared so gently, in such elegance and wealth, love a rough, ignorant logger who didn't even know what a finger bowl was for? How could she give up all this to follow me into camp?

But there had been that wild, pleading look in her eyes. He couldn't forget that.

The meeting went well, smoothed by the fine dinner, the charming ladies, and later by Compton's excellent cordial, which he dispensed with a lavish hand. Compton and his lawyer, Deming, Johanssen, McGraw of Snohomish did most of the talking. Matt Regan had little to say, except to nod and ask a question or two. Because of his presence there, Johanssen and McGraw took for granted his agreement to the merger, and without waiting for his word, which they all felt was implicit, struck hands with Merritt over the deal.

"Mr. Deming has drawn up a tentative merger which I won't ask you to go over tonight, since it encompasses all we've agreed on here. We can meet in my office Monday morning to settle the formalities, eh, gentlemen?" smiled Compton, looking about the room confidently.

Matt Regan met his smile with stony eyes, and Merritt said, genially, "Well, Mr. Regan? You've had very little to say, but silence gives consent, so they say."

"Not always." Matt's voice was deliberate, and he pulled out his pipe and began to fill it.

Compton's face reddened and he leaned against the mantel under Terry's portrait as Matt had done earlier. "Do I understand you to mean, sir, that you have some objections to the way we've set up the merger?"

Matt answered him in his own way. "The idea of a merger to protect Western lumber against the Eastern monopolies is fine. I think I told you when we first discussed the matter last spring that I was all for it." He spoke slowly, filling his pipe in an unhurried way, tamping down the tobacco with his broad thumbnail. "But I'm not sure you and I can come to an agreement, Compton."

Merritt gave him his long, hooded look. "Just what are your reservations, Matt?" he asked sharply, aware that Johanssen, who had been beaming into his glass, had begun to sit up and take notice.

"They have nothing to do with the idea of a merger, nor the way you've set it up," replied Matt. He pulled on his pipe and waited till it was going well before continuing. "My reservations, as you put it, are personal and private."

"I see." Compton chewed on his cigar a bit. "In that case, suppose we have a private talk in my study later, after my other guests have gone."

The others left soon after, and Compton led Matt into his walnut-paneled study where a low fire of logs burned cheerfully. He indicated a leather armchair, and seated himself behind his formidable mahogany desk.

"Now, Regan," he said with a cold smile, "what's this bee in your bonnet?"

" 'Tis no bee in me bonnet, Compton," replied Matt quietly, crossing his long legs. "I just don't think I want to do business with a man who would lie to me."

After dinner, Terry went to her room, but she found it im-

278

possible to stay there. Seeing Matt again had left her in a curious state, alternating between excitement, which made her heart pound and her cheeks flush, and a sense of not being quite in touch with her surroundings or her own body. One minute she could feel the hot blood rushing to her face, the rapid tattoo of her heartbeats, the next, she seemed to be light as air, as if she were disembodied.

There was a quality of unreality about the whole evening. She could not quite believe that Matt was actually there, that she had seen and talked to him. She did not feel real herself. She saw herself passing biscuits and sherry, answering questions, accepting food, meeting Matt's eyes across the table, but it seemed like a dream, or like a play in which she had been both actor and spectator.

Hearing Mac barking in the back yard, she put on her light wool cape, slipped down the back stairs, and let him out. He leaped about her, whining eagerly, his tail whipping, and she decided to take him for a walk.

The night was dark, without moon or stars, and though it was mild, there was the smell of rain in the air. The autumn equinox was due soon, but there might be a few more days of blue October weather. Leaves drifted over the sidewalks, and in the next block someone had raked them into small piles beside the curb and had started to burn them. They had burned down to glowing inverted cones now, and incense-like fingers of smoke rose from each pile.

The meeting would probably drag on for several hours. She had made her father promise to keep Matt after the others had gone so she could see him alone. He had agreed reluctantly and had once more told her flatly that he had not changed his mind about Matt as her suitor. He's stubborn as a rock, she thought, but I'm stubborn, too.

Lost in her thoughts, she walked farther than she intended and was suddenly panicky lest Matt might have left before she got back. She whistled for the dog and ran the last few blocks home. All the lights were out in the big house, except the one she'd left on in her bedroom and a lamp in the study. She quickly shut the dog in the back yard and hurried through the dark kitchen, where the good rich smell of the beef roast lingered, and into the front hall.

Hearing voices, she paused before opening the study door. She recognized the low rumble of her father's voice and then another's that sent a wild rush of gladness sweeping over her. Thank God, he's still here!

She heard Matt, very clear and controlled and proud, saying, "I know you don't think me good enough to marry into the Compton clan, sir, and from yer standpoint ye may be right. But what about Terry? I don't give a tinker's dam what ye think of me, Merritt Compton, if she still loves me. And I don't need yer merger, either. I'll make out on me own, even if I have to fight the Weyerhausers and you, too, single-handed!"

Ah, God love you, Matt Regan, that's all I need to hear, she thought, and opened the door. The two men, who were on their feet glaring at each other, turned as she stepped into the room, closed the door quietly behind her, and looked at them.

"Well, Terry," said her father with a wry smile, "I kept my word, you see."

"Thank you, Father." She went up to the big Irishman and put her hand on his arm. "I was standing outside just now, Matt. I heard what you said. I still love you. How could you have ever doubted that?"

"'Twas not me heart doubted, Terry lass," he cried, enclosing her hand in both of his. "'Twas me blind, stubborn pride, me ignorant mind."

"Ignorant you are not, Matt Regan, but blind and stubborn you may be. Whatever you are, I love you, and if you still want me, I'll marry you," said Terry calmly. It was odd; she had been faint with apprehension and excitement all evening, but now peace and certainty enfolded her. She felt stronger than both the great, tall men staring at her.

"Your father will never consent to it."

"Then we must marry without his consent."

Matt was looking at her with a half smile and his eyes were bright with pride in her. "Will ye leave home and family to go with me, girl?"

"I will." She turned to her father. "You're a stubborn man, Father, but I am stubborn, too, when my happiness is at stake. I don't like going against you, but this is my life."

"Everything I've ever done for you was out of love and the hope of making you happy, Terry," replied Merritt heavily. "I've done everything in my power to give you the proper background, all the advantages to help you make a suitable marriage. Are you willing to throw all that away on this son of poor immigrants, who probably doesn't even know who his grandparents were?"

Matt moved impatiently, his lips tight with anger, but Terry pressed his hand quickly, indicating that this was a thing she must settle herself with her father.

Her voice was soft as a dove's, her eyes cold as stones, as she held his gaze and said, "Oh, but aren't you forgetting something, Father? I don't know who my grandparents are, either, on my mother's side. But perhaps you haven't told Matt about my mother. Maybe he won't want to marry me at all when he finds out that the Compton blue blood you're so proud of doesn't run pure in my veins, that there's a good bit of common red blood from Maizie La Tour, of the Variety Theater, my mother, who died in Bess Fuller's boardinghouse on Yesler Avenue."

Merritt Compton's face drained and he sat down heavily in the chair behind his desk. Terry let Matt's hand go and stood apart from him, as if she would, at this point, press no claim on him.

"Terry, I realize that perhaps I was wrong in having lied to Matt, and in not having told you the truth about what happened between us that last night in camp," said Compton painfully. "But must you humiliate us both before a stranger?"

"Matt is not a stranger to me, Father. He is the man I love and want to marry. I want him to know everything there is to know about me." She gave Merritt a strange, pitying look. "I'm sorry that it humiliates you for Matt to hear that my mother was Maizie La Tour. I'm not ashamed to have him know. I'm not even ashamed to tell him that Mother was so unsuitable as your wife that you divorced her before I was born."

Compton met her implacable gaze, in which he read not the hatred he had reason to expect but a pity and an alienation that cut him to the heart. I've lost her, this lovely girl who has given whatever meaning there will ever be to my life. And it is my own fault. Knowing her honesty, how could I have been less than honest with her?

He pushed himself up from the chair wearily, all at once feeling that forty-five was no longer the prime of life, and wishing that he did not have to go up to the bedroom he shared with Isobel and that Maizie was still in this world, for he knew if she were, she would ask no questions, make no demands, but open her arms to him and hold him on her warm, generous breast.

Matt had gone to Terry and taken her hand again. Merritt heard him say to her, "I'm proud of ye, my girl. I think I love ye more for what ye just told me than even before, if that's possible. I shall always revere the memory of your mother, for she brought *you* into the world. I'm proud that ye're not ashamed of her, in spite of yer blue blood, and I'm grateful for the touch of earth she gave ye, darlin', for that makes ye easier to love."

Terry looked up at her lover with her grave, steady glance and murmured, "Thank you, Matt."

282

Compton stood looking at the two young people, his dark eyes hooded and inscrutable, and he thought, Why didn't I see it from the first? This is the man for Terry. This big young man with his independence and his nerve, giving me the lie in my teeth, challenging my merger, though he's not shipped more than a few thousand feet of timber to the mills yet, ready to fight for the girl he loves, knowing that I have the power, if I choose, to crush his new small company. This is not only the man I was hoping would emerge to give Terry the husband who could satisfy her, but the one to save the lumber industry from the small, frightened men who want to run away from the big challenge, the big fight.

I think, he mused, with a faint smile softening the sadness of his mouth, that if Matt Regan had not taken my daughter away from me, I could have loved the black devil of a cocky Irishman.

Matt turned and spoke to him, his voice curiously gentle, almost respectful. "We've had hard words between us this night, sir. There is no need for either of us to take back what we said. They have been said and we meant them at the time. But 'twould be a sadness for Terry, and for both of us, too, I think, if we should part as enemies. You can't find it in your heart now to think well of me, which is no more than natural. But I hope you will come to think well or at least more kindly of me. I promise to give my life to making Terry happy. I stopped praying years ago, but I will start in again, and my one prayer will be that she will never regret casting her lot with me."

"I believe you, Matt Regan," said Merritt in his tired, beaten voice, and put out his hand. Matt gave it a hard, strong clasp. "And we don't part as enemies. I hope, too, that some-day we may come to be friends."

"Thank you, sir. As I once had occasion to tell you, you are a generous man, Mr. Compton."

"I'm afraid, Matt," sighed Compton wearily, "that I am,

283

like most of us, generous only when it suits me to be. But believe me, if you can, when I say that I have never before been dishonest in any of my dealings, in business or in personal relations."

"Love makes us all do strange things, sir. As it has turned out well for me, I can afford to be generous, too." The Irishman smiled and his blue eyes lit up. "If you're thinking of the merger, Mr. Compton, rest easy. I'll go in with it, and I'll have a little talk with Robertson at Chehalis, too. He's an old friend of mine, sir. We mushed over Chilkoot Pass together. I may be able to swing him round."

"Good. I'm glad I can count on you, Matt. I think we're going to need men like you." Merritt turned slowly and looked at his daughter. His face was kind and sad and he put up his hand in a small gesture of benison or farewell. "God bless you, Terry girl, and try to forgive me for being quite stupid and blind."

He moved toward the door, but turned at a small, stifled cry from Terry. She suddenly darted away from Matt and rushed up to him and caught his hand. To his utter surprise, she was weeping. Not trusting himself to embrace her, he patted her shoulder and touched her cheek gently. "Oh, Father, I didn't mean to hurt you so much," she whispered. But he smiled and took both her hands, squeezed them hard and let them go. "Don't you worry about me, kiddie. Just be happy, please," he said, and let himself out of the study and closed the door.

Terry stood where he had left her, staring at the shut door and wishing she might have said more, some kind, special, intimate thing to comfort him. For she knew quite well, though in this last moment she realized how much he loved her and how deep her bond to him went, that there would probably never again be a time when they could come close to each other.

Matt had watched her as she went to her father. In his intuitive Irish way, he sensed something of what she must be feeling, as she stood with head bent, before the shut door. Though he burned to leap forward and take her in his arms now that they were alone, he waited until she turned slowly, her face grave, her eyes seeking his.

"He loves you very much, Terry darlin'. Whatever he did, it was because of his deep love." His eyes were full of compassion and his voice was gentle and warm.

"Yes, I know. I'm so sorry for him. Poor Father. We can forgive him, can't we, Matt?"

"We can, indeed, my heart. We can forgive all the world for its sin and sorrow, since we're together at last," he cried. And now he could wait no longer to hold her. "Ah, darlin', let's forget the poor man and the sad, sinful world altogether." And he held out his arms to her.

She went to him gladly, grateful that he, too, in this moment of their victory, had understood and had been sorry for her father's sorrow and defeat. She went toward her love and her fate, feeling for the first time in her life quite free of her father, her tragic mother, poor, frustrated Isobel, free of all the restrictions and obligations and hollow duties of her whole life.

Matt Regan took her into his arms, gently at first, but as he felt her softness and warmth against him, tightening his arms as if he would never let her go. He did not kiss her at once. He laid his cheek against her soft, fragrant hair and savored the ecstasy of the moment when all that warm, scented, silky glory would lie unbound on the pillow for him to sink his face in. He could not believe that she was his, and he whispered against her cheek, "Ah, me darlin', can it be true? Are ye truly willing to put yer life into me big, clumsy hands? Are ye willing to give up all this luxury and ease, the maids serving the dinner, the fine house, the jewels, the elegant clothes, to chance it with an ignorant logger who's started out on his own on little more than a shoestring, and who can give ye no home but a camp in the woods for a few years?"

She raised her steady, gray eyes to his intense blue ones, dark with his love and concern. "Yes, Matt. I'm leaving nothing that means anything to me, except Father, and I would have to leave him someday. I was never truly at home here. I think I have never been truly at home except in your arms. I think that's where I belong."

"Ah, Terry, it is, it is, indeed. From the first I laid eyes on ye I knew ye belonged no place but here, close to me heart, forever and ever." He put his mouth to hers then, gently, and she gave him her lips, and it was as sweet as it had been so long ago on the trail, and yet sweeter, because when his arms tightened round her and his mouth pressed hard, she could meet his ardor with her own, unafraid.

"Oh, Matt," she whispered, when he held her away to smile down at her, with tenderness and humility, "it's so nice to know where I belong, at last!"

He laughed and squeezed her till she wondered if her ribs weren't cracked. "Ah, sure it is, love. But oh, me darlin', it took a devilish long time to get ye there for keeps, Terry."

Matt Regan's Lady